UNIQUELY MINE

A FITZ SERIES

THERESA SEDERHOLT

Uniquely Mine
A Fitz Series

When the latest string of murders, sweeping New York City, lands on Detective Fitzgerald S. Rodriguez's desk, the signature evidence hits too close to home. Being unable to stop the murder of his own mother has made Fitz a jaded man. Now he will stop at nothing to protect the one he loves.

Serial killer, Mark Chambers, is like a cat that preys on unsuspecting mice for sport. When a fresh kill no longer quenches his sexual appetite, he sets his sights on Makenna Justice. The fiery-redhead, with her emerald green eyes, ignites a fire in him that he hasn't had since his first kill.

Time is of the essence for all three of them.

Mark must feed into his desires once more without leaving a trail.

Fitz has to dig himself deep into a killer's mind to catch him.

And Makenna?—She just has to stay alive.

Uniquely Mine, A Fitz Series
Copyright© 2015 by Theresa Sederholt

All rights reserved. This book or any portion thereof may not be reproduced or used in any manner whatsoever without the express written permission of the publisher except for the use of brief quotations in the book review.

The author acknowledges the copyrighted or trademarked status and trademark owners of the following wordmarks mentions in this work of fiction: Starbucks. 61st precinct. Kings County ME. ScanStation. Thalamotomy Surgery. Sinemet. Harley Davidson. Dragonfly Sleeve. Ninhydrin. Luminol. Duke of York. War of Roses. Wikipedia. FBI. BAU. Superman. Lex Luther. GPS. Google. Aventus by Creed. Kryptonite. The Post. Page Six. The Daily News. Mercantile Exchange. Honda. Weeping Wanda. Howard Johnson's. Thomas Kincaid. East River Ferry. Quantico. iPhone. iPad. Fabio. Charlie Brown. Playstation. Dior. Chanel. Cross Fit. Daniel. Helmut Lang. Avengers. BMW. IRS. NYPD.

Music '3 Doors Down "Kryptonite," 'Breaking Benjamin "Angels Fall," 'The Veronicas "You Ruin Me," 'Parachute "The Mess I Made," 'Daughtry's "Waiting for Superman," 'Lee Brice "Always The Only One," "Kenny Chesney "Always Gonna Be You," 'Lee Brice "I Don't Dance," 'Justin Moore "Til My Last Day," 'Chase Rice "Ride (featuring Macy Maloy)," 'Bon Jovi "Superman Tonight," 'Creed "One Last Breath."

This is a work of fiction. Names, characters, businesses, places, events, and incidents are either the products of the author's imagination or used in a fictitious manner. Any resemblance to actual persons, living or dead, or actual events is purely coincidental.

This book contains strong language, graphic sexual situations, and violence. It is not intended for anyone under the age of 18. Warning, might be a trigger for domestic violence.

Publisher: Theresa Sederholt ©
Cover designer: Robin Harper Wicked By Design.
Editor: Jacquelyn Ayres.
Formatter: Stacey Blake, Champagne Formats.
Photographer: Eric Battershell Photography/FITography
Models: Tessi Conquest and Burton Hughes

ISBN: 978-0-9862598-7-6

DEDICATION

In memory of Faye Schackne.

If Only

If only I could have one more moment with you, I would stand beside you again on Windham Mountain, admiring the view. I would utter those words to you all over again, *breathtakingly beautiful, like living inside a Thomas Kincaid painting*. When I close my eyes, my mind plays though the many memories we've shared. If only I could live them all over again, I would with you. You guided me when I needed it, yet, you never held me back. I could list all the things we did together, but they would never be enough. If only I could have one more moment with you, I would hold you tight and tell you how much I love you. If only one wish could come true, I would wish to spend another day with you.

CHAPTER ONE

Mark Chambers

WOMEN MAKE IT SO EASY for me. They think I'm broken and want to fix me. I let them try, but I'm not broken, so there is no fix for me. I have a need that only they can fill. I need to feel my hands around their throat, feel their bodies come to life with every smack on their ass. Every gasping breath makes my cock harder. If I close my eyes, I can feel each pulse of my blood surging forward. Women see me as the bad boy. The boy that needs to be rescued. *They* are the ones that need to be rescued—rescued from me. This one tonight is no different. New York, just another city filled with desperate women. It never ceases to amaze me how women are so nurturing. I'm beyond redemption, beyond repair and that suits me just fine.

Chicago, Los Angeles, New York, they were all the same. A big city filled with lonely hearts waiting for their prince charming to come. Only to find out I'm not their dream come true; I'm their worst nightmare. I've been watching this one for a couple of days. I first spotted her coming out of a gym in Chelsea. The day I met her I pretended to be lost, and she'd been more than happy to help me

1

find my way. I had to go right past her place, so she offered to share a cab. Right about now, she's probably regretting that decision. In a matter of ten minutes, I knew where she lived. By the time she left that cab, I had her number in my burner phone. So easy, it's laughable.

I look down at her bulging eyes, lean in, and whisper in her ear. "Do you fear me, yet? Like the fear you feel when stepping into a dark room."

I tighten my hands around her neck, and with each squeeze, my cock gets harder. She needs to feel what it's like to be on the brink of death and then come back over and over again. She will never experience that rush again. It won't be much longer; I have to time it perfectly. The ultimate rush, followed by my release, which can only happen just as she is about to pass out. It's all in the timing. It has to be perfect. One hand around her throat and one hand pumping my cock. This is the hardest part; I feel the blood racing through my veins. She's there; I release my grip and give her the air she craves.

She gasps, and then I pound my cock into her and squeeze my long fingers around her throat, yet again. Even with her hands tied behind her back, this one hardly puts up a fight. I thought she had more in her, more of a need to live. She hasn't realized this is the end of the line. Her eyes are beginning to bulge and roll back, and I know she will pass out soon. That's my cue. My blood is hot, racing through me. Everything is heading to the finish line. I come, and my entire body feels like it's burning, a burn I can only achieve right before I kill her. She's not dead. Unlike television, it takes a long time to strangle someone. They pass out at least five minutes before they die. I don't have the time to wait around. I snap her neck. Let's face it; it's the humane thing to do.

Now comes the clean up, making sure I leave no trace behind. Except, of course, the *rose*. I leave it so I can claim the kill as mine. *Uniquely mine.* The thought makes me hard again, but I have no time for that. I place the collar around her neck and stroke her beautiful cheek. I wish I could have kept her a little longer.

Eleven minutes. I look around the room, making sure every last trace of my presence is gone. Oh, how I love the smell of bleach. So crisp and refreshing, like the dawn of a new day. I wonder how long before the city starts to panic? How long before they connect the dots? I take one last walk around before locking the door behind me. After all, I wouldn't want anyone to break in and contaminate a perfect crime scene.

FITZ

I'm the defender of those who can't defend themselves. I'm jaded by humanity, the humanity I see on a daily basis. I try to be the best I can be, but sometimes it's hard. Most days, I look in the mirror and I'm okay with the guy looking back at me. I wonder how many people in the world can say the same. Unfortunately, today is not one of those days. Today, I've been called to the scene of yet another murder, the third one this month. The pattern has formed, and as a detective who specializes in these types of cases, that's why I'm here. Even though I'm based out of the 61st Precinct in Brooklyn, I go where I'm needed. Lately, that is anywhere but home.

My captain is already waiting—and yelling—when I get to the scene. I haven't even finished my first cup of coffee, and he's already rambling on. Why can't he just shut the fuck up for five minutes? All the yelling in the world will not make my brain move any faster. Captain Jack Hart is tall, like basketball player tall, yet, he has two left feet. He's barking orders to anyone who will listen. Until he sees me, that is. There is no avoiding him at this point. I just cleared a major case and should be celebrating, but not in this city.

There is never a time for celebrating. Hell, I'm supposed to have two weeks off between cases and I haven't even had two days before this case was thrown in my lap. "Hey, Captain, do we know a time of death yet?"

Hart's jaw ticks when he's stressed, and lately, that's all the time. I could probably tell time with his ticking jaw. "Yeah, Fitz, this one is fresh, only a few hours old, so I'm hoping we can get something more from her. Maybe this sick bastard left something behind. Her name is Sophia Hall and, Fitz, she's one of us."

I'm about to enter the scene. Four words no cop ever wants to hear. "A cop?"

"She was a data analyst at One Police Plaza. I explained to the chief medical examiner about the other two, and he has agreed to let Gail run lead on this. She's inside waiting for you."

Another crime scene, another pair of protective booties and gloves. The crime scene unit is just finishing up and Gail O'Connor, the Chief Medical Examiner for Kings County, is waiting to talk to me before she leaves. Gail and I have worked together before, so she knows I like to look. Yeah, she calls me a creeper, but I have a way of getting inside the killer's head, so no one ever tries to stop me.

I like to walk the scene in silence, absorbing all the little details and smells. No forced entry; keys are on a hook by the front door. No pets to contaminate the scene. Very clean, possibly a little OCD. I head over to the body where Gail is, looking ready to leave. "Talk to me, Gail. What's different?"

She hesitates for only a second. "How do you know me so well?"

I smile, as always, trying to charm her, but it never works. "It's what I do. What's got you biting the inside of your cheek?"

She instantly releases it. "You know I'm not going to say anything until I get her back to the lab, but, Fitz, look how clean everything is. It's like he feels so confident that he's taking even more time cleaning the scene and not just the body. Look around, nothing is out of place, at least from what I can tell." She waves her hand around the room, trying to force her point. "Hell, there isn't even a damn dust bunny. Who doesn't have a dust bunny?"

I look down at the victim, and I'm taken back by how beautiful and young she is. "Are you done with her?"

"Yes, but make it quick. I want to get her back to the lab while she's fresh."

I squat down and smell; the smell of bleach is overpowering. "He bleached everything?"

"Yes, and it seems he even brushed her teeth with it, but CSU couldn't find a toothbrush. Could it be his trophy?"

I shrug my shoulders. "I've seen stranger things; you never know what the trigger is for these guys. Tell me the truth, Gail, did you take a sniff?"

Her face flushes even though she knows I'm playing with her, trying to lighten the mood. "Yes, Fitz, I'm getting as bad as you."

"I keep telling you, Gail, become one with the crime scene."

She rolls her eyes. "What are you, some kind of Zen Master today?"

I'm no longer squatting. I'm on my hands and knees, my face inches from Sophia's neck. "I see she has a collar around her neck, and it appears to be the same as the others. Is the rose in place?"

"Yes, it's one of the first things I checked. And, Fitz, if you put your face there to look, I will smack you." I look up, and she has her hand out ready to follow though with her threat.

"All right. I'll finish up here and meet you back at the lab. I know you're eager to get started on her." By waving at the tech, I let him know I'm done with the body.

"Fitz, how about I call you when I'm ready to deliver? The pressure of knowing you're outside my door is not going to push the results through any faster."

I smirk at her, knowing the only thing it will get me is her usual eye roll. "Yeah, yeah. I get it." I wave at her as I begin methodically working my way around the apartment. It's a junior one-bedroom, which is bigger than a standard studio, yet smaller than a one-bedroom. By New York City standards, this one is rather large. It's a walk-up, three floors with only two apartments on each floor. The first floor is a café that's only open for breakfast and lunch, closed by two p.m. They might be of some help, depending upon what time they come in to prep.

This place is directly opposite the United Nations building. I'll make sure Hart pulls footage from all available cameras. Sophia has her bed in the small alcove with beads hanging in the doorway, working as a makeshift divider. I sniff the wall next to the divider and smell bleach. Christ, he even washed the walls. I go to the other side and sniff—no bleach. I race outside and catch Gail before she pulls away.

"Hey, did CSU take pictures of the walls? Specifically the doorway leading into the alcove?"

"I know they did a scan with the ScanStation, but I'm not sure if they took actual photos of the walls. Why?"

"Only one wall smells of bleach. What do you want to bet he had her up against that wall?"

She puts the car in park and reaches in the back seat pulling out a camera. "I always keep one with me. Now, show me what you're talking about."

Ensuring we don't cross-contaminate, we re-don booties and new gloves, head back inside, and start taking pictures of both walls. "You're like a bloodhound, Fitz. You know that, right?" Gail mutters.

"I've been called worse. Don't suppose you want to leave me that camera?"

"You know I can't. If you find something, use your phone. Chances are, CSU already got these shots. Now may I please get to

6

my lab?"

I shoo her away and go back to what I was doing. Sophia has the type of desk that pulls down from the wall. CSU already bagged her laptop, phone, and tablet. She has very few personal pictures, except for her graduation picture from the academy, class of 2011. I snap a picture of it and pull out a pad from my breast pocket to make notes.

Yeah, I'm old school. Oh, shit. Where the hell is my pen this time? Grabbing a pen off the desk, I begin to draw the wall in relation to where Sophia was found. If he killed her up against the wall, why not leave her there and walk out? Why stage the scene? What is he showing me? What is he trying to conceal?

I twirl the pen around my fingers as I run everything through my mind. The name on the pen hits me like a brick between my eyes. *Mystik*...oh, *fuck* no!

Mystik is a high-end BDSM club owned by my best friend. Coincidence? Maybe; if I believed in coincidences. But, one of our own...possibly a regular at my friend's club, doesn't sit too well in the "coincidental" department for me. This bastard's entered my world now, and he's going down.

CHAPTER TWO

SOPHIA'S APARTMENT IS NOT THAT far from Chelsea, where Mystik is located. I don't know what time they open, but I quickly text MJ to meet me there. Andy owns the club, but since he got sick, MJ has taken over the daily operations. Sophia is the third victim this month, but this is the first one with a tie to the club . . . that I'm aware of. If the press gets wind of the murders, they will play up the BDSM aspect. The captain has been able to hold back any information about the rose and specifically where it was found.

The BDSM lifestyle has become more mainstream. Yet, religious leaders are calling it the work of the devil. Others call it domestic violence. However, as long as the safety guidelines are followed and the sex is consensual, it's not violence. As for me, I really don't know much about it, but if you're safe and it makes you happy, then to each his own. I'm just trying to make it through the day, while keeping the nightmares at bay.

I get to the club and take a quick look around outside before I enter. It's nothing like I expected, not that I knew what to expect. I've never been to a BDSM club. Oh, I've had plenty of opportunities to come here, if I wanted to; I've just never felt a desire. I pull my

8

phone out, about to call MJ, when the door flies open and she walks in. "Hey, I was just getting ready to call you. I'm on a case and the victim had a pen from your club in her apartment."

"That's the reason for the urgent text? Fitz, I give out that promotional shit to promote business; there are thousands of them out there. It must be pretty important to you if it got you to finally step foot in here."

"There is a BDSM feel to the crimes, and if the press gets wind of this, I'm afraid this could come back to you."

"What do you mean *a BDSM feel?* Why the hell would it come back to me?"

My mind is racing over how much I can talk about. "You know I can't give you all the details; collar, ropes, that kind of stuff. I don't know enough about your world to know if it's real or if it's staged to look real."

"What do you want from me?" She seems more agitated with me today than usual.

"I need your client list and any video footage you have for the entire month."

She stops walking and pushes me up against the wall. Her face is only inches from mine and every freckle seems to be getting darker. "Have you lost your fucking mind? This is a high-end club that offers the utmost privacy. I have to keep it that way to cater to my client's extreme needs. You need to solve this right now, and you need to leave my clients out of it, Fitz!"

"Makenna Justice, you've had my balls in a grip since you were five years old. You have been ordering me around from the first day we met. Unfortunately, this is not something I can solve overnight. I need time, and I have a plan. Let's head into your office, and I will give you the details." As I watch MJ walk away, I realize—yep, in a grip—always has and probably always will.

We head down the hall toward her office. The first thing that

9

strikes me is how dark everything around me is. I begin making notes. This place is completely out of my realm. I guess I'm what you would call a vanilla kind of guy, with a few sprinkles thrown in for good measure. We never talk about sex; her brother is my best friend. I feel the knot in my gut getting tighter; some things are better left alone.

We step into her office, and I'm taken back; everything is bright with a warm comfortable feel. I walk around the room, quietly taking it all in, when a hard smack to my ass snaps me back to reality.

"Fitz, get your head out of your ass. Sit down and tell me your plan. It better be good, because if this gets out, it will be a major hit to my bottom line."

I sink into the white leather sofa (which has to be the most comfortable thing my ass has seen in a long time). "My plan is pretty simple. You sign me up as a new member."

She tosses her phone and keys on her desk and spins around to face me. "That's your big plan, Fitz? Please, tell me you have something more than that. My business and reputation are both on the line here. Everything I've spent years building hinges on your *big plan!*"

I take a few deep breaths and prepare myself for the fight ahead as she sinks into the couch next to me. MJ is a lioness in sheep's clothing. I squeeze her hand, knowing what I have to tell her next will probably put her over the edge. "Calm down and give me a chance to see if it works. In the mean time, I'll need a membership list from you, along with full access to all your video surveillance. And, MJ—I mean *every*thing. Everyone that has come in and out of here for the past month." I wait, because I know what's coming; an explosion of epic proportion.

Three, two, one...

"Have you lost your *fucking* mind all together? My list is private for a reason; some of my members are from society's elite. We're talking top political candidates. Fuck, there is even a Pastor and a Rabbi that are members. If that gets out, I'm done. Besides, what would make you think that you can just come in here and fit right in? This is not a job; it's a lifestyle choice. It takes years of training to be a Dominant or a submissive. Do you even have any idea what goes on here?" her voice has gone up about ten levels, and her freckles seem to explode with the fire brewing just under her flushed skin.

"Look, MJ, you know this is not my thing. I only know the little bit Andy told me when he purchased the business years ago. This is not my first choice; however, I don't see any other way. For Christ's sake, at this point, we don't even know if it's a man or a woman. I'm at a loss here. So, if you have a better idea, I'm all ears."

She closes her eyes for a moment, as if trying to gain some sort of control. Either that, or she is going to belt me one. She gets up and heads over to the coffee bar. From the way she's acting, I'm starting to think I'm going to need a lot more than coffee, if I'm going to pull this off. "Fitz, coffee?"

"Yeah, my usual, please," my words are a little more gruff than usual.

"What does your captain think of your harebrained idea?"

"Look, I get that it's not the ideal situation. First, I want to go though your member list and any video available. Who knows? Maybe we will get lucky."

She hands me my coffee and sits next to me. "Your captain doesn't know, does he?"

I quietly sip my coffee giving her all the answers she needs.

"Fitz, I could never be in the same room with you, ever."

"Why? We've been best friends since you were in kindergarten, so why can't we?"

Maybe I'm not getting what it is she does here. As far as I know, she manages the day-to-day operations. She gets up and heads toward the desk. "I can't even talk to you about this. I'm going to show you a scene from the other night. While you watch, I will get the list, along with the security footage you wanted." She hits play and walks out.

M J leaves and I refill my coffee, getting ready to watch the "*scene*." How bad could this be? The screen is dark, but the music is very sensual. The lighting is low, yet I can see that the room is set up like an old Tudor style library. A man is sitting in a large, leather chair behind a very ornately carved desk. So far, everything appears to be normal . . . as normal as it could be, considering where I am and what I'm about to watch.

The door opens, and a woman walks in; she is naked except for the thick, black leather collar around her neck. From what I can make out, it's not the same as the killers. The one on this lady's neck is much wider, and the ring is thicker. The video is black and white. The lighting makes it hard to see any faces, which is probably intentional.

The man loosens his tie and begins speaking in a very deep, stern voice. "Come, sit at my feet and suck my cock. If you please me, I will spank you, and I might even let you come."

She scurries up to him and sits at his feet. She unzips his pants and pulls out his cock, taking him into her mouth. Slowly, she begins working her way up and down. Going deeper with each thrust. The man wraps his fist around her ponytail, slowing down her movements. She is taking all her cues from him. They seem to be in sync as he reaches down and pinches her nipples hard.

Every time he pinches, she stops. He reaches into the desk drawer and pulls out what appears to be some sort of riding crop. He lets go of her ponytail and again pinches her nipples. When she stops to adjust to the pain, he uses the crop. I can hear the swishing sound of the crop before it hits her skin. Every time the crop makes contact with her skin, it gets louder.

I can't help cringing. I can barely make out his facial expression, but his body language doesn't seem to change. This happens repeatedly until the man finally finds his release. As the woman cleans him completely with her tongue, he impatiently taps his fingers on his desk. Finally, when she is finished, he puts his cock away and straightens his tie. The woman is still on her knees, never lifting her head to make any eye contact with him.

The man reaches into the desk drawer again and pulls something out, placing it on the desk. "Stand up," he commands. His voice seems deeper and more gravelly. "I'm not pleased with you tonight."

What the hell? He got off, so what's his fucking problem?

"Play with each nipple and then put the clamps on; I will adjust them." The woman begins kneading each nipple, never once looking at him. She puts each clamp on; her head remains downward, the camera never getting a glimpse of her face. He slowly begins to tighten each one. Her legs start to shake, and her breathing quickens, as she seemingly fights crying out in pain. Who wouldn't? My hand instinctively rubs my own nipples, and I wince as if I can feel the same pain she must be feeling. Finally, he stops, and I let out the breath I was unaware I was holding.

"You may sit at my feet and play with yourself, but do not come. Clearly, you need more training."

She drops to her knees and begins to slide her fingers slowly down her torso to the apex of her thighs. She lets out a little moan as her fingers work their way very slowly in and out. Her hand begins to move faster, and if she doesn't slow it down, this won't end well for her. My heart is beating so fast; I don't want her to get into trouble. She lets out another little moan. "Jesus Christ, lady, stop

13

before you can't!" The man pushes his chair back just a little before commanding her to stop.

"Show me your hand now." She lifts her hand up toward him, and as the light hits her fingers, I can see they are glistening with her arousal.

"Very nice, continue."

What the fuck? Is this guy serious? What he's doing is cruel, letting her get to the edge and then stopping her. This goes on for another twenty minutes, and it's making me sick; my stomach is in knots, and my chest is tight. Finally, he tells her to stop and lay across his lap. He holds both her hands behind her in one of his, at the small of her back. He takes his right hand and strokes her ass. With each stroke, he swipes a finger up the center of her core, front to back, which elicits another small moan from her.

When she seems to relax, he begins to spank her, never in the same spot. He's not just spanking her ass, but her thighs too. Swish and a smack, over and over again. After about ten smacks, he, very abruptly, shoves his fingers into her, causing her to gasp and cry out. He pulls out and starts the spanking all over again. I don't know how much more of this I can take.

Maybe MJ is right; maybe this is too much for me. Finally, he stops and orders her to stand up. She stumbles to her feet, visibly shaken. He orders her to lie on her back across his desk with her feet in the air. He instructs her to turn her face away from him.

He doesn't even take the time to remove his pants. He unzips, takes his cock out, rolls on a condom, and then slams into her, hard. He's pounding into her repeatedly. He slows down and removes the nipple clamps at the same time and gives her permission to come. He pulls out, removes the condom, and comes all over her breasts. He puts himself back together and then dismisses her.

As she gets up to leave, the camera finally catches her face. I barely make it to the trash and throw up the remains of my coffee. I don't know where to begin or know how to process all of this. As I try to regain my composure, MJ walks in.

I'm still leaning over the trash. "Makenna, please tell me *why*? Make me understand what you got from that."

She rubs her hand slowly up and down my back. "Do you still think you can do this, Fitz, now that you have seen a small sampling of what goes on here, or do you want to try to figure out a different way to find this killer?"

CHAPTER THREE

FITZ

MJ AND I SIT FOR a long time, neither of us saying a word. I've seen so much bad and evil in my short life, I don't understand why she needs this. "Can you please make me understand why, or is that too personal?"

"There's no simple answer. Why does someone like a certain taste or a certain smell? It's a lifestyle choice for me. I get that you don't understand it, but respect that I entered into this freely. Respect my choices, Fitzy, *please*." She very rarely calls me Fitzy anymore, and the sadness in her voice breaks my heart.

"Can I ask you questions?"

"Ha, since when do you ask permission? If it's about the lifestyle, then yes, but if it's personal, then no."

"Does your family know?"

She cocks her head to the side and gives me her typical *what the fuck is wrong with you look*. "What did I just say? Would you discuss your sex life with them? Would any of your friends discuss their sex life with their family? If so, then you need to start hanging out with different friends."

"You are my family, and this is more than your sex life, MJ; this is also a business. Let me rephrase it for you. Do they know what type of club this is, and how involved you are in all of this?" I wave my hand around for emphasis. My jaw is tight, and I'm praying they don't know.

"You know Andy was the original owner, but when he was diagnosed with Parkinson's, he transferred it to me. Mom and Dad have no idea, and I would like to keep it that way. Before you ask, they think it's some sort of social club for young people to meet up and have good, safe fun."

I roll my eyes at that one. "Wait, Andy is no longer the owner?! Am I the worst detective in the world? So much has changed in my best friend's life and I've been clueless."

She's giggles and raises her eyebrow; I'm glad she finds it amusing. "Andy wanted to tell you but, honestly, he was so overwhelmed by the changes he has been forced to make because of his Parkinson's. Plus, he knows your taste, and he didn't think you would understand any of this. Besides, you can't keep a secret, and since you live downstairs in Mom and Dad's house, it could be a problem."

"I can too keep a secret, besides, Andy is worse than me! Anyway, I still can't help but feel so out of touch with everyone."

"Don't be so hard on yourself; when you're investigating a case, you become lost in it. You go into that zone, and then afterward, it takes you a bit to come back to us mentally. That's what makes you so good at what you do. Lately, you haven't had any down time; you're always working."

"You are always so strong and so domineering in everything you do, how do you turn it off when you're in a scene? Your whole demeanor was so different, I had no clue it was you." This has me so baffled; the last person I ever expected to see in that scene was MJ.

"I honestly don't know. Maybe that's why I enjoy the role of a submissive. What you didn't see in that scene is the aftercare. When I walked out of that room, he eventually followed. He took care of me and tended to all my needs. That's part of his role as a Dom.

"When I'm outside of this club, I'm everything for everyone. I handle my parent's finances and everything they need. I help Stephen take care of all of Andy's health care needs. I do it all, and maybe the need for someone else to take the lead and take care of me is what drives me, I'm not sure. Either way, it doesn't change the problem at hand; you have a killer to catch."

"Don't try to change the subject. Is Andy doing any better after the surgery? I feel bad that I haven't checked in on him more. Unfortunately, my last case lasted almost a year."

"You know there is no cure for Parkinson's, but the thalamotomy surgery helped. He's still taking Sinemet to help with the symptoms, but the expenses are huge, even with healthcare coverage. Please, don't be mad at him for not telling you. He really was going to at some point, but that point never came. This club has helped save my parent's home, and it pays for all of Andy's medical needs." She grabs my hands and squeezes them. "I never wanted to see that look on your face; that's why I never told you."

"What look is that?"

"Pity, shame, hurt, all of the above. I never wanted that."

She cries, and I pull her into my arms. I can deal with just about anything, except her tears. "MJ, I'm hurt that you didn't feel you could come to me. You're my best friend; hell, your mom raised me and kept me on the straight and narrow when my mom died. I don't understand why you wouldn't come to me for help. I could have at least helped with Andy's medical bills.

"I know I've been wrapped up in work. The past ten months, I've kept everyone at a distance. But I needed to stay focused, and I've had back-to-back bad cases. My only sanity is knowing that my family is safe and removed from all the ugliness I deal with on a daily basis."

She lifts her head and wipes her tears with the back of her hand.

"It's not your cross to bear; it's mine."

"You are the most stubborn woman I have ever known! For Christ's sake, MJ, you should be able to lean on me."

She slightly pulls away from me. Her whole demeanor seems to change. "Can we get back to the business at hand, please? I put a copy of the security footage on a thumb drive for you. I also gave you a member list, but if the person came in as a guest, then it wouldn't be in there."

Gentle and kind is gone, and Ms. Business is back. I'll back off for now and give her some space, but this is far from over. "How do you keep track of a guest? I would think there is some sort of release form they would have to sign."

"I've included my standard release package that every guest must sign. When a member brings a guest, they can only be in a scene with the person who brought them. For health and safety reasons, they can't have any bodily contact with anyone else.

"Every guest is given a yellow, rubber bracelet with Mystik on it. That lets everyone know who they are; and it's hands off. They can walk freely around the club and observe other scenes, except in the private rooms. Those rooms are off limits. That is where the scene you watched took place; they are by invitation only. Members know that anyone with a yellow band can't be invited to join a scene.

"Each guest is allowed to visit the club two times. After that, if they want to come back, they have to join. I also have pictures of every guest attached to his or her release package. There is a computer copy and a paper copy; I've included both. Fitz, maybe the person is not a member here, or even a guest. Maybe she just picked up my pen from somewhere. Hell, I would think that before jumping to the conclusion that she's a member or a guest."

"All three victims were found with a black leather collar around their neck. All of them had their hands tied behind their backs, and the last victim had the ropes intricately worked around her breast.

I looked online at different ways to use ropes during sex and it seemed pretty classic. I know the killer could have looked all this up on the Internet. I get that it could just be a coincidence, but this is all I've got so far. When someone is a member of a club like this, do they generally stick to one club or do they frequent others? Are there a standard set of rules that every club must follow?"

She closes her eyes and takes a deep breath. "You need to understand this world is not all black and white. It's a matter of preference. Generally speaking, members usually stick to one club. If they travel, some clubs have reciprocal arrangements. Many people that come here come as a couple. There is a singles night only, but you have to have a sponsor to even get invited to that. Mystik is a private club, so I set the rules. The type of play involved in clubs varies from club to club. Look, why don't you take the information I gave you and run with it. I will make up a basic list of Mystik's rules and membership privileges. Then let's meet tonight and see what you've got."

I know when to back off with her, and right now, staying focused on work is what's best for both of us. "I have to get to the coroner's office, and then I'll start reviewing all of this. I'll call you later." I grab the package and head out the door.

I open the door and get hit with the sweltering August heat. Ask any true New Yorker what the worst month of the year here is and they will tell you August. I will take the snow and rain any day of the week; I hate the month of August. I don't have a car; I take the train when I'm working. When I'm not working, I'm on my Harley. Life in New York City is not like what you see on TV. There is never a spot to park, and all the sirens in the world won't get you there any faster. Not having a car has been a bone of contention with my captain for years.

Sitting on the train affords me the time to think and to people watch. In my line of work, it's the best place to connect with people from all walks of life. This time of day, the number 2 train is a local, so I have plenty of time to think. I need this time to run through everything in my head. The first two victims were found in Brooklyn, but this last one was in a nice section of Manhattan. Is he spreading out by choice or is he striking wherever he finds opportunity? Why did he brush her teeth with bleach? Why the rose and why a white one?

I researched the meaning of the white rose, and I was surprised at what I found. In some cases, it's a sign of innocence and purity. It can be a way to express hope for the future or a way to say goodbye. From all I read, the white rose has the most uses, so I need to get inside this guy's head and figure out why.

Why does he put it inside her vagina? What does the vagina symbolizes to him? If I take the sexual meaning out of the equation, then I'm left with what?—reproduction, womb, and shelter. None of this makes sense and nothing ties the pieces together.

My stop is next. Maybe Gail will have some answers for me. The train finally comes to a stop in East Flatbush, and I race out of the bowels of the city, heading toward the Medical Examiner's office. The ten-minute walk in the August heat sucks. This really makes me rethink the whole car issue. By the time I get there, I will need a shower. At least I know Gail's office will be freezing; the medical examiner's office always is. I duck into the men's room to clean up a bit before finding Gail.

As soon as I walk into her office, she takes one look at me and rolls her eyes. What is it with everyone and their eye rolling today? "Hey, what did I do now?"

"Fitz, are you ever going to requisition a car? You look like hell?"

"Can we please forget that I'm an ass for taking the train in midday August heat, please? What do you have for me?"

"Follow me; I have a lot to show you." We head into the autopsy room and it's even colder in there.

"Let's start with the ropes. They are the same type of rope used on the other two girls. The rope is very common, the type that is sold at every big box hardware store. The way the ropes were tied is called the *dragonfly sleeve*. This is different from the other two girls. The other two only had their hands bound behind them. The dragonfly takes time to tie. It is a very common type of knot in the BDSM community."

She pulls up a video showing exactly how the *dragonfly sleeve* is done. If the killer were used to doing it, then it wouldn't take as long as I thought.

"The rose was white and smaller than the first two, I'm not sure if that means anything to you. The stems were cut exactly the same length. There were no thorns. There was quite a bit of vaginal tearing in this victim. It was not from the rose, but do you have any thought as to why he places the rose in the victim's vagina?"

"Not yet, but apparently it has some meaning for him. I'm making sure that fact is being kept out of the press. What else do you have for me?"

"There was no semen or any other bodily fluids, not that I expected to find any. There was a lot of tearing in the anal canal, more than in the others, but Sophia was a small girl. He cleaned her vagina and rectum with oxygen bleach before he placed the rose. He even brushed her teeth with the same bleach. He cleaned under her fingernails with it. He also applied a coat of polish over her nails, although I don't have any idea why.

"I am going to try to use the Ninhydrin to see if he left any prints behind. I don't think I will find any, and I won't bore you with the method. I just wanted to let you know why her hands are bagged and sealed. The first two victims were strangled, but he snapped this victim's neck, which is new. Do you think he might be escalating? I mean, the time between each kill is coming quicker."

"Either he's escalating or time was a factor for him, which, going by the rope work, makes no sense. Why did he use oxygen bleach?"

"With oxygen bleach, all traces of blood are gone. Not even Luminol will show any blood."

"Jesus, what else did you find?"

"She had some abrasions on her back that matched the wall cleaned with the bleach. The collars are all the same, almost like he purchased them in bulk. They came from the same run of leather. I have a call into the manufacturer, but they are based out of China. They are not collars that would be found in an adult toyshop, these are supplied to large pet stores and feed shops. Just like the first two victims, the collar was put on after he killed her."

"Did any of the victims have a yellow rubber bracelet? You know those bands that are very popular."

"None of the girls were wearing any jewelry at all. That doesn't mean that they didn't have one. Why?"

Trying to avoid her question, I hit her with some more of my own. "What about the stomach content; was there anything unusual or different in this one?"

"No, all the girls had a full meal before they died; she had pizza and red wine about four hours prior to her death. There was no se-men in her stomach, only food. She was in excellent physical shape. Nothing out of the ordinary."

I rub my temples, trying to fight off the growing headache I feel coming on. "Okay, I need to get back to the precinct and sort this all out in my head. Let me know what you find out with the nail polish."

"Don't think I didn't notice your avoidance about the bracelet. When you're ready to run it past me, I'm here to listen."

She gets up and squeezes my shoulder. "If you want to wait, I can give you a lift."

"Thanks, but I do some of my best thinking on the train. Besides, I need to take another look at Sophia." Thankfully, she doesn't question me.

I head over to the autopsy table and stare at Sophia. The tech steps back to give me some privacy. "Oh, Sophia, I really wish you could talk to me. Why did you have that pen? Was it a coincidence? Give me the damn answers!" The tech clearing her throat snaps me back to reality. I look up and realize I was talking out loud.

"Sir, if she answers you, I might stroke out right here."

I smile and thank God they all know me, otherwise I'm sure I would be committed. "Thank you very much for your patience; I'm done. Please remind Gail to send me the report when you're done with her hands."

I step outside into the heat and walk to the train station. My precinct is located in the south end of Brooklyn, so it will take me some time to get there. I'll have to change trains, but I need this time to myself. If I hurry, I can beat the rush hour commuters. Rush hour on the New York City subways is not for the faint of heart.

I finally get to my last train, the Q, and work my way to a seat on the last car. I put my earphones on to drown out the noise from the rails. "Angels Fall" by Breaking Benjamin is blaring as I mindlessly run through everything Gail said. I need to see the crime scene photos from all three victims. Not just the victims themselves, but also the stuff around them.

Why would he take the time to polish her nails? Were any of the other girls members or guests of Mystik—or for that matter— any other BDSM club? Is he trying to make it look like the kills are

BDSM related to throw the police off track? I would think that since the collars are not from an adult toy store, he's staging the scene. I can't assume anything or rule anything out. There has to be some sort of link that I just haven't found yet.

The commute was quick for a change. I look around and realize I'm the only one in this car. When the doors open, I'm hit with a blast of hot, humid air. Jesus, maybe I should get a car.

I head into the precinct. At least the AC is *finally* working. I'm barely in the door five minutes and Hart's yelling. I swear that's all the man does. One day he's going to give himself a heart attack. I see him racing toward me, but there's no time to hide. "Fitz, what did Gail have to report?"

"Can you at least let me get in the damn door? There were some differences from the other two victims, but the signature was still there. I need to look at all the photos from the scene and the evidence log."

"I know that look, it's the look right before you tell me you have something. Please, dear God, tell me you have something for me."

"Maybe, not sure yet, so let me do my thing. I promise as soon as I have something, I will get with you."

"Okay, I already set you up in a room upstairs, let me know if you need anything from me. Oh, and, Fitz, before you bitch, I had nothing to do with it. You have a partner on this one. The FBI sent her over. Her name is Alfie Shaw, so deal with it." He walks away mumbling about getting a partner and a car all in one day would be some sort of divine intervention.

I hate working with a partner. I hate explaining my way of thinking, probably because I don't understand it myself. I head upstairs and find the shoebox of a room, no money wasted on frills here—that's for sure. I pop my headset back on, so I can ignore everything else and set up my stuff. When I finally look up, I see I'm not alone. Standing in the doorway is a very tall, beautiful lady, who stops me dead in my tracks. I pull off my headset. I want to introduce myself, but for some reason, I'm at a loss for words. I finally snap myself out of my self-induced fog and attempt to introduce myself. "Umm, hello you must be Alfie Shaw; I'm Fitz."

She smiles and her entire face lights up. I'm so fucked here. "Hi, Fitz, you can call me Al. Do you want to bring me up to speed on what you have so far?" She walks in and pulls up a seat right next to me, Jesus Christ, why the hell am I being tested? This is why I don't want a partner. Alone, I can keep my head in the game, *his* game. She snaps her fingers. "Hello, Fitz, are you okay?"

Snap the fuck out of it, Fitz. "Yeah, I don't usually work with a partner."

"Why?"

"Honestly, I find it distracting. I like to stay focused."

"Maybe you need a woman's point of view. You know you're not expected to be the white knight, racing in to save the day."

"Trust me, Al, I'm no one's hero. Haven't been for years. I was just going to pull up the photos from all three scenes." I need to put her out of my head and focus on the case. I begin to run through all the evidence with her. Step by step, we sort it all out. I explain to her my connection to Mystik and the pen found at the last victim's apartment.

"So you're thinking there might be a BDSM link to all the victims? You know, it could just be a coincidence. She could have gotten that pen anywhere. How many times have you walked off with someone's pen? Plus, you said yourself that the collars are standard collars from a big box pet store not an adult toy store. This could all be a set up, and we could be walking right into it."

"I get it, but I still can't get that feeling out of my gut that this is somehow linked."

She gets up and walks over to the whiteboard. "What do the women have in common? Have their paths crossed at all?"

"Not sure yet; I just got the case this morning. I also have the footage from MJ and her member list to go through."

She is frantically making a list on the whiteboard. I organize in my head, and it seems she organizes on paper, this might work out after all. "I'll have my tech go through the member list along with all the victims' information. I'll also have him look at their social media accounts to see if they've crossed at all. Do we have all the victims' computers, cell phones, and any other electronic gadgets?"

"Yeah, we have everything we could find."

She pulls up the autopsy reports from each victim and puts them on the computer screen side by side. "Why snap the neck of the third victim? The first two are exactly the same: suffocation due to strangulation. Was he rushed or is he elevating?"

"Are you asking me or talking out loud?"

She laughs. "Both, I always talk a case out loud. It brings it into perspective for me. Don't worry, I will tell you when I need you to answer me. So, everyone ate before they died, but the meals were all different. Everyone had the same black leather collar around their neck. Each one had a white rose in their vagina. Every one was cleaned with bleach. He even brushed the last victim's teeth with bleach, why? The M.E.'s test for semen in the stomach was negative. Why did he only polish the last victim's nails? What is the significance of the rose? Why a white one? Feel free to answer me now." She steps to the side of the board, so I can see all of her notes.

"I was waiting for you to come up for air. The white rose, historically, is a symbol for purity and innocence. It dates back to the Duke of York and the War of Roses." She cocks her head and lifts her eyes in shock. "Yeah, I'm not an authority on roses, Wikipedia is a Godsend. Anyway, playing on the purity angle, bleach to kill the crime scene or to purify? None of the girls had semen in their stomachs, but maybe since the last girl's teeth were brushed, he took it a step further. I'm thinking maybe Sophia gave him a blow job."

27

"Could be both. Did you check Wiki for all the meanings behind bleach?" She finally sits down but her eyes never leave the whiteboard.

"Actually, I did, but I won't bore you with it. The oxygen bleach erases all traces of blood. The bastard knows his shit. Can you have your tech check the FBI database and see if there are any similar cases in other states or even other countries?"

"Sure, now that a pattern has formed, I can narrow the search within the parameters that we have. The rose should help narrow it down even further. A white rose seems like a unique calling card."

I stare at the whiteboard, and something is bugging me. Finally, it hits me. "Nail polish."

"What about it?"

I turn the computer screen toward her. "Look, only the last victim had polish on her nails. Why? Gail is going to try some technique to lift prints from under the polish. I don't think she will find anything. I mean, let's face it; the guy brushes their teeth with bleach."

"So, then, why polish her nails?"

"Hold on, Al, pull up the scans from each of the girls' apartments. Now, only put the pictures up from the scene around each body."

"You want the long shot?"

"Yeah." I'm looking back and forth between the three and it hits me. "Do you see it?"

"See what, Fitz? They look exactly the same."

"Yeah, very neat and very clean. Almost like everything has a place. Extremely organized, even in the placement of the bodies. Gail said Sophia's place was so clean that there wasn't even a dust bunny. He's doing the cleaning, not the victims."

I grab my phone and begin to dial Gail, but I freeze as something in one of the pictures catches my eye. "Al, zoom in on the second victim's night stand." *Fuck!* I point to the yellow band on the nightstand, "There's the connection. She was a guest at Mystik."

I finish dialing Gail and put her on speaker. "Hey, Gail, you're on speaker; my partner, Alfie Shaw, is here. Were you able to get anything off the nail polish?"

"No, there was nothing."

"A dollar says the polish underneath was chipped."

"Yeah, what are you, psychic now, Fitz?"

"No, I told you our guy is extremely OCD. The bodies were all placed the same way. It looks like he cleaned their place after he killed them."

"If he is so OCD, then why is the third rose a different size? And, since when do you have a partner?"

"Maybe because the third victim is much smaller than the other two. I'm not sure we'll know that answer until we find him. I wasn't given a choice; FBI wants in on this one, so now I have a partner."

"I uploaded the final report for you. If you need anything else, call me. Good luck, Alfie, you're going to need it."

"Thank you, Gail, but I think I will be just fine."

"Hey, Fitz, does she have a car?" She laughs.

"Goodbye, Gail."

Al is staring at me wide-eyed. "What?"

"You don't have a car? How do you get around?"

"I take the train or I walk. If you lived in New York City, you would understand why. Let's get started on the footage from Mystik. I want to see if we can see any of the victims on there."

"Okay, you set it up and I will get the coffee. You want anything?"

"Yeah, coffee regular and grab me a bagel, please."

She gets up to leave, and I can't stop myself from watching her hips sway. Damn, her ebony skin and hazel eyes are a major distraction. She looks back and smiles, probably feeling my eyes watching her every move. I quickly avert my gaze and set up the footage, the whole time thinking how fucked I am with this one.

After spending hours going through endless videos, we came up with nothing. The videos mainly focused on exits, the main entrance, and the back offices. I really wanted to believe MJ was right; Sophia just picked it up randomly along the way. Maybe I'm looking for a connection that doesn't exist. As much as I would love to believe that, the second victim did have the bracelet. There are only the guest profiles left, so I send Al home, assuring her if I come up with anything, I will let her know. I open the next file which has all the guest profiles and release forms scanned in alphabetical order. I know the second victim had the yellow bracelet, so I load her picture into the file and do a facial recognition search to look for a match.

Sure enough, her profile picture is there, under a fake name. I cross reference it with the member that brought her and it's bogus. The member's profile puts his name as Lex Luther. *Really?* Is this some kind of taunt for me? For Christ's sake, that's Superman's archenemy. I run the guy's picture through Google images and find those models you see in generic picture frames. This guy was able to upload the bogus file to Mystik's computer system, how?

There are hundreds of guest files, and even though she didn't have the yellow band, I have to keep checking. I upload the first victim's photo, no matches. Now, I upload Sophia's picture, and there is a match. I find her guest information, which is also a fake. I gather everything, grabbing my phone as I head out the door.

When I call MJ's cell, it goes right to voicemail. I call her at the club, but they tell me she is on her way to Andy's house. Perfect, I want to talk to both of them. I call Andy, and he picks up on the first ring. "Hey, Fitz, you in town?"

"Yeah, I'm heading to the train now. I called MJ; she is on her way to your place. There is a problem, and I need to speak to both of you. I'll see you in thirty."

"What happened?"

"My train is here; I'll see you soon." I hang up, not waiting for a response. This is not something that I want to talk about over the phone. Two out of the three are confirmed; it's no coincidence. I put my ear buds in and hop on the train. At this time of night, it's not so bad.

CHAPTER FOUR

Makenna Justice

SHOWING FITZ THAT TAPE WAS one of the hardest things I've ever had to do. We have been best friends since we were kids. I've always wanted more with him, but he's always treated me like his little sister. After today, seeing the look of pity that crossed his face, I know nothing will ever be the same. He asked me why. How do I explain it? It was never my choice. I just became so overwhelmed with everything: life, Andy's illness, my parent's constant need for me to help them. *Makenna this and Makenna that, Makenna can handle it all.*

Every day I found myself having to become stronger. Slowly, I began drowning in everyone's need for me to carry his or her load in life. My strength for them became my weakness. Then one night, I met him and that night changed my life. I found an outlet for all my pent up frustration. A place for me to just be me: Makenna Justice. No one's savior, no one's helper, just me: a woman waiting for a love that I know will never happen. After that night, I knew there was no turning back. I didn't have to feel or even think for myself anymore. I was in too deep; there was no way out. Now, the lifestyle has become a drug—my drug of choice. One that lets me forget *him*

. . . at least for a little while.

I need to see my brother; I have to tell him that Fitz knows everything. Secrets never really stay buried, do they? They always seem to rise to the top. I grab my keys and let my club manager know that I'm leaving for the night. When I open the back door to the club, a blast of hot, humid air hits me. *Ugh, New York City in August.* Even though my car is parked in the alley, the shade doesn't help it cool off any quicker. It's not until I get to the tunnel that I feel some sort of relief.

The ride from the club to my brother's house is eleven miles and my GPS says it's supposed to take twenty-seven minutes. By New York City standards, that calculates to, at least, an hour. Just once, I wish that bitch inside my GPS was actually driving my car so she could see it's not twenty-seven fucking minutes. I only turn it on so I can see the traffic reports, not that it matters, since everything is bumper to bumper.

I finally get through the tunnel and it's clear sailing. I shut the GPS off and lose myself in my music. How fitting, The Veronicas sing "You Ruin Me." I wipe away my tears as I pull up to my brother's brownstone in Bay Ridge. Thankfully, the parking gods are with me today.

I love Andy's home. He restored the old brownstone back to its original splendor, even down to the butler's pantry off the kitchen. He created a master bedroom with an ensuite. The main floor has the kitchen, living room, dining room, and a small powder room. The guest rooms and full bath are upstairs. He paid a lot of attention to all the little details that makes this house a real home. In the main bathroom, he was even able to save the original claw foot tub. Restoring it gave him purpose.

Before I reach for the front door knob, Stephen, my brother's husband, steps out. "What's the problem now?" I hug him and he holds it a little longer than usual. I finally pull away, and he squeezes my hand.

"He's not having a good day. Fitz called. He said there's a problem, and he's on his way. I know you tell Andy everything, but if it's bad, you might want to think about sugarcoating it a bit."

Rolling my eyes at the idea of me, sugarcoating, I offer him a soft smile. "I'll try."

He looks up to the heavens, probably for some sort of divine intervention. "Oh, why do I bother?" he grumbles under his breath, opens the door, and ushers me in.

I get into the kitchen and find Andy setting stuff up to grill. I take a moment and notice how tired he is, moving a lot slower than usual. Christ, if this nut is getting his victims from our club, this will really hit him hard. I know why he purchased the club; it's just another weight on my shoulders.

"I know you're there lurking, MJ. What is the problem that Fitz wants to talk about? I know you know, so just spill." Before I can answer, the buzzer sounds.

"Finish getting everything ready, I'll let Fitz in." I don't give Andy a chance to answer; I head into the hall and hit the button, releasing the door latch. Fitz is dragging his ass up the steps and when he gets closer, I notice the dark circles under his eyes. Before I can say a word, Andy is pushing me out of the way.

"What the hell took you so long to get here? You look like shit. Are you ever going to get a car? What the fuck is going on? Why didn't you use your key?"

"Hello to you, too, Andy. I need a shower first, and then we'll talk." He pushes his way past us without another word, waving hello to Stephen as he heads upstairs to the bathroom.

Andy glares at me. "What the fuck are you hiding from me? He looks really bad. I'm worried, MJ. It can't be work; he never talks to us about it. Is he sick?"

Stephen takes all the food and heads out back to start grilling. I squeeze Andy's shoulder. "Listen, I only know part of the story. Wait till he can fill us both in on everything he knows, please."

He grabs me and hugs me tightly, then pulls back and kisses my forehead. "Fine, I can wait."

I wish I could, but the look on Fitz's face was very grim. "Why don't you help Stephen with the grill so everything doesn't get burnt?"

He laughs. "Yes, my wonderful husband can't cook to save his life. I'll meet you outside; you can get the beers from the fridge."

He heads out and I grab two beers, making my way upstairs to the bathroom. I hear the water still running, so I head into the bathroom and take a seat on the edge of the tub. Since we were kids, Fitz has never locked the bathroom door. It's a real fear that he lives with every day. I don't know why; no one would ever tell me. Just another facet of this tortured man. The bathroom is full of steam, and I swear he takes longer than a girl. He finally shuts the water and swings open the shower curtain.

"Jesus Christ, MJ, you could give me a little privacy." His hands instantly try to cover his goods. I toss a towel at him.

Fitz has a Superman tat on his right hip. "I see you got your tat freshened up; it looks good. Relax, it's not like I haven't seen what you've got." I smirk. He towels off and then wraps it around his waist. He sits on the edge of the claw foot tub and takes his beer. If I had a penny for every time I wished I was this close to his naked body, I'd be a millionaire.

"Stephen is worried about Andy and what we tell him tonight might do to his health. I told him I would try to *sugarcoat it* a bit," I inform him. He cocks his head to the side and raises his eyes before taking another long pull on his beer. "I told him I would *try*," I emphasize. He puts his arm around me, pulling me closer to his bare chest. My heart flutters and I have to fight to keep my breathing under control. If I tilt my head, ever-so-slightly, my lips would be on his chest. A place they usually land only in my dreams.

"I won't pull any punches. Even though there are still more guest profiles to go through, it looks like there is a connection to the club. We need to keep Andy in the loop, but, MJ, if you think it gets to be too much for him, just give me some sort of sign. The last thing I want is Andy to get worse over all of this. I know that stress can aggravate his PD and I don't want to be the cause of that."

As much as I don't want to pull out of his embrace, I know I have to or this won't end well. I get up and head toward the door. "Get dressed, dinner is almost ready." I leave, not giving him a chance to answer and head into the kitchen to get the beer Andy wanted.

FITZ

I know she is stressed about all of this, but something is off with her, more so than usual. Maybe it has to do with the video she had me watch today. I don't think any less of her; we all need what we need to make it through the day. I only wish I could understand *why*.

I wish for a lot of things, but there are certain things I just can't risk. Family is one of them. I pick my clothes up off the floor, thankful that even though I only live around the corner, I've always kept a change here. I throw on my shorts and t-shirt and head out back.

The smell is wonderful and makes my stomach rumble. I realize the only thing I had to eat all day was a bagel. Andy is working the grill which means dinner won't be charred. I grab another beer, have a seat next to Stephen, and finally try to relax.

"Fitz, he's not having a good day physically, please keep that in mind." Stephen always puts Andy's well-being first, he loves him that much. Andy is lucky that he found someone as special as Stephen. Not everyone can handle the day-to-day life of someone who is ill. Once Andy was diagnosed with Parkinson's, Stephen insisted they get married. He wanted to make sure he could take care of Andy in every way.

"Don't worry, I will tread lightly. However, he does need to know what's going on."

Before he can answer, Andy comes over with a huge tray filled with steaks, ribs, chicken, and sausage. MJ passes me the salad, and my only focus right now is food. "What were you expecting, an army?"

He says grace and then begins piling meat on my plate faster than I can eat any of it. "I know what you're like when you are working a case. You forget to eat for days on end. I'm making sure you stay nourished. You're in that quiet, deep-thought mode, so apparently, you've been put on another case. You just finished one. Why did they put you right back out there again?"

"The kills are coming fast on this one and they don't want to send the city into a panic like when the Son of Sam killer was on the loose. I'm trying to keep the press away from this as much as possible, though I'm not sure how long that will last."

I start tackling all the food on my dish, grateful for the silence. I finally feel myself relax, and when I come up for air, my plate is clear.

"So, Fitz, now that you've finally eaten, you want to tell us what the problem is?"

I glance over at MJ, but she quickly looks away. "There have been three murders in the city, and it looks like there might be a link to Mystik. Right before I left the station, I confirmed that two of the victims were guests of the club. Their profiles were bogus, along with the member that brought them. My partner is running the guy's MO through the FBI's database to see if she gets any hits. The last victim had a pen from the club. The second victim had the yellow guest band, so there is a connection," I spell it out. MJ gets up and gets another beer. Her back is toward us, but I know she is rattled and probably doesn't want Andy to see it. I turn my focus back to him. "Andy, I was hoping that the pen was just a fluke, but then I found the bracelet. Right before I came here, I found the fake profiles. I don't know how he was able to upload it into the system. I'm going to have the FBI's tech check into it. I know there is a connection, now I need to dissect it all, so I can figure out how to stop him."

Andy is a lot calmer than I expected him to be. "Tell me how I can help?"

"My partner and I need full access to the club, not just the files and the computer. I want us to basically take up residence there." I push my plate away, unable to eat another bite. Before Andy can answer, MJ spins around so quickly, she drops her beer bottle. Stephen rushes to clean it up while MJ stands frozen in place.

"Partner, full access, what the fuck, Fitz? I warned you that your *big plan* wouldn't work and now you want to subject your partner to the same thing I'm trying to keep you away from?! Since when do you have a partner?"

I jump up, my face inches from hers. "MJ, I told you this was a possibility. What the fuck is your problem? I'm trying to stop a killer, and I don't give a royal fuck if it inconveniences you. Bottom line: I need in, and I need it now, Goddammit! Someone was able to access your computer system. Did you stop to think that person might work for you? Maybe you're in his fucking crosshairs, MJ. All of this has been happening right under your nose!"

"Fitz—"

"MJ, you are not going to win this one; just stop, right now," I bark. She quickly turns and storms into the house. This is far from over, and as I chase after her, I hear Andy tell Stephen to stay out of it. I catch up to her and slam my hand against the front door, just as she is about to open it.

"Fitz, so help me God, you better let me out of here, right now!" She's pounding on the door, and her skin is as flushed as her beautiful, red hair.

"Not until we hash this out, so untwist your damn panties and talk to me—*now*!"

She stops and her whole body begins to shake. I can handle anything except MJ crying; her tears are my weakness, like Superman's kryptonite. I spin her around, lift her up, and take her into the guest bedroom. I haven't seen her this upset since her cat, Bubba, got hit by a car. I hold her and rock her until she finally calms down.

"Now, do you want to tell me what the hell is up with you? What am I missing here, MJ?"

She begins wiping my shirt. "I got mascara all over your shirt."

I take her hand in mine, and I lift her chin so I can see her beautiful, green eyes. "I don't give a shit about the shirt; talk to me, *now*."

"If I give you unfettered access to the club, then you will be there all the time. The same way you couldn't take seeing me with that Dom, I won't be able to take seeing you with anyone."

I'm looking in her eyes, trying to figure out what she is trying to tell me, without telling me. Oh shit, no *fucking way*. It hits me like a brick and I gasp. I can't seem to catch my breath. My chest is tight, and I think I'm having a heart attack.

"I have loved you from the first day my brother brought you home. I tried to tell you over and over again, but you blew me off. I really thought the night you took me to my prom, I might have a chance, but you've only ever seen me as Andy's little sister. I'm not that little girl anymore, Fitzy. I'm a woman, and I'm in love with you. I have been for a very long time."

I jump off the bed, and she nearly topples to the floor. I'm pacing around the room like a caged animal. How could this be? What fucking planet have I been on? "When did this happen?" Oh, that was a stupid question.

"Really, Fitz, you need to know when? Well, if you must know, I was five years old, and I came home from school crying. You found out that Johnny Fazzio made fun of my red hair. You went to his house, rang the bell, and when his mom answered, you told her you were sorry. She asked you why, and you told her that you were going to have to punch her son in the face, and you wanted to apologize. She asked you why you felt you needed to punch Johnny, and you told her what he did. She dragged his ass across the street to our house and made him apologize to me. After that, he never called me another name. No one ever bullied me again. I fell in love with you that day. My hero, coming in to save the day. You've been my hero ever since."

I'm in total shock. How could this be? "You were five years old, and I stopped a bully from calling you names. You can't love me, MJ. I'm a jaded man, not good enough for you. I never was. You deserve someone who is going to make you happy. I can't be that man." I grab my stuff and storm out the door without giving her a chance to respond.

CHAPTER FIVE

Mark

WHEN I CLOSE MY EYES, I can still smell her sweetness. The sweet scent of the rose mixed with the crisp smell of bleach. I always leave a white rose for them to take on their journey. Whether it is to heaven or hell, I don't give a fuck. Sophia: such a sweet name and a sweet girl. I relive the events, and I feel my blood begin to heat up my body. I close my eyes and remember getting her to the point that she couldn't take anymore, when she was about to pass out. That's when I feel it, the beauty of her falling from extreme pleasure into deep fear. My balls tighten and my blood surges, finally allowing my body the release it craves. I reach over and grab some tissues off the nightstand to clean up my mess.

Three this month, alone—even for me—that's a lot. I'm so glad I found Mystik; it's like a candy store for someone like me. I didn't meet Sophia there, but she was intrigued when I took her there for a date. Some women are always looking for something or someone to take them further, past their self-imposed limitations. At least, now that I found Mystik, it might make it easier for me. I can't get too comfortable there, that's how things can go wrong. Especially, if

41

I'm going to have my ultimate prize.

I climb out of bed and head into the shower; my mind keeps reliving the thrill. I turn the water on as hot as I can stand it and step in. The water hitting my skin sets my nerve endings on fire. I turn and let the water pulse on my cock. I need to get off again, or I'll never make it through the day.

I close my eyes and pump my cock slow, at first, twisting and pumping just the way I like it. In my mind, I hear her crying and begging for her life. All of their cries blend together as one. Sophia's plea was so beautiful, like the song of an angel. It's barely a whisper as my hands tighten around her neck. I feel chills running up and down my spin. My hand closes even tighter around her throat, cutting off her air supply. I'm almost there, pumping hard, ready to explode.

I hear a knock on the door, "Mark, your breakfast is getting cold."

"I'll be right out." *Fuck,* go away; I can't lose it. I'm so close. *Pump harder, faster,* I tell myself repeatedly. I close my eyes and remember her heart pounding, the fear that overtook her. I reach down and squeeze my balls. I finally come, rivulets shooting everywhere. I flip the switch to cold, trying to cool off my nerve endings.

Slowly, my racing heart begins the calm down as my mind comes back to the real world, not the one I want to live in, but the one I have to live in. I step out of the shower and continue to get ready for work. I keep myself very fit and trim. I know I have the looks, however, I try not to draw too much attention, just enough to intrigue. I step into my walk-in closest, which, by New York City standards, is huge, and decide on the darkest navy suit I own—my power suit. I feel it today, the after effects of the thrill of the kill… *Beautiful.*

I head into the kitchen to get my post-workout shake. My workout this morning being the whack off I gave myself in the shower.

My wife is getting ready to send Mason off to school. He is in a private school for gifted children. When he's not in school, he's in soccer camp, anything to keep the kid busy. Fifteen minutes tops and I'm out of here, which makes me smile. "Good morning, everyone."

"Mark, I don't know what took you so long, but your eggs got cold. I threw them away. Don't forget Mason has a soccer game today. Will you be able to take him?" She is more sarcastic than usual.

"Of course, dear, what time do I need to have him there?" I smile, trying not to give way to the simmering hatred that has been growing on a daily basis.

"The game starts at four-thirty, so you need to have him at the field by four."

"Okay, I need to run if I'm going to leave work early. Mason, I will pick you up at three-thirty." I make a show of kissing him goodbye and head toward the door as quickly as possible.

"Mark, did you forget something?" *I didn't forget, I just don't want to.*

"I'm sorry, Nicole. Please, *love*, forgive me." I hurry back into the kitchen and kiss her goodbye. Before she can say anything more, I grab my gym bag from the hall closet and run out the door.

Summer in New York City is horribly humid; they don't call this the concrete jungle for nothing. I walk just about everywhere, or take the train. I took a chance sharing a cab with Sophia; I couldn't resist, but it will never happen again. I need to have more control.

I don't know what happened with her. She intrigued and captivated me. Sadly, that was short-lived, and then I had to snap her sweet, tiny neck. After all, she wasn't *the one.*

I can't think about that right now; I have to stay focused on work. If I don't make my clients a lot of money, then I can't keep up my lifestyle. I have my Series 3 and my Series 7 license, but I only trade commodities. I also have my Master's Degree in Computer Science, which is coming in quite handy, but it's trading that I love. It's hard and fast paced, exactly what I need.

I head downtown toward the Mercantile Exchange, trying to stay focused on work. When I'm in the trading pit, I need to have only the trading in my head. If I make an error, it will cost me money, and, ultimately, my job. Last night gave me the fuel I need to deal with today. Lately, I'm finding that I need to kill more often to keep that level of intensity I need to have at work.

If I could keep them for a while, I wouldn't have to kill them so quickly. I would love to find a place that I could keep the girls longer than just one night. Actually, there's only one girl in particular: Ms. Justice, the girl with the flaming, red hair. Her face is like an angel, and her eyes sparkle like emeralds. I found her by accident, one day at the gym, and from there, I followed her to Mystik.

Who would have thought such an angelic looking girl would be the owner of a club like that. I really need to find a place for us, where I can keep her all for myself. In this day and age, anyone can find you, if they try. It's hard to find someone that will let you rent an apartment without any paperwork. I don't want to waste the documents I had made just for an apartment, but if needed, I can make more.

Maybe I can find an apartment in one of the boroughs . . . something in a private house for rent. After all—cash is king. I feel excited and renewed as I head into the exchange, ready to take on a new day.

My day is progressing along nicely; the markets are on a steady upswing. When I finally have a break, I pull up one of the many online classified web pages that's available. It always amazes me what some people will put on there. There is way too much personal information online. People don't realize how dangerous it can be. I laugh at that thought: me, worrying about danger.

I need to find a place, but it's hard; my needs are specific. There are a few possible ones in Brooklyn. My first two kills lived there, but those were in different sections than I'm looking in now. I've only been in New York City for two months, so I would have to do a lot more research before I jumped on some of these. However, the thought of keeping her locked up for my own personal use makes my cock throb. I close my eyes and try to gain control.

I have to be in control; it's how I survive. Getting a hard-on at work is not control. With my eyes closed, I take a few deep breaths and resist the urge to stroke myself. I open my eyes. I look at the time and realize I need to leave if I'm going to get the kid to his game on time. I gather up my stuff and quickly head out to pick up Mason from school.

If Nicole wants a mother of the year award, then she should be running the kid to all his activities. Anyone looking at us would think we are the perfect family. We both have very successful careers and a perfect child. Looks can be deceiving, that's for sure. My wife is a bitch and my son is a spoiled brat. Nicole's way of dealing with him is to not deal with him; the nanny deals with everything. She buys him whatever he wants to shut him up.

Now that she made junior partner at her firm, she has even less time for Mason. I'm only there to service her when she decides she is in need. Lately, it's become less and less, which is fine by me. She is becoming more domineering with each passing day. I'm not her submissive, no matter how hard she tries.

CHAPTER SIX

Andy

STEPHEN HATES ANY KIND OF confrontation; he avoids it like the plague. The fact that it's MJ and Fitz makes it even worse. There is an awful lot of yelling, banging, and now, silence. "Stephen, why don't you start cleaning up, and I will see who is left standing."

He gets up and starts the task, all the while, talking under his breath. "I, for one, hope she finally told him." If I'd let him, he would have blabbed it all to Fitz years ago. He's still muttering away as I go assess the damage.

I finally find MJ in the guest bedroom, curled in a ball, crying, and Fitz is nowhere to be found. I crawl into bed, open my arms, and she crawls into them. "Did you finally tell him?" She doesn't answer, only a slight nod. I push her hair from her face. "I gather he didn't take it well." Again, nothing but a nod. "Eventually, you will have to tell me what happened. Look you know how clueless he is, or maybe he just wants to be."

She finally stops crying and pulls away from me. "He freaked out, grabbed his stuff off the dresser, and ran out the door."

I wipe away what's left of the mascara running down her cheek.

46

"You stay here with Stephen; promise me you will spend the night. I don't want you driving home upset and alone. I'll go find Fitz." I look up and Stephen is waiting in the doorway. He puts a cup of tea on the nightstand and climbs into bed.

"Go, Andy, I've got this. MJ, your brother will find him, and if he doesn't kick his ass, I will."

I leave my sister, knowing she is in good hands, and head out to do some damage control.

Fitz

I walk down the block and head toward home, thankful that I don't live too far away. What the ever-loving fuck is she thinking? In love with me, why? I can't wrap my mind around this. She is so beautiful, kind, and gentle. When she's not squeezing the life out of my balls. Why would she love me? I round the corner, and I see Andy sitting on the stoop. "How the fuck did you get here before me?"

"Asshole, I took our shortcut through the alley, and you're the slowest cop on the force."

"I might be slow, but at least I'm a deadeye shot." I need answers and only he can give them to me. "Did you know?" He looks down, almost embarrassed to answer me. When he looks up, I snap and punch him in the jaw. "What the fuck is wrong with you? Why didn't you tell me? How long have you known? Why tell me now? Fuck . . . Andy, fuck, just fuck!"

He's rubbing his jaw and now I feel bad. "Are you done with your rant? Or do you want to take another swing at me?" he asks. I wave my hand at him to continue and I sit on the stoop, next to him. "What exactly did she tell you?" He gives his jaw one final rub and lets his hand fall from his face. I close my eyes and lean back, retelling him the whole story.

"I knew as a kid she had a crush on you, but I blew it off. When her prom date stood her up, and you stepped in to save the day, I realized it was more than a crush. I told her to move on, and honestly, I thought she did. Then, I found out about the club and the man that introduced her to the lifestyle. I realized it was her outlet for a lot of pent up feelings."

My eyes fly open at the realization that this club was not Andy's idea. I hold my hand up. "Wait, hold up, I thought you purchased the club, that it was initially your idea? I honestly thought when you got sick, she took over as a manager or something."

"It was my idea, but not for the reasons you thought. Look, Fitz, she was going to that place every night. The guy was hardcore, and I wanted him away from my sister. I mortgaged my home and my parent's home to the hilt to buy the club. Essentially, I paid him to go away. I was the sole owner of Mystik.

"I felt I could put some key people in place and keep a close eye on her. I was never going to keep it for very long. I thought maybe I could get her away from there, and then eventually, I'd sell the place. It all sounded good, until I got sick; that was the game changer. If I didn't get the club out of my name, my medical cost would have put us all out on the street.

"I did a quick deed with a title transfer. Stephen's law firm handled the entire thing. Honestly, with nothing in my name, I'm able to get some sort of assistance with the rising medical cost. I didn't know what else to do; MJ is now the sole owner of the club. About six months ago, she was at the house and got pretty wasted. Stephen put her to bed, but not before she confessed everything about how much she still loves you and always will. When Stephen told me, I knew I had to confront her. She was drunk and said some pretty hurtful stuff," his voice trails off and he rubs his eyes.

"She said she hated me for finding you and bringing you home.

She accused me of being more concerned with saving you than saving her from a world of heartache. That broke my heart. I know she didn't really mean it, but it still hurt all the same. I don't know what to do for her. It's like she is going though the motions of life, just not living it."

I'm stunned, but looking back, not really. My heart has feelings that I won't let my head believe. Why believe them when they could never be? I'm damaged goods. "Why the hell didn't you tell me any of this? You know I would give you everything I have."

He grabs my arm, "Don't you think I know that? It's a lot of money, more than your pay can handle. I know it's rare that PD has struck me at such a young age but please understand it's my sickness, my problem to deal with. I'm a proud man, and so much has already been taken away from me.

"You've never made me feel like less than a man, even when I had to stop driving. I have to feel like I haven't totally given up my man card altogether. It's hard to explain to a healthy person, what it feels like when your head says yes, but your body is laughing at you. Besides, if I told you about her feelings and you'd acted upon it, she would wonder why, maybe we all would."

I keep trying to wrap my mind around all of this but finding it difficult. "Why didn't you tell me about MJ and the guy that started this all?"

He looks down, almost as if he's embarrassed to answer me. "She begged me not to, and honestly, I really didn't think I would keep the club very long. Sadly now, we don't have a choice. My medical costs are literally out of control. I do get some money from disability, but that really doesn't cover much. The money from the club pays a large portion of my medical expenses that are not covered by insurance. I'm a young guy and I want to live. Stephen is working so much, trying to help me cope with all the expenses. It's a terrible burden that I don't want to put on anyone else."

"Andy, we're brothers—maybe not by blood, but in my mind— that doesn't matter. It's *never* mattered." This is so fucked up; I don't know where to begin. "How much of this do your parent's really know?"

His eyes grow wide with fear. "Oh, dear God, nothing. Mom and Dad think it's a place that helps keep kids off the streets. You know, like a social club of sorts. Please, Fitz, I'm begging you, don't say anything to them."

"Do Mom and Dad know what MJ told me tonight?" I can't even bring myself to say it.

"Knowing Mom, probably, but again, what could she say? As far as Dad is concerned, I'm not sure. My relationship with him has always been strained. Hell, you have more of a relationship with him than I do."

"That's only because we have the job in common. Since he was shot, he's closed himself off from everyone, Andy, even me."

"Fitz, now that you know everything, what are you going to do?"

My head is spinning, I need out. I get up. "Go home, Andy."

He jumps up and grabs my shirt. "That's it: *just go home, Andy*?"

"Yeah, I need to go for a ride and process all of this. Go home and make sure she's okay. I'll talk to you tomorrow." I smack him on the back and walk over to Wanda. Yeah, my bike has a name. I named her after the character "Weeping Wanda" from an old television show. The character could cry at the drop of a dime. My hog, on the other hand, won't make women cry, but after a ride on her, they will need new panties. I hop on, not giving him a chance to answer; I need time. I watch Andy cut back through the alley before I start my hog I head out. Traffic is light, which is great. I don't look back. I can't. Doing so will only bring me a world of pain and regret.

Andy

I get in the door, and Stephen is waiting for me. "How is she?"

He pulls me into a much-needed hug. "She's finally asleep; how are you? What the fuck happened to your face? Did you find him? Why do I even bother to ask, of course you *found* him."

I finally let go of him and head to the kitchen for a drink. "Let's go up to bed, and I'll tell you everything." I grab an ice pack and a couple of bottles of water and follow him up the steps. After a quick shower, I climb into bed. I know he's worried about me, but I'm more worried about MJ. He hands me the ice pack, and I give him the run down on everything that happened.

"So he hit you because you knew and didn't tell him? Well, that was the adult thing to do, now wasn't it? Putting aside the fact that I'm your husband, I'm also the attorney for this family. That being said, you have a bigger problem than Makenna's love life. There is a serial killer, and he has the club in his sights, which means Makenna could be on his radar."

I feel my chest tighten, and I grab Stephen's arm. "Ah, oh no, I was so busy worrying about her heart that I overlooked her safety. What should we do?" I ask, my fear escalating. He rests his forehead on mine, and I close my eyes. He tenderly kisses me, and I thank my lucky stars for him.

"Look at me, Andy," he urges. My eyes open and find his. "We will get through this and keep her safe, I promise. You know the effect stress has on your health. I won't have you getting worse because of this."

"I know, let's get some sleep." I toss the ice pack down, and he wraps his arms around me. He holds me and gently strokes my back, reassuring me that she will be okay. I only wish I believed him.

FITZ

I've been driving for hours, and I find myself zipping along on the thruway toward Albany. I decide to get off exit 20 for gas and see a Howard Johnson's. I'm tired and I need to think, maybe even get some sleep.

The room is clean, but sleep never comes, my thoughts are all over the place. Have I been so removed from life that I can't even see what is right in front of my face? I've had feelings for her; who am I kidding? I love her. I have always loved her, but I forced myself not to go down that road. All these years I believed if I did, I would lose the little bit of stability I had left, the family I'd craved so much. And now, my fear of losing them might have cost me someone I hold so dear.

Since I was six, I have lived with the horrors of the world. When I became a cop, I thought if I kept everyone at a distance, I would be protecting them from all that evil. All it did was create an unwanted distance between us and now Makenna could be in danger because of it. If I had done things differently, and not let fear take center stage, she would have never been in that club.

I head to the shower and turn the cold water on full blast. The stinging pain is a shock on my skin and something I need. My body needs sleep, but I know my mind will never shut off. Why waste my time? I'd rather drive. I get dressed and head to the office, dropping the keys in the express check out.

I know this area very well. In the winter, Andy and I would come up and go skiing on Hunter Mountain. In the summer, we came up for the festivals and county fairs. If only I could turn back the hands of time and know what I know now.

I get gas, pop my headset on, and take the back road up the mountain. It's very scenic but also very dangerous. There are no guardrails and the road is very twisted, kind of like how this whole situation feels. Funny how some songs just happens to come on at just the right moment. "The Mess I Made" by Parachute is blaring in my ears, and when I get to Kaaterskill Falls, I open it up. The sun rises just as I reach the top. The view is breathtakingly beautiful, like living inside a Thomas Kincaid painting. I pull over, cutting the engine to take it all in.

I need this time to think and process everything. My first priority is to catch this killer, and then, I need to get her out of that club. Was she in there because of me? Was I her catalyst like she is mine? I finally faced the fact a long time ago that I became a cop because of her.

Since she was five, I've wanted to be her hero, coming in to save the day. I couldn't save my mom, but I vowed I would always protect Makenna. My hand instantly rubs my tat, remembering the day I got it, the night of her prom. She never knew that I'd made sure her date wouldn't show up that night.

Her days at that club are over, but am I ready to let her know my feelings for her? Do I have the guts to risk it all? I honestly don't know. What I do know is that time is not my friend. I need to get home, and I need to check in with Al. I have a plan. No one will like it, but that's just too fucking bad.

I start Wanda up and make my descent around the winding curves down the mountain. The long drive gives me the time I need to think my plan through before I tell everyone.

CHAPTER SEVEN

Mark

I LEAVE THE HOUSE THREE hours before I need to be at work. I told the bitch I needed to go in early to bust a trade. She was more worried about getting the brat off to school. I don't know why since the nanny always does and today was no different.

I head downtown to catch the East River Ferry. I need to time this perfectly if this is going to work. I did some research last night and it looks like the Dumbo section in Brooklyn is going to be a great fit. I have a few apartments to look at. My biggest concern is privacy. One boasts no neighbors on either side. I run through my list of everything I will need to have in order for this to work.

I spent hours on line last night figuring out how to soundproof a room. I'm not a carpenter, but it didn't look too complicated. When I get to the first apartment, I don't even bother to go in. There are way too many prying eyes.

I don't have time to waste, so I head over to the next one. This one has a private garage, not that I have a car, but I can store a lot of tools and stuff in there. A little cottage type house, the garage is attached. *Perfect.* The owner is a widow, and with enough flirting, she accepts my cash only offer. I make her day when I offer to pay the first six months in advance. She probably thinks she won the lottery; she should only know. I show her a fake driver's license with the name Mark Daniels and inform her that my hobby is building stuff so she doesn't panic or snoop when the supplies are being delivered. I let her know that I will be using the garage as a workshop, since I don't have a car. She doesn't care, since the only thing she has in there is a large freezer.

I get everything squared away with her and head to work with a renewed vigor. I love it when a plan comes together. It's the thrill of the hunt, the build up to the kill that excites me the most. I could keep finding different women (hell, they are a dime a dozen), but they're not *her*. Besides, the more I kill, the greater my chance of getting caught. Like trading, it's a numbers game, and I need the numbers to be in my favor.

Before I know it, I find myself back on the ferry. This really isn't that bad of a trip. I pick up the *Post* from the bench next to me, and I check every page: nothing. Haven't they figured out that it's the work of one man? Even in the crime blotter, there's no mention of the murders. I really thought this city would be more on top of things.

I'm amazed that I accomplished so much this morning and am able get to work with time to spare. After getting another coffee, I begin the process of setting up an account with a hardware store. I have numerous fake identifications, the benefits of higher education.

By noon, everything is arranged, and I'm getting same day delivery. As much as I would love to find someone new right now, I need to take a little break while I get the house set up. I must have everything perfect for her. After all, she is the ultimate prize. I have a new sense of excitement as I head into the trading pit to finish out the day.

Makenna

The early morning sun is peaking though the blinds. The realization that I finally told Fitz how I feel hits me like a rock, turning my stomach. I barely make it to the bathroom and heave. How can I ever face him again? I curl up in a ball on the cold tile floor and cry. "Oh, dear God, what have I done?"

"You told him what's been bottled up in your heart for the past twenty-five years." My eyes fly open at the sound of Andy's voice.

"I didn't realize I said that out loud, or that I had company," I admit. He sits next to me and hands me a wet washcloth, and it feels good on my tear stained face. He doesn't say anything; his face etched with pain, my pain. "Don't you get it? Nothing will ever be the same. I probably lost my best friend, all because I couldn't keep my mouth shut! What happened when you went after him?"

He rubs his jaw. "He punched me in the face."

I instantly remember that little boy coming to my rescue, my hero. I begin to laugh and I can't stop. My laughter quickly turns to tears again. "Oh, Andy, what should I do now?"

He pulls me into his arms, holding me tightly. "First thing you will do is get your shit together. More than ever, you need to be on your guard; there is a crazy man out there. Your safety is everything."

I know where this is going, and I know I can't do it. "I can't have him in the club. I can't see him with another woman. He needs to find another way."

"MJ, he can go in as security or a bartender; we'll figure it out. Go home and get cleaned up. I'm going to meet with Fitz later, and we will come up with a plan, I promise."

"You know, you're the best brother in the world."

He kisses my forehead, "It will always be *us*, MJ."

He gets up and pulls me with him. "Get dressed. I'll make a pot of coffee and meet you in the kitchen."

He leaves and I hurry up and get dressed, then head directly toward the wonderful smell of fresh coffee. He's at the kitchen table, glued to his laptop. "I'll grab my coffee to go."

"Sit. Who else has access to the computers at the club other than us?"

I grab some coffee, and of course, he has ten different flavored creamers. "Do you really use all of these?"

"Yes, it depends upon my mood. Now, who else, MJ?"

"I have a new tech guy, but his credentials are top notch." I rub my temples, feeling a major headache coming on. He gets up and begins packing up his laptop. "Where are you going?"

"I need you to drop me off at the precinct. I have some things I need to talk to Fitz about."

I know my brother, and I know when I need to shut up and do what he wants. This is one of those times. I get up and put my cup in the sink. "Fine; let's go."

Fitz

I hate taking my bike to the precinct, but I have no choice right now. I'm not in the door two minutes, and the captain is on my ass. I hold my hand up, "I have a plan, and if you would lay off my ass, I might be able to put it in motion, *sir*. As soon as I have any kind of lead, you'll be the first to know."

He hands me a cup of coffee. "That's nice, Fitz, but what I was going to tell you is that Andy is here and Al took him upstairs.

She came back for day two, so, apparently, you haven't scared her away—yet."

I grab the coffee and grumble as I head upstairs. What the fuck is Andy doing here? I can't give him answers I don't have, and I know he's not going to like what I have to say. I get to the door and I hear the two of them laughing. Now is not the time for laughter, not when there is a killer on the loose! I need to calm down before I step into the room. They both look up when I walk in. "I see you met my partner, Al."

"Yes, turns out we both were married at the same court house on July 24, 2011, the day New York passed the Marriage Equality Act."

Well, you probably could blow me over with a feather right about now. I had no clue that Al was married. She doesn't wear a wedding ring. The room is dead silent. "Al, you'll find that when Fitz is on a case, he goes into a different zone. It's hard to explain, but it works," he informs her then brings his attention back to me, "I brought my computer in. I thought maybe your tech would want to look through it."

Al gets up and takes the computer. "Travis, our tech, arrived here today from Quantico. I'll take this to him and see how he wants to handle it. I'll give you guys some privacy." She leaves, closing the door behind her.

I take a deep breath, reining in my temper. "I don't want MJ left alone, where is she?"

"She dropped me off here, and then I sent her home. She sent me a text that she was home safe. I came here to go over some ideas I had and to drop off my computer. You look like shit. Have you slept, yet?"

"Forget about me. I have a plan, and whether you like it or not, this is what's going to happen. MJ will never go back to the club again. Al and I are the new owners of Mystik. You will do a newsletter, or however you communicate with your members, letting everyone know that Makenna Justice is taking an extended vacation abroad. She has a manager there and he will stay on; I checked him all the way back to grade school. Al will run all the office and personnel stuff that needs to be handled. I am the new floor manager." I have to keep the stress level low for Andy's health.

He gets up and begins to pace, "Are you going to tell her or do you want me to?" Before I can answer him, Al comes back. She hands Andy his computer.

"Travis said your computer is clean. I would like to take him to the club and have him check out that one, if it's okay with you?"

That works out perfect for my plan. "Al, take Travis to the club. I'll let the manager know you're on your way. I'm going to drop Andy off at MJ's and I'll meet you at the club later." I quickly fill her in on my plan before heading out the door with Andy racing behind me.

I hop on Wanda and hand Andy his helmet. He hates my bike, so I'm sure he will complain. "Look, Andy, I know you hate Wanda, but I came straight here."

"If you had a fucking car, like a normal person, I wouldn't have to have my balls vibrating for the next thirty minutes," he gripes. I laugh for the first time in days as we speed toward MJ's place.

Makenna

I love living in Brooklyn. I've lived here my whole life, and I don't see that ever changing. Every thing is within walking distance, and, if it's not—they deliver. Why would anyone live anywhere else? I have the best view of the Manhattan skyline.

I head into the shower and contemplate what the hell I'm going to do next. I still can't believe I blurted it all out to him. Of all the times to grow a set of balls, last night wasn't it. There is a crazy killer on the loose, I probably lost my best friend, and my brother is so stressed out, which will take a toll on his health. I can't walk away from the club; it's my outlet for so much pent up frustration. Truth be told, I tried moving on without Fitz in my life, but it always came back to him. That's how I ended up in that club. Have I put him so high up on a pedestal that no one will compare? I don't know how not to; he came to my rescue when I was only five, and he's been doing it ever since. When my date stood me up for my prom, he came running in the door in my father's too-big suit with a beautiful corsage, professing to be my hero. Riding in like the white knight to save me, little did he know that he would break my heart. My tears begin to fall like the water cascading all around me. I crumple to my knees, praying for some sort of strength and guidance.

I don't know how much time passed, but the water is cold, and now I hear banging. I get out of the shower, grab a towel, and head out of the bathroom. I hear my brother and Fitz yelling for me to open the door. I barely get the dead bolt unlocked and they come barreling through.

"What the hell is the problem?" Andy grabs me in a bear hug.

"I can't breathe, Andy!"

He lets go, and the look on his face is a look filled with fear. "Thank God, you're okay."

"Why wouldn't I be? I was just in the shower."

"Go get dressed; Fitz and I want to talk to you about his plan." He shuffles his hand out for me to get going. Something tells me I'm not going to like what's coming. I look back and forth between the two of them, and I know when I'm fighting a losing battle. I throw my hands up and head into my room. I emerge five minutes later, and Andy is making coffee while Fitz stares out the window.

"So, who is going to tell me what you don't really want to tell me?"

Andy hands me my coffee and orders me to sit. Fitz's phone rings and he answers. I'm not sure whom he is talking to but his answers are very curt.

"Now, MJ, hear me out before you get all crazy on me. Fitz has come up with a plan, and I think it's a good one. It will keep you safe and ultimately that's all I really care about. As of today, Fitz and his partner, Al, now own Mystik. There will be an announcement at the club and a short press release to the members. You sold the club and have decided to travel abroad. Al will take over the back office operations and Fitz will work the floor. Do you do any business from your laptop here or only from the club?" Everything he says sounds like white noise.

"I'm not giving up the club!"

Before he can answer, Fitz grabs him and pushes him toward the door. "Go for a walk, *now.*"

Andy is barely out the door, and Fitz is already up in my face. He sits on my coffee table directly across from me, his legs trapping mine. "You will do this, and you won't fight me on it. It is too dangerous for you to be in that club. He got into your fucking computer system to upload those fake member profiles, which means this might be personal. For all I know, you could be his target and you're acting so nonchalant about the whole fucking thing. You're going to turn over your laptop to my tech today."

"What if I don't want to go along with this plan? Have you thought of that?"

He leans in, his face inches from mine. "Makenna Justice, I have protected you and watched over you since you were five years old. I will protect you till my dying day. You will do as I tell you, or so help me God, there will be hell to pay!"

With his face inches from mine, I can feel the heat coming off of him like a raging inferno. "What about the white elephant in the room? Are we going to address that?"

He closes his eyes and takes a deep breath, "No, it will hang between us until this case is over. My head needs to stay in the game—*his* game—if I'm going to catch a killer and keep you safe in the process."

"Am I, at least, allowed to leave the house?" With my question still lingering in the air, his phone rings. He gets up and takes his call; everything is either yeah, no, or fuck, none of which sounds good. Andy comes back and when he sees Fitz is on the phone, he sits next to me.

"Well, I half expected to come back in here and find only one of you still standing."

I glare at my brother, "Well, obviously you came back too soon."

"Don't look at me like that; you know this is for your own safety."

"You're both being ridiculous. None of what is going on has anything to do with me. So many people have come and gone through the club, it's probably just coincidence."

Fitz finishes his call, his jaw is tight, and his eyes are dark as coal. "There is no such thing as coincidence. Your OS drive on the club's computer has been cloned. You are not to leave this house. Andy will stay here with you until the guard gets here. Where is your phone?"

"You are not leaving me here without a phone!" No phone? He's fucking nuts. He doesn't answer me, his jaw is ticking, and then he pulls out his phone. He is glaring at me with his *don't fuck with me* look. Oh. My. God. He can't hear my ring tone. I get up and run toward the kitchen where my phone is in the charger. I try to get to it before it goes off. Fuck—too late. Daughtry's "Waiting for Superman" begins to play. If there was a hole big enough for me to crawl into right now, I would. Before I realize what's happening, my hands are cuffed behind my back, and he's got me pushed against the fridge, face first!

He spins me back around, "Really, MJ, I'm not fucking joking around. You're in the crosshairs of a killer. He's been in the club, he's been in your computer, and, for all I know, he has cloned your phone. Andy will stay here with you; he has a phone. When I come back, I will have a new one for you."

I'm looking into his eyes, and I know there's more. "What are you hiding from me?"

He grips my arms. "There was an encrypted file on your computer. He's taunting and leaving a breadcrumb trail. I don't know if it's for you or me. Hell, it could just be part of his sick game. If I take the cuffs off, do you promise not to fight me?" he asks. I nod, and he lets go of me. I silently turn around so he can unlock them.

"I'm not an idiot; if there is danger, I will listen. I promise I won't leave the house until you get back here. But, I think you're wrong. The club is closed today, and it would be the perfect day for me to go with you to help make the transition go smoothly."

Suddenly, there's a knock on the door. He checks and lets the guard in. "There's been a change of plans. I need you to take Andy home. Makenna is coming with me."

Andy stopped driving eight months ago, and we've all taken it in stride, especially Fitz. For a man, it is hard to admit at thirty-eight that you can no longer drive. Especially Andy, since he worked on cars for a living. Andy grabs me and gives me a big hug. "MJ, you do everything Fitz tells you to do, no matter what. Remember, I'm still able to kick your ass. And, Fitz, so help me God." He brings his attention to Fitz, who shoos him out the door before he can finish his warning.

"Gather up your laptop, phone, and any other electronics you've used here and at the club. The tech is waiting for us."

I gather up everything and hand Fitz my car keys while I lock up. He takes them and shoves them in his pocket. When we get into the elevator, he punches the street level button. "My car is in the garage."

He smirks. "Yeah, and that's where it will stay."

When we get outside, I see the dreaded bike. He hands me a helmet to put on while he loads my stuff in the saddlebag. "Keep your arms around me and make sure you lean with me."

"Why can't we just take my car?"

No answer, he gets on and starts up Wanda. I get on and try not to get too close to him. He reaches back and pulls both my legs forward—*hard*. I let out a yelp as my coochie hits him dead center. "Squeeze your legs into mine and keep your arms tight around me," he yells back to me before whipping out into traffic, causing me to hold onto him like a vise grip. He's weaving in and out of the grid like a mad man, but all I can concentrate on is the vibrations on my ass as my coochie bangs up against him. If this ride lasts any longer, I swear I'm going to need new panties.

We pull up to the club, and he cuts the engine. I quickly climb off, trying to gather my wits and hide the discomfort between my legs. He climbs off, removes his helmet, and then takes off mine. He's smirking at me. "What the hell is so amusing?"

He brushes his thumb up my cheek. "Now, you know why I call her Wanda."

He leaves me there with my mouth open while he gets my laptop and phone and then rushes me in the door.

CHAPTER EIGHT

Fitz

WE GET INSIDE THE CLUB, and the memory of what I saw, the last time I was here, hits me like a sucker punch to the gut. She will never be in that position again. I don't want her to need this; I want her to need me as much as I need her. If I could turn back time, I'd go back to being that gawky teenage boy on prom night. I would tell her how I really feel. Instead, I'd let my fear of losing so much stand between us.

When this is over, I'm going to tell her the truth, a truth I have been afraid to admit. Right now, I need her safe. Mental pep talk time, Fitz. *Stay focused on the here and now. There will be plenty of time for all this later. Right now, catch this sick fuck.*

We get into MJ's office and Al is already brainstorming on a white board. She looks up from what she is doing and heads over toward us. "Hi, I'm Al, you must be Ms. Justice." Al has a warm and inviting way about her, and she must sense how hard this is for MJ. Who wouldn't? It's not every day your world gets turned upside down and you end up in the crosshairs of a killer.

"Hi, you can call me MJ. I see you've already settled in. Did you meet everyone, and is there anything I can get you?"

"You've got a great coffee set up here; I don't think you'll be getting rid of me anytime soon. Your manager showed me around, and our tech, Travis, is working on your system now." She reaches over and takes the laptop and phone from me. "I'll take these to him and then I will go over with you what I've found."

She quickly heads out the door, leaving us alone. I look at MJ and see her eyes are filled with tears. She is fighting so hard to keep it together. "Hey, come on, this is just stuff." I wave my hands around, trying to make light of it. I know her space has been invaded, and she is trying not to freak out. "I know it's been your home away from home, but it doesn't define who you are. Keep your head screwed on straight and help us do our job."

Just then, Al comes barreling through the door with Travis. "MJ, this is Travis. He has a few questions for you." MJ grabs a cup of coffee and has a seat.

Travis seems a little uneasy and fidgety, bouncing from foot to foot. "When you have your laptop here with you, where do you keep it?"

She takes a deep breath, "I keep it here in my office. My phone, on the other hand, is all over the place, but it does have a password on it. Why?"

He doesn't answer her. Knowing MJ as well as I do, I know this must really be pissing her off. "Did you ever have any security cameras set up in here?"

She puts her cup down rather abruptly. "No, this is my sanctuary, and if you don't answer my questions, you will not get any more answers from me. Why do you need to know this? What's happened?"

He looks between Al and me before explaining. "I figured your phone would be cloned, since most people don't think twice about putting it down. People generally think that because it has a password, it's protected; it's not," he informs me. "Your computer has a

66

Backdoor Trojan Virus, which allows the user to operate it remotely. Since you're telling me you only use it in this room, then someone has had unfettered access in here. I've covered up your webcam with duct tape. It's very simple, and stops anyone from looking at you. I was able to trace the source, however, the signal is being bounced all over the world. I am in the process of creating a clean computer that can be used for business. The existing one should be left active, but do not use it. I want to be able to see when he logs in and out.

"I've also set you up with a password manager. I can't stress enough to you how important it is that you use this. It only took me two minutes to gain access to all your banking and personal records. With the new system, you only have to remember one password, the program will keep changing it for you. I know this must seem like a lot, but I promise, I've seen worse."

MJ is very quiet, and the awareness hits me hard; someone could have eyes on us as we speak. "Travis, has this room and the adjoining restroom been swept?"

MJ gasp and instantly pales. "It was the first thing I did when I got here. I can assure you the place is clean. The only time he was able to see anything was when the computers were on."

Her hands are trembling as she tries to focus on everything Travis is saying. "Oh my God." She gets up and races to the bathroom, and I'm not far behind her. I hold her hair back and then hand her a wet washcloth. The realization that a madman has been watching her must have finally become a reality.

"Fitz, he watched me in my home, my office. I feel so violated." She stands over the sink, scrubbing her hands as if that will help.

"Why would he be so focused on me? What could I have possibly done to make him pick me out of the crowd? I don't bother anyone. I go to work or the gym and, once in a blue moon, an occasional date. Nothing that would attract this type of attention."

"Who knows why? It could be something so simple to us, but

to him, it means everything. For all we know, it could be something from his past, and seeing you might have triggered it. We'll get to the bottom of this, I promise."

She takes a deep breath and squeezes my hand. "I want to look at the footage that I gave you. Maybe if we can find one of the girls, I will recognize him. I know it's a long shot, but I have to do something," she pleads. As much as I would love to shield her from all of this, I know I can't.

"When you're ready, you can sit with Travis and go through it. I need to go over some stuff with Al."

We head back to the office and while MJ sits with Travis, Al and I take a walk. "So, what haven't you told me?"

"Travis found a file embedded on MJ's computer. After looking at it, I had him run the profile of everything we already know. There have been some similar cases in Los Angeles and Chicago. No arrests were made in any of them. No DNA left behind—nothing. The only difference is he found the woman on dating sites or classified ads. He seems to be progressing and getting a little bit more daring. I mean, watching her without her knowing it turns this up a notch."

My stomach is twisting in knots. I want to take MJ, get on Wanda, and never look back. "He's not just progressing; he is perfecting his skills, one dead woman at a time. What was in the file he found?"

"Some very twisted pictures, and, Fitz, all the women in the pictures have red hair. He captioned each one with some little note for MJ. I definitely believe she is his target, his ultimate goal. Everyone else leading up to her is just to satisfy the beast. The question is why MJ?"

"Make sure she doesn't see that file. I need to get her into a safe house."

She cocks her head and raises her eyes. "Good luck with that one. She doesn't seem the type to walk away quietly. Maybe Andy can help you out with that," she suggests. I hesitate, not sure how much she knows. Andy's health is his business, and if he wants to disclose it, that's totally up to him. "Fitz, Andy told me. He wanted to be upfront with me about the club and about his health. After talking to him, I know he would do anything for his sister. I also know what stress can do to any illness. If he doesn't know where his sister is, it will only compound the problem."

I know she is right, but I'm so used to playing everything close to the vest. I work alone for a reason, and this camaraderie shit is getting on my last nerve. "I'll talk to her. Anything else I need to know?"

"No, let's see if she made any progress with Travis."

We head back to MJ's office and find Travis alone. "Where is she?" I feel bile rise in my throat.

"She's in the restroom. I showed her the pictures of the three victims. She said she felt that there was something familiar about the last girl. After a bit, she remembered she spoke with her in the restroom the night she was murdered. Small talk, it was all very brief."

Jesus, she was right there. He could have gotten to her anytime he wanted. My stomach tightens even more. I head toward the restroom, and I hear her crying. I never lock the door, but she always does. "MJ, please unlock the door and let me in." Nothing, *fuck*! I feel around the top of the frame for the key—*nothing*. "MJ, open the fucking door right now, or I'm kicking it in. So help me God, you know I'll do it." I hear the click and quickly push the door open, only to find her on the floor next to the door, crying. I lift her up and put her on the counter, kicking the door shut in the process.

"Look at me, stop crying; you know what it does to me. You're the strongest woman I know, don't fail me now."

"I remember speaking to the girl the night he killed her. I caught a quick glimpse of his back when she left the ladies room; it was fleeting, at best. I wouldn't recognize him if he was standing right in front of me. God, she was so young and innocent." Her eyes are searching mine. "I don't know why you think you can hide stuff from me, you never could before."

She's right. I'm going to have to tell her. "You're right, but you have to keep it together for me. I think *you're* in his crosshairs. The file that was found on your computer had some sick pictures and they were all redheads. We believe he could be responsible for killings in Chicago and Los Angeles. He's leaving a breadcrumb trail, and it's leading back to you."

She's trembling, and I pull her tightly in my arms. When all this is over, I'm going to tell her. I'm going to hold her and never let her go. No more lost times. "I'll always be your hero, MJ, no matter what. I'd give my life to protect you. Please be strong for me. Don't fail me now."

She finally stops crying and wipes away the last of her tears. "Okay, Fitzy, I will do whatever you need me to . . . *promise.*"

"I'll give you a few minutes to get cleaned up. I'm going to discuss the arrangements with Al. When you're ready, we will go to Andy's house and go over everything with him." I catch a glimpse of her in the mirror as I leave. The look on her face is a look that will haunt me forever.

Mark

I leave work and head out into the brutal heat. I need to head to the gym and try to work off some of this frustration. I have to stay focused, but the constant throbbing in my balls is deafening. At least, I don't have to worry about the token kid, the nanny has him. My gym is right near Mystik, that's how I found the place and the angelic Makenna Justice. I hope she puts up more of a fight than Sophia did. She was good, but not good enough. In the end, she was just like all the rest. Just another silly girl, thinking she'd found her prince charming. Too bad I was her worst nightmare come true.

The gym is packed at this time, which is good; it affords me the time to look at all the available meat. I head over to the rowing machine and take a seat. I have a perfectly adequate one in my building, but I joined this gym because it's *hers*. I haven't seen her here in a couple of days. I can't jump the gun. I need to stay focused on the prize. Makenna Justice, with the beautiful, long, red mane, will be mine. I will keep her, play with her, and take her over and over again. The possibilities are endless. Hmm, my balls tighten at the sheer thought of it. She has an obsession for all things Superman. Not sure why, but it has inspired me to leave little clues for her everywhere. I wonder if she found some of them? Can't wait till she realizes there is no Superman—only me.

An hour on this rower and still no sign of her. I head over to the weight area and work out there for another hour. There are a few possibilities, but none compare to her. I knew from the first day I saw her in here that she was the one—the ultimate prize—and she was waiting just for me. Finding out she was the owner of Mystik was the cherry on the tip of my dick.

The other women, in all the different cities, were just a passing fancy. None of them stacked up to her. I knew the minute our paths crossed in here that I had to have her, and not just for one night. She deserves so much more than that. She deserves to be worshiped like a goddess, for however long it takes me to get my fill, if I ever do. I glance around the room one last time before I hit the showers.

After a quick shower, I figured I would head home and convince Nicole that she needs my cock for a while, but she texts me that she is pulling another all-nighter. The nanny's got the brat, so I can go to my new apartment and start my project. I grab my stuff and head toward the train. When I round the corner, I see her and instantly freeze, which gets me cursed out by the guy behind me.

Stepping into the doorway, I remain in the shadows . . . *watching*.

Her beauty is undeniably breathtaking. Who the fuck is the guy with her? He turns her around and pulls her hair into a ponytail. From the shadows, I can tell her eyes are closed and her head is bowed. She is in a beautiful submissive state, and I feel the dull throb begin in my cock. The vein that runs root to tip is pulsating. I try to steady my breathing; I don't want to get caught.

He turns her around and hands her a helmet. Who is this guy? She seems so comfortable with him, in sync, which tells me they are not new to each other. I checked her computer; she hasn't been with anyone on a regular basis since she purchased the club. He leans in and whispers something in her ear before they climb on and he pulls her closer to him. Within seconds, they pull out into traffic and instantly, they're gone.

I don't know who she was with, but now I need to step up my plan. If need be, I will take him out to get to her. I head to Brooklyn to start on my project with even more urgency than before.

Andy

Fitz sent a text that he and MJ were on their way, and Stephen should be home any minute. When I'm nervous, I cook. When I'm happy, I cook. When I'm upset, I cook. Fuck, I cook a lot. But, what I can do is limited, and this helps. I hear the front door and look at the security monitor. I'm happy Stephen is home first. I want to fill him in on everything I know, which, right now, is not much. He walks into the kitchen, and his smile instantly fades. He hugs me and then kisses me hard. "Babe, what happened? You've cooked and baked enough food for a small army."

I take his hand. "Let's go upstairs and shower. I'll fill you in on everything I know before Fitz and MJ get here."

We head upstairs, and I tell him everything. "Wow, I can't believe she agreed to Fitz's plan so quickly. Maybe, by some small miracle, she realizes this is no joke. Maybe she should stay here with us until this whole thing blows over."

I sit on the stool, watching him undress before he climbs into the shower, pulling the curtain closed. His body is perfection with his sculptured six-pack and that delicious V. I've worked out my whole life, and I don't have it. I'm sitting in my self-induced daydream when he pulls the curtain back and laughs. I'm light-skinned and blush easily, being caught daydreaming about my husband always causes me to turn bright red. I've always been a little shy and my husband loves it.

"Andy, instead of daydreaming about me, you should have just joined me. What time will they be here?"

I get up and hand him a towel. "We don't have enough time, or trust me, I would have. Make no mistake, later, you are all mine." I give him a long hard kiss while both my hands are cupping his beautiful, sculpted ass. I finally pull back and look into his crystal blue eyes. "Look who's blushing now?"

I turn and leave, giving him some privacy to finish up, and giving myself a chance to gather my scattered wits. I get back downstairs to the kitchen just as the oven beeps, letting me know the roast is done. I pull it out to give it a chance to rest, grab a beer out of the fridge, and when I turn around, Stephen is standing there. He has on my favorite jeans and no shirt. He is talking, but it all sounds like the teacher in the Charlie Brown cartoons. He was wearing those jeans the first day I met him. They hang just below his V, and they have rips in all the right places. Over the years, the rips have gotten better. Like a fine wine that ages with time.

"Hello, Andy, are you with me? Did you do laundry? I can't find any shirts."

I take a long pull of my beer. "You know damn well what those jeans do to me, yet you chose to wear them when there's nothing I can do about it. Don't even think of telling me otherwise. Yes, I did laundry. I just didn't get a chance to put it away yet."

He takes the beer from my hand and places it on the counter. "How much time do we have before they get here?"

"Not nearly enough for what I want to do to you. We will continue this later." Just as he begins kissing me, we hear the front door open. He breaks away, heading into the laundry room to get a shirt, leaving me in the kitchen a hot mess.

MJ comes in with Fitz right behind her. "Andy, are you feeling okay, you're all flushed."

I grab my beer and try not to turn any redder than I am. Fitz is laughing, probably over how clueless my sister can be sometimes. "Fitz, I cooked all day, you are staying for dinner, right?" my tone means he has no choice.

Before he can answer, Stephen comes in and demands to talk to Fitz in private. They step out back, and MJ sets the table while I carve the roast. Something tells me it's going to be a long night. I look over at MJ, and she is trying to set the table, but her hands are trembling . . . bad. I stop what I'm doing and take her in my arms. "You'll be okay. I promise we will get to the bottom of this." I've protected her my whole life and, sick or not, I always will.

Fitz

I'm not in the house two minutes, and Stephen is already pulling me out back. By the scowl on his face, I venture to say I'm in a world of trouble—so, what else is new? "What's the problem now?" I glance in the window to make sure everyone's okay and, when I turn back,

Stephen sucker punches me in the jaw. He's shaking his hand, cursing up a storm. "I gather that was for the other night?"

"Fuck, you're like a tank! Yeah, that was for the other night. I know that you and Andy go back over thirty years, but that doesn't give you the right to hit him. He is doing the best he can. You know how sick he is! This is no joke, Fitz. I'm trying to give him the best possible life. He can't have stress; it will only make him worse. He's worried about MJ, his parents, and his health. Add a deranged killer in the mix and I'm not sure how much more he can take."

"I know he's worried and stressed, so am I. Did he tell you I've taken over the club?"

He's still rubbing his knuckles, and I feel bad. "Yes, he told me everything he knows."

I know anything I tell Andy is a direct pipeline to Stephen, as it should be. "The computer tech found a file on MJ's computer. She knows about the file, but not the details. She's this guy's target. He's killed in Los Angeles and Chicago. She has now become his obsession. I want to put her in an FBI safe house, but I don't think she will go along with it." I run my hands through my hair. "She'll never leave her brother or her parents. Andy is going to freak out, and I don't know what I'm going to do about Mom and Dad. On top of all of this, I find out that the woman, I thought was so far out of my reach, has been in love with me all these years." I take in a deep breath and blow it out aggressively. "I'm sorry. I don't mean to dump all of this on you. I know you're worried about Andy, I am, too."

He sinks into one of the chairs at the realization that this just got a whole lot worse for everyone. "Fitz, please don't tell Andy about the details in that file. I honestly don't believe he can handle it."

"I agree with you. For now, it's only between us. I'm not letting MJ go back to her place without me. Stephen, he's been watching her through her computer and not just at the club."

"Oh my God, have you had her apartment checked?"

"Yes, it's clean, but I still don't want her there. We better get back inside before they wonder why we have been gone so long."

He gets up and squeezes my arm. "Leave her here with us. Andy is here all day and Mom and Dad are only around the corner. At least, you know she will go for that. That's really your only option. You know she won't go for anything else."

Stephen is on the outside, looking in. He's family, but the emotional ties are different for him. Plus, he's a lawyer and a damn good one. He has one of the most logical minds I've ever encountered. "Do you think I'm the reason she got mixed up with that guy and ended up in that club?" I'm not sure I want to hear the answer, but I know I have to.

"Honestly, I think you are part of it, but only a small part. Makenna carries so much weight on her shoulders. When Andy got sick, she took over his health care needs like a lioness, protecting her cubs. I had to remind her on several occasions that I'm Andy's husband.

"Her parents rely very heavily upon her, and not just for the big things. I really think she needed an outlet, and he came along at the right time. In the end, Fitz, you can't look back. Can I ask why you never told her how you feel?"

I usually play everything very close to the vest, but Stephen is always so honest and easy to talk to, maybe it's finally time. "Fear. I was very young when my mom passed away. My dad, a vicious drunk, who beat me daily for no damn good reason, but I'm sure you know all of that. Andy brought me home with him and his mom and dad took care of me. They protected me from my own dad and kept me from going down a bad path in life. It was a second chance for me to be loved the way any kid dreams of being loved and accepted." I take a deep breath and continue. "I watched Makenna grow up and become the most beautiful, kind, caring woman I've ever known. I never thought I was good enough for her; I still don't. I didn't want to lose what I had with her and the only family I've ever really had. The only people who ever loved me. I know I'm strong, but God help me, she's my weakness. The scary part is she has no clue how much power she holds over me. She is the only person who can destroy my whole world. It's that fear of losing her, and everyone else that has kept me at arm's length."

I turn to go inside, and he stops me. "Eventually, you will have to let that wall down and let her in. If you don't, you will die a lonely, broken man."

I'm already broken and lonely. Right now, the only thing I have to do is keep my head in the killer's game.

Andy

Stephen and Fitz step back in and Stephen is rubbing his knuckles. Makenna quickly wipes her tears, so Fitz doesn't notice, I'm sure. I go to the freezer and pull out a bag of peas for Stephen. He probably decided to get even with Fitz for hitting me. Unfortunately for Stephen, Fitz is built like a brick wall. There is not an ounce of fat on him, and he has a body that makes women weep. He's never been serious with anyone, and after the other night, I think I've finally figured out why. We've always teased him that he's clueless, but in reality, I think I've been the most clueless of all.

"Come sit down. Dinner is ready and no talk of anything bad right now," I demand and watch as they all take their seats. Stephen says grace and everyone digs in. It must be good because everyone is very busy eating.

"Stephen, how was work today?"

"Good. That reminds me, we have a dinner party to go to this week. A few of the attorneys were promoted to junior partners, so we like to have a little social event for them. Kind of 'welcome to the fold. Now, work your ass off' type of party. MJ, why don't you plan on coming with us?" He brings his focus to her. She is pushing the food around her dish and not really paying much attention to any of us.

"Fitz, I made your favorite dessert: strawberry shortcake and homemade Guinness ice cream." I throw him a wink. He has a grin from ear to ear. Well, at least, I've made someone's day.

He gets up and begins clearing the table. "Andy, why don't you and Stephen go into the living room while MJ and I clean up and make coffee?" He's not suggesting, he's demanding, and I know when not to fight him. Besides, I'm tired. Stephen and I head into the living room, leaving them to deal with the mess.

Fitz

I sit back down and pull her chair around so she is facing me. "Listen to me, you better pull it together right now. There are a whole new set of rules coming your way. You will listen to everything I tell you, and you will not fight me on any of it. Andy is worried sick about you—we all are."

"What the hell kind of rules, and what makes you think you can tell me what I can and cannot do?"

"I've been protecting you your whole life. That will *never* change. No matter what happens, I need you safe, this whole family does." I push my chair out and continue to clear the table. I'm not ready to have this conversation yet.

She gets the coffee going, and before I know it, it's finally time for dessert. Andy knows my weakness, and he's hitting me with both of them tonight. We take everything into the living room. Now, I need to let them know the plan.

I take a deep breath and begin. "MJ, you have two options: you can go to an FBI safe house or you can stay here on lockdown with Andy."

She puts her dish down and glares at me. I swear flaming arrows are shooting at me. "You're suggesting I run and hide?! Will staying here put everyone else in danger? What about my parents? Who is going to take care of them? Just because you're trying to put my life on hold, doesn't me that the world comes to a crashing halt. Like it or not, Fitz, life goes on one way or another." She has a death grip on both sides of the chair, probably to keep from throwing something at me. I've never been able to say no to her, but right now, her safety trumps everything.

"You only have two choices, be thankful I'm giving you that. Maybe you don't understand; you've somehow become the target for a lunatic! You have no idea what this guy has done. Trust me, he is very sick!"

I get up and walk over to the window, trying to calm the fuck down. No one has ever been able to push my buttons like she can. Andy and MJ begin yelling back and forth. Finally, Stephen gets up and takes the lead.

"Enough, everyone, calm down. MJ, Fitz and I spoke earlier, and it is in everyone's best interest if you stay here. You and Andy can continue to look after your parents and look after each other. Fitz, I think when you are not at work, you should be here, too. If anything else happens, we will move Mom and Dad in here. Keeping everyone safely under one roof is the best thing," he finishes. I turn and look at MJ, and she's holding back the tears. I'm not sure if it's anger, fear, or both.

"Fine, but I will need to go home, and get some of my stuff and my car!"

I pull my keys out of my pocket. "I know you're just aching for another ride on Wanda."

She is calling me all sorts of names under her breath, and I don't know who is laughing more, Andy or me. When we get out to the street, I hand her a helmet. "Anyway you spin it, babe, Wanda will be helping you release some of your pent up frustration tonight."

I climb on and start her up. When MJ gets on, I pull her body tightly against mine and pull out into the night. The sooner we get this over with, the sooner I can concentrate on catching this bastard.

CHAPTER NINE

Andy

THE FRONT DOOR SLAMS SHUT, and I know my sister is scared. She puts up a brave front, but I know better. Fitz is trying his hardest not to show how worried he is. Stephen quietly begins cleaning up the dessert dishes. He has his trial lawyer face on, no emotion at all. "Are you going to talk to me or do I have to pry it out of you?" I inquire.

He stops, looks over at me, and graces me with the most beautiful smile. "That, my love, would depend on how you plan prying it out of me," he teases. I know my mouth is hanging open just thinking of the possibilities. "Why don't you run a bath for us, and I will finish cleaning up here, then you can work on prying it out of me."

He doesn't have to tell me twice. I grab a couple of bottles of water and head to our room while he finishes up. I try to erase all the bad things from today and focus solely on Stephen. The bath fills, and I pour a little of his favorite shower gel, Aventus by Creed, in the tub, and soon, the entire room smells like Stephen.

I shut the water and turn around. He is standing there, his shirt is gone, but he's kept the jeans. My eyes trail along the edge, noticing his bulge, which I so desperately need right now, but I can't rush

81

this. He's not moving, merely looking into my eyes with a mixture of love and lust that just might melt my jeans right off me.

"Babe, now that everyone is gone, I think you need to fulfill those promises you alluded to earlier." I'm happy to oblige, but I pray I can give him all he wants and needs. Slowly, I get undressed, watching his eyes beg me for more. I work out every day, and although my body is failing me in some ways, I haven't totally lost my damn man card yet.

The scent of Stephen all around me is overwhelming. Time to turn the tables for a bit. He needs to be the one to fight for self-control. I take my thumb and gather my own pre-cum. His eyes track my every move as I swipe my thumb across his tender lips. He follows it up with his tongue, very slowly, back and forth. "Tell me how badly you want to taste more of me."

He smiles, and there's a glint in his eyes. He slowly kisses me from my lips, down my neck, and to my chest, paying a lot of attention to my pebbled nipples, right before he drops to his knees. He takes a hold of my cock and gives the tip a kiss before he swirls his warm tongue around the head, teasing me very slowly. He doesn't take me deep; he knows that would be a game changer. I wouldn't last, and tonight, I need this to last. I want to be able to give back to him. Sometimes my meds, coupled with stress and exhaustion, make it hard for me to focus, hard for me to maintain a full erection. Tonight, is one of those times. Maybe if I relax, things will get better.

"Stephen, babe, the bath water is getting cold."

He stands up and pulls me into a tight hug. "My love for you is fierce. I didn't sign on just for the good times, Andy. I love you, no matter what. And I always will."

I don't know what I ever did so right in my life to have such a wonderful, beautiful man love me so completely. He slides out of his jeans and climbs into the tub. I climb in and sit between his legs, his front to my back, his legs hooking around mine. The hot water is very relaxing and finally, I feel myself unwind.

"How's your hand?" I'm rubbing his knuckles and he barely moves.

"Is that your way of asking me what happened out back with Fitz?"

I turn so I'm sideways, my head resting on his shoulder. "Of course, I want to know, did you think otherwise?"

"I told him I don't care how far back you go, he is never to raise his hand to you again. You're not children, for Christ's sake. We talked about the situation at the club and MJ's safety. He asked me if I thought he was responsible for some of her lifestyle choices. I was honest with him. I believe that by him keeping his distance from her played a part." He plants a soft kiss on my head. "What shocked me was that he confessed that he's been in love with her all these years. I asked him why he never told her, and he said fear has held him back. That's so sad; two people love each other, and fear is standing in the way. I know that he lost his mom at a young age and has basically been considered one of the family, but what makes him think that he would lose everyone if things didn't work out with him and MJ?"

I hand him a washcloth and some shower gel so he can wash my back, while I prepare to tell him the one thing I've never shared with him . . .the story of Fitz, my best friend.

"Fitz's father beat him and his mom, Mary Elizabeth, on a daily basis. He was a violent drunk and when he went into a rage, Fitz usually got the worst of it. One day, he came home from school, and his father was in a bad way. His mom made him go into the bathroom and she locked him in there to protect him. She told him no matter what happened, he was to keep very quiet.

"He stayed in that locked bathroom for three days. His father beat his mother to death and Fitz heard the whole thing. When all was said and done, his father was taken away and Fitz was alone.

His father was sentenced to life in prison and the courts awarded custody of Fitz to my parents. We are the only family he has ever had. That's why he will never lock a bathroom door. He used to panic at the sound of any lock clicking. He's gotten better, but it took years. He fears losing everything, and honestly, I get it. However, Fitz and MJ are going to have to come to terms with this. They can't go through life just existing because of a fear that's keeping them from having a life."

"What happened to his father?"

"He got into a fight and died in prison." I lean my head back so he can wash my hair.

"I know he lives in the apartment downstairs from your mom and dad, but why? I mean he's living right across the street from where his nightmare began."

"He claims he stays there to keep an eye on Mom and Dad, but I think they're his safety net. He's never been close with anyone other than us. He is loyal and faithful to a fault. He became a cop to try to save all the Mary Elizabeth's in the world. He's like a bloodhound with a scent, and that's what makes him so good at what he does. I worry, because every time he has a case, he quite literally becomes a part of it. Each case takes something out of him, and when he has one case right after another, there is no time for him to come back."

He finishes rinsing my hair and then helps me out of the tub. He is always so attentive to my needs, and I know how lucky I am to have him in my life.

"Andy, between all of us, we will keep MJ safe—I promise. Now, let's shut all this off for tonight and concentrate on us." He's right; I've had more than enough stress for one day. I need to make Stephen my main focus right now. We head into the bedroom, and tonight, I take the lead. I need to feel in control. He understands that and even though he loves to be in control, he never complains. My tremors are not that bad tonight, but my movements are slow.

One of the sexiest things about Stephen, besides his beautiful body, is how he whisper kisses, and tonight is no different. My fingers stroke his abs as he peppers me with those kisses that make my heart skip a beat. He works his way down my body, never rushing, making sure he pays attention to all my needs. Circling my nipples and then down my core.

When he reaches my cock, he swirls his tongue around the head, and then slowly takes me deep. His mouth is warm and velvety smooth. I reach over to the nightstand, grab the lube, and pass it to him. As much as I think I want to be in control tonight, what I really need is for him to take me. "Top me tonight, please."

He works his tongue around my sac and finally hits the most sensitive area on any man, the proverbial highway to heaven. He works a lubed finger inside of me while he strokes with his tongue. When he hits my prostate, it's like the pearl of the oyster. My cries of ecstasy echo throughout the room. I'm lightheaded with pleasure, and I don't even realize he's entering me. When I finally open my eyes, he's smiling, his face only inches from mine.

"I'm going to move now, real slow and easy." He leans down and begins to kiss me, soft at first, but as he's getting closer to the edge, his kisses get harder. Finally, he throws his head back and his body begins to shake. He pushes my knees up higher as I beg him to move deeper and harder. That's all it takes for both of us. He's kissing me again with his declaration of love, and I know I'm truly blessed.

I must have fallen asleep for a bit, when I wake up, Stephen isn't in bed but everything is cleaned up. I'm about to get up and look for him, when he comes back into the room with a tray.

"I made some tea, and I wanted to make sure MJ got back okay. Everything is fine, Fitz went back to work, and the house is locked up tight."

"Thank you for all that you do for MJ and me."

"I'm your husband, and I love you, now drink your tea before it gets cold."

"How is she? Did Fitz say anything?"

"Fitz was his usual disconnected self and MJ, well, she was typical MJ." He chuckles. God only knows how much she put poor Fitz through.

"Come on, babe, you need to get some sleep, your case starts tomorrow."

I pull him close to me and stroke his back, and before I know it, I hear his gentle breathing. I say a silent prayer, thanking God for putting Stephen in my life. With that, I drift off to sleep.

Makenna

Thank God the ride from my brother's house to mine is only twenty minutes. I don't think my coochie could take much more. I feel safer knowing Fitzy is with me. The thought of someone watching me makes me feel sick all over again. The elevator ride is very quiet, and with his dark aviators on, I can't tell if he's looking at me, or if it's just my mind playing tricks on me. "Who the hell wears dark sunglasses inside?"

"Someone who wants to keep you guessing."

When the doors open, I freeze. I don't know that I can go back in there. I feel a wash of fear flush over my entire body. His hand instinctively holds the doors open as my heart begins to race.

"You're safe, I promise. While we were at the club, I had the entire place swept. The only place he watched you was through your laptop." I try to put on brave face and step forward.

When we step inside, I keep looking around, expecting the boogie man to be lurking around every corner. I know I'm being ridiculous, but the fear is real. Fitz is on high alert. The tension so thick, you can cut it with a knife.

"What happens when I have to take Andy to his doctor appointments?"

"There will be a plain clothes officer outside at all times. He will accompany you and Andy wherever you have to go."

I feel the room start to spin, and he grabs me before I hit the floor. "I'm okay, really, I didn't eat much today." I try to shoo him away, but he lifts me up and carries me into my bedroom. He puts me on the bed and kneels down in front of me.

"Look, I get that you're scared. I'm scared, too. I'm going to protect you, I promise. You need to let me do my job and don't fight me. I'll help you pack. Just sit here, please." His plea and knowing he's scared nearly brings me to tears. If Fitzy is scared, this is bad. "Where is your suitcase?"

When I get up to go get it, he lifts me up and tosses me in the middle of the bed. "Are you nuts?"

"This is what I mean. Why can't you, for once in your life, do as I tell you? I'll pack; just tell me where the suitcase is. You almost passed out. Now, do as I tell you!"

I point toward the closet. "Top shelf." Before I can warn him, everything comes crashing down on him. I begin to laugh, and I can't stop. It's got to be the stress, but seeing him sprawled on my bedroom floor covered in my winter clothes leaves me in hysterics.

"I was taking my winter clothes to Andy's house for storage. I didn't close it because I wasn't done stuffing it," I explain. He's not saying a word. "Fitz, are you okay?"

"Yeah, I'm enjoying the laughter." He tosses everything on the bed and I start folding it all.

"What about Mom and Dad? Are they safe? Can Andy and I go to their house?"

He sits on the edge of the bed and squeezes my hand. "I've already put a plain clothes officer on them. You guys can go visit them whenever you want."

His grip on my hand gets tighter whenever we talk about my parents. "What is it? Besides the obvious, what are you worried about?"

"I can't keep a secret from your mom. She busts me every fucking time. I swear that woman has a third eye or something."

"She does nail your ass every time. I'll mention that you're on a big case and you won't be around much. Do you want Andy and me to get some of your clothes and take them to his house?"

"No, if she sees that, she will nail my ass for sure. I'll go home in the middle of the night, when I know she's sleeping, get my shit, and take it to Andy's myself." He pulls me up off the bed and we begin to pack. Working together in silence, we quickly get it all together.

"Fitz, should I go to that dinner party with Andy and Stephen or would it be better for me to stay home?" I turn to him. He has a far away look in his eyes. I wish I knew where he'd mentally wandered off to. "Hello, Fitz, where did you go?"

"Sorry, yeah, go with them . . . safety in numbers. We need to get going. I'll follow you back to Andy's house."

I reach up and stroke my fingers along his beautiful face. "I only hope one day you will let me in your heart and your head."

He grabs my wrist and pulls my hand away. "Not now, I can't. Let's go before it gets any later." We finish in silence and head to the parking garage. I drop him off at Wanda and he follows me to Andy's.

We get to Andy's house, and he introduces me to the officer parked across the street. He explains that Lucas will always be with me. Fitz also informs me that he will be the only one who can change my guard. When we get upstairs, I decide to settle into my favorite guest room before I head into the shower. I finish in the bathroom and return to my room. I find him sitting on my bed. "Is everything okay?"

He's quiet, his eyes growing dark, lingering over every inch of my body. Holy Hell, I could combust from the look alone. He gets up and is only inches from me. His eyes never leave mine. My body is betraying me; my nipples display my desire for him.

He rubs his thumb over my bottom lip. "Breathe, Makenna, I have a new phone for you. Travis will have a new laptop for you tomorrow." He puts it in my hand and I swear my body is quivering. How the hell is that even possible?

As he heads out the door, I look down at the phone; it's password protected. "Wait, what's the password?"

He looks back over his shoulder and smiles. "You'll figure it out."

He's gone, and I'm staring at the phone. What the fuck is the password? I hate riddles about as much as I hate charades. I type in my birthday, Mom's birthday, Andy's birthday, nothing. Then it hits me.

I laugh as I type it in: Fitz. I stare at the screen saver and begin to cry. It's my prom picture; I can't believe he kept it. I crawl into bed and look to make sure my contacts are all there. Then I hit photos and gasp. I can barely see through my tears, there is an endless array of our life in pictures.

When did he find the time to do this? Could he feel the same way I do? Why won't he talk to me? What is he afraid of? I look at every picture, and I know I will never love anyone like I love him. The club and everything associated with it has been a way to separate me from the loneliness. I can't sit back and waste any more time; we need to clear the air. I get up and head out to find him, only to find a note taped on to the front door. He's gone, and once again, I'm alone.

Fitz

What the fuck was I thinking? Setting up her phone with the pictures from mine just put it all out there. At least I was able to get into my place, get my stuff, and get out before Mom woke up. She is not my mom by blood, but in my heart, she will always be. She became a foster parent to keep me out of the system. She saved me and the thought that I might have hurt MJ in some way makes me sick.

The very family I have fought to protect and never lose might now be lost to me for good. My train finally comes, and I put my headset on, 3 Doors Down's "Kryptonite" is playing. I put it on repeat to drown out the sound of the trains and the pounding in my heart. I close my eyes and speed off into the night.

CHAPTER TEN

Mark

I GOT A LOT DONE on the room tonight. It always looks easy in a video, until you actually try to do it. What I thought I could get done in one day will probably take a lot longer. If I could spend one whole day here, I could get it done sooner, but Nicole will wonder where I am. Besides, I need to be totally prepared for her. I will only have one shot at getting and keeping her here. First, I need to figure out who the guy was tonight —she looked too comfortable with him.

I fire up my laptop and log into her home computer. First, I look through her endless folders, but she keeps very little personal stuff on here. Hell, there are more pictures on her phone, most of which are selfies and girlfriends, than on her computer. I log into one of her social media accounts, and she has over a hundred notifications. Why hasn't she been on here today?

I scroll through her pictures. Finally, I find a picture with three guys holding up beer bottles. No one is tagged. I check the date: 2011. I copy the image of the guy that she was with and do a Google image search…nothing. I check all her other social media accounts. Odd, there is no activity today. Next, I log on to her work computer, nothing at all, very quiet. Everything is just as I left it. I know the club is closed today, but she was there—I saw her. So, why no activity?

I log out of everything and pull up the endless videos I have of her. They. Are. So. Perfect. She has no idea she was being filmed. I made a special one that I placed in one of her files. I wonder if she's found it? I alternated with pictures of her in the privacy of her bedroom, pleasuring herself while I get myself off. The final shot is me, coming endlessly with her.

I pull up one of my favorites, and her beautiful body graces my screen. Watching her rub the lotion all over her body makes my heart race. I stroke my cock root to tip, just like her fingers glide all over her body. I have it on a continuous loop; her fingers glide so effortlessly, yet she always stops when she gets to her tiny Superman tat. Why does she linger there? Her delicate fingers always stop and tremble when she reaches it. It's so small, if she didn't always stop there, I would have easily missed it.

I'm there and I can't hold back, seeing her in this state takes me to a higher level. The thought of claiming her and making her mine puts me over that invisible line. I come with such a force, I feel like my balls are being sucked back in. When I finally catch my breath, I realize I need to step up my plan. My hand is a sad substitute for her beautiful mouth. I've never wanted anyone like I want her. I want to own her, keep her, and fuck her endlessly. I clean up and formulate a new plan, one that will get me Makenna Justice a lot sooner.

I get home and Nicole is already waiting for me. She is sprawled on the sofa with a glass of wine. I glance at the bottle, and it's half empty; this could be nasty. "How was your day, Nicole?"

"Where have you been? It's nearly ten, you couldn't be working."

I sit next to her and pour myself a glass. "I took a potential client out to dinner. You said you were going to have to pull an all-nighter, did I miss something?"

She smiles, surely it's the thought of more money coming in. "No, I was just surprised you were out so late. We have a dinner party to go to for work on Friday. Maybe you can pick up some new business since you have to be there."

This might cut into my new plan. "What time and where?"

"It's on the East side, a place called Daniel. We need to arrive promptly at eight. Did you get the business?"

I'm looking at her like she has three heads, until it hits me. I need to keep my lies in order with her. "They are still undecided; I will have to wine and dine them some more." She picks up her papers and gets back to work. "I have an early day tomorrow, I'll leave you to finish up. Try not to stay up too late." She is already focused on her work; I kiss her good night and head to bed.

This is also a sign that I have to step up my plan. I quickly shoot an email to my boss letting him know I need to take emergency leave. My grandfather passed suddenly, and I need to go back home to settle his affairs. I let him know I'll be back on Monday. This will give me almost two full days to work on the apartment. If I'm lucky, I might actually have her in my arms by this weekend. The thought makes my cock throb, but I need to stay focused. I fall asleep, excited about my new plan.

Morning comes and I can't get the hell out of here fast enough. I speed through my morning rituals and head out to the kitchen. Nicole is on the phone, trying to solve some crisis at the office, while Mason is playing a game on his PlayStation. It's the perfect time for me to pretend I'm late and leave as quickly as possible. I grab my coffee, make my goodbyes, and race out the door. Finally on my way, I have to fight my excitement.

I grab *The Post* and hop on the train. I skim through it, still nothing about the bodies. What the hell is wrong with the cops in this town? In LA, I was just perfecting my craft, learning from my mistakes. By the time they put the pieces together —that it was one person—I had already moved on.

In Chicago, I was at full stride and they figured out quickly that it was one guy doing it all. I thought, for sure, New York would be quicker than the others. Especially, after they found the rose. So, I have to ask myself, why are they holding back?

I know I scrubbed everything with oxygenated bleach. I've left nothing of me behind. I learned from LA; I wax my entire body, and I scrub everything. If she's had my cock in her mouth, I even brush her teeth.

I look up and realize I'm at my stop. When I reach my apartment, my landlord is sitting on the front stoop having coffee. Great, peering eyes, just what I need. I wave good morning, hoping I can skirt on by.

"Good morning, Mark, you're here early today?"

What the fuck? Is she watching my every move? "Yes, ma'am, I have a few days off from work. Will you be home all day?" God, I hope not.

"No, I'm going to my son's home at the Jersey Shore. I'll be back Sunday night. Will you keep an eye on the place? Feel free to take the paper, too."

Oh, luck be a lady tonight. "Of course, you have a great weekend." I wave and head into my place. Everything is lining up perfect. Saturday will be the day I have her.

94

Fitz

I get to the precinct and it's still quiet. I arrange a makeshift bed on the floor in the corner of my office and try to get a few hours of sleep before the day starts. My dreams become the nightmares of my past. I hear the screams, but I can't get the door open; she locked me in. *"Mira perra malparida." I hear the smacks, over and over again. "I work hard all day, I come home and that esa media raza de mierda is always up your ass." Smack, crash, smack again. "He left his bike out—again. How many times do I have to beat the little bastard before he does what he is told?"*

I try the door, but it's locked. I hear her crying and begging him not to hit her. I can't get out and I can't help her. I curl up into a ball on the floor, sticking my fingers in my ears trying to muffle her cries. Another loud crash makes the walls shake, then nothing. Night turns into day and night again. It's cold and very quiet, she's not crying anymore. Will she ever come let me out? I lie on the cold tile floor and try to look under the door. I see her lying on the floor. "Mommy, open the door please. I promise to put my bike away. Daddy, please don't hit her, please." I try to be brave and not cry, big boys don't cry, but I can't stop my tears.

Daylight comes again; finally I hear a noise. Oh dear God, please don't let it be him. "Mommy, please, I'm still in here." I hear a click, and the knob slowly turns. I'm holding my breath praying as the door opens, and a policeman is standing there. Andy's dad crouches down in front of me. "Son, are you okay?" His voice is deep, yet it cracks when he speaks to me, why?

"Where is my mommy? He was hitting her, and she locked me in here." He is big and blocking me from getting out of the bathroom.

"Do you know who was hitting her?" I want my mommy and he won't let me pass.

"Yes, my daddy. He beats us both, a lot, but you know that. Where

95

is my mommy?"

"You need to come with me and let the doctors check you out." He scoops me up and rushes me out of the house. I see Andy's mom, and she's crying. Why is she crying? I reach for her, but I'm rushed into the ambulance. The doors quickly close and we take off. The flashing lights are all around me.

The lights in the office come on, and I'm startled out of my nightmare. My eyes fly open, and Al is crouched in front of me. I quickly wipe my face.

"Hey, are you okay? Why are you on the floor?"

I quickly scramble to my feet. "I needed to close my eyes for a bit. I'm a mess. I'm going in the shower. I'll be back." I don't give her a chance to drill me. I grab my backpack and head out the door.

Fuck! I haven't had that dream in years, why now? I peel my wet clothes off and climb into the shower. Probably because so much of the past is being brought to the surface. The shower turns cold very quickly. I finish up, get dressed in a hurry, and head back into my office.

Sleep is highly overrated, that's for sure. Especially, when you wake up worse than when you went to sleep. I stop by the coffee machine and cringe. What the fuck is that shit? I head back into the office and Al is waiting for me. "Hey, grab your stuff. We are going across the street to the diner to work. I need food and coffee."

She gathers up her stuff and races out the door with me. The diner is always crowded, but the owner keeps a couple of booths empty for anyone from the precinct to use. Eugene comes by and I order my usual, which makes Al cringe.

"Are you really going to eat all of that?"

"Yeah, I can be a bottomless pit at times. Before you even ask, I work out five days a week. So what is on the agenda for today?"

She picks at her bagel while I inhale my food. "First, I know you're paying for the round-the-clock protection on everyone. Were you afraid that the captain wouldn't approve it?"

I stop in midstream. "How did you find out?"

"Never mind that, answer the question. You never even tried to put it through proper channels."

"They're my family and all I have left in this world. I'm not about to take chances with their lives. If it was your wife and kids, what would you do?"

"Well, Travis is done with MJ's new computer," she changes the topic. "He made her social media accounts mirror what she already has. He has some fancy name for it, but what I gathered from him is that she can go on, but he would rather she stayed off completely. He said the guy is very tech savvy, and he doesn't want to give him any other opportunities."

"I agree, I'll talk to her and Andy about it. Neither of them needs to be on there. What else do you have?"

"I put a timeline together for the murders in Los Angeles and Chicago. He started in LA and then moved to Chicago. It looks like LA was where he was practicing and perfecting his MO. By the time the police put it all together and called it the work of a serial killer, he'd moved to Chicago. In LA, he used different color roses. When he got to Chicago he switched to the white rose. Once they figured out that it was the work of one man, they leaked it to the press, and just like LA, he vanished. Now, he is here, and I think if we let it out that it is the same guy, he'll run. If that happens, we have to start all over again."

"I agree. The press needs to stay out of this if we are to have half a chance at catching him. Was there any evidence from LA that could be helpful?"

"The first victim always gives us the most evidence in any serial case. That's where the killer starts to learn what works and what doesn't. I won't bore you with all the science; there was a hair left behind, but it was not from the root. It was useless."

Eugene brings over a new thermos of coffee and clears the plates. "So, what makes victim number one so helpful?"

"He used duct tape, not the intricate ropes that he uses now. He was sloppy whereas now he is OCD with the cleaning and the bleaching. The first victim helps us to build a profile and, coupled with the other victims, we can see where he was and, hopefully, where he is going."

"So, you built a profile, do you care to share?"

She glares at me. "Don't be a wiseass, Fitz. I think he is mid-thirties. I believe his whole body is now hairless, possibly even his head. He is highly educated and has grown to detest any kind of filth. I wouldn't be surprised if he worships his own body, treating it like a temple. I'm not sure if he is into the whole BDSM lifestyle, or if it is a ruse. Either way, he has some sort of experience in the lifestyle."

"Wait, what makes you say that?" So far, we're both on the same page, now I'm not so sure.

"Putting the collar on afterward. The collar is one of the most important symbols in the BDSM world. Psychologically and emotionally, it is similar to a wedding ring to some people. It can have other meanings as well. It could be for play, or it could symbolize the Dominant/submissive. We can't rule it out, yet."

I top off my coffee and stare at the cup. Was that collar around MJ's neck because she belonged to that man? I feel my chest tighten. Part of me wants to know, and the other part of me wants to snap the guy in half. When this is over, I'm going to have to talk to her about everything. Fuck, I don't even know if she is in a long-term relationship with the guy. So much time has gone by, yet, for me, time has stood still. Fear crippled me for so long, and I wasn't strong enough to fight it off.

"Fitz, hello where did you go on me?" I look up and realize Al is still talking to me.

"I'm sorry, I was processing everything you said. I lost you after the talk of collars."

She takes my hand and squeezes it. "I don't know what the situation is between you and MJ, but you need to put everything aside until this guy is caught or remove yourself from the case. You won't do this case any justice if you're not paying attention to all the details. Now focus, please.

"I watched that video you found online on the *dragonfly sleeve*. It's not that difficult once you get it started, but it's not something that we see in everyday life. Like I said earlier, I don't think he is a novice, the ropes and collars would suggest he is experienced."

"But, why is he putting the collar on afterward? If it is so important, why not have them wear it all the time?"

She throws some cash on the table. "Come on, let's go back to the office. I have some stuff to show you." We walk into the precinct and the captain doesn't even try to stop us.

"Thanks for breakfast, but next time it's on me."

"Shut up and pay attention. I stopped at the store on the way home last night." She reaches into her bag and pulls out a collar, very similar to the ones found on our victims. She puts it around her neck and tightens it.

"What the hell are you doing?!"

"Calm down, I want you to try to strangle me," she instructs. I think she's lost it. "Don't look at me like I've lost all reason, just try."

I walk up to her and place my right hand around her throat, but I can't get a good grip. I try both hands, but the collar is in the way. It's not easy to strangle someone; it takes time.

"I get it. He needed the collar off to strangle them. Take that thing off and let's get back to the profile. Tell me about the other victims." I take a seat while she heads to her whiteboard, which is where she is the most comfortable.

"All of them were on some sort of social media. All were single and white. The first victim was a single parent. We think she answered an online ad for employment. She is the only one whose mouth was taped shut. No prints could be lifted off the tape. He's probably somewhat good-looking and has charisma. He is able to charm them. Hell, Sophia was never at Mystik until she hooked up with him."

I'm rubbing the back of my neck, trying to ease my frustration. "Was Travis able to put together Sophia's movements for the two weeks leading up to her death?"

She flips through some papers until she finds exactly what she wants. "Yeah, sorry, I knew I saw it earlier. She was a pretty routine person: work, gym, and occasional dinners with friends. She frequented a club called The Village Underground. She always went out with the same group of friends. When they were interviewed, every one of them said she would have never gone to Mystik."

"Where is her gym?"

"Her gym is in Chelsea, why?" She shoots me a quizzical look.

What the fuck? "Wait, she worked at 1PP and lived by the UN, yet, she went to a gym in Chelsea, why?" I ask. She's looking at me and I know she doesn't get it. I jump up and draw it out on her whiteboard, a huge horseshoe. "Why go to a gym that is clearly out of the way for her, but close to Mystik?"

"Hold on, I remember seeing something about this in her file." She spreads out the papers and then finds what she is looking for.

"She used to live in Chelsea, she only moved into her apartment four months ago. Before that, she had a roommate who we already questioned. She had nothing new to add, what are you thinking?"

"We need to get to her gym; let's go." I grab my backpack and hold the door for her.

"Have you all of a sudden gotten a car?"

"No, but I bet you have one."

She reaches in her bag and tosses me her keys. "It's a rental; please don't kill it." We get to the car and it's some small economy box car. *She can't be serious.* We get in. I look over and she is laughing. "At least I have a car, Fitz."

I give her a huge smile. "Well, just wait till I put you on Wanda."

"Oh, hell no! I've seen you drive that thing! And poor Andy, his balls are probably still vibrating."

"After Andy had to stop driving, I thought about getting a car, but I knew it would piss him off. He complains about Wanda, but truth be told, he loves that I've made him feel like he hasn't lost his man card. For that reason alone, I would never get rid of her."

"How long have you been friends?"

I'm comfortable talking to her about Andy, which is strange, since I usually play everything close to the vest. "We met in kindergarten, served as altar boys, and went through Catholic school together. When we graduated, he went to NYU for business and I went to John Jay for Criminal Justice. He ended up becoming a Master Auto Mechanic. His first love has always been cars."

"I know you graduated top of your class, did you ever think of joining the BAU? You are so good at what you do, it seems like a logical progression."

"As long as my family is in Brooklyn, I will never leave." We pull up at the gym and the probing into my life is over with.

It's midday, and the gym is not that crowded. I let Al talk to the manager, while I have the receptionist, Rhonda, show me around. I blend in quiet well here; I don't look like a typical cop. I work out five days a week, two hours a day. She is going on and on about the different types of equipment they have and a variety of classes for every level. She explains that the Cross Fit classes are usually booked up pretty quickly. I let her go on and on as I look around the room. Could I be looking at a killer and not even know it? The thought sends a chill down my spine. She finishes her tour. I thank her and find Al waiting out front for me. We get into the car and head toward Mystik. "What did you find out?"

"Sophia was a regular member there for the past two years. She was very well liked and continued her membership because she loves the boxing classes. She was never seen in there with a man. Do you still think he might have found her there?"

"Hell if I know, but it's really the only place she has been that is close to Mystik." My thumb taps at the wheel to the beat of my racing thoughts. "We need to open the club tonight, are you sure you're ready for this?" I can tell by the way she is twisting and pulling at her shirt, she is uneasy about the whole thing.

"We will do what we have to do. In what capacity do you want me there tonight?"

We pull up, and I park in the alley. "Well, Travis will be monitoring the computers. I think the manager can keep an eye on the different rooms. You can walk the floors, keeping an eye on everyone. Make sure you wear a collar so no one bothers you. I'm going to tend bar, along with the regular bartender. Andy put a notice in the business journal and he leaked it yesterday to the *Post* Page Six." I turn and look at her and I try not to laugh, she has that squished face look.

"What the hell is *the Post* Page Six?"

"It's the rag—you know—the gossip page that everyone turns to first." I glance over again, noticing it doesn't seem to ring a bell with her. "Oh, come on! Don't tell me you don't look at that shit. I asked MJ once why she always turned to page six and she said it makes her own fuck-ups seem not so 'royal' anymore. Makes sense to me, some of these people are in the spotlight and, the reality is, they put their pants on one leg at a time, just like the rest of us." I cut the engine off. "We need to head inside to brief the staff, and then I want to check in with the detectives watching everyone."

We're barely in the door when the staff starts peppering us with questions. Al and I assure them that their jobs are secure and nothing will change. I watch to see who seems the most rattled, but there is nothing out of the ordinary. I let Al finish up with the staff while I head into MJ's office to make some calls. My phone rings and it's Kevin, the cop I have watching over Mom and Dad.

"Kevin, what's the problem?" My heart feels tight, and as much as I try, I can't stop the fear.

"Fitzgerald, why do you have this young man following me? I told him my son is a cop, and I have watched enough of those shows to know when I'm being followed," a familiar female voice greets me. I let out a deep breath and begin to laugh.

"Mom, I'm working a case, and since I can't be around all the time, I wanted to know that everyone is okay. I swear it's not a big deal."

"Well, you should have told me. You know I hate surprises. I'll give you back to him and make sure you show your face soon. I love you. Oh, and you might want to explain to this nice young man that I go to mass every day and tonight is Bingo."

Before I can say anything, Kevin is on the line. "Look, she is a tough one. I don't know how she figured out what I was doing. I sat through mass but do I have to sit through Bingo too?"

"Yeah, you do, and be thankful. She will probably make you dinner, so don't complain." I hang up and check in with Lucas. He informs me MJ and Andy never left the house. Knowing they are safe, I need to get everything ready for this club to open.

CHAPTER ELEVEN

Mark

I'VE BEEN AT IT ALL day, and I'm closer to finishing then I thought. I decided to paint the new soundproof walls a very pale green. I lay out the *Post* and put the pan with the roller on top. That's when I see it. Page Six of the rag talking about Mystik and Makenna Justice. I sink to my knees and read the story. *Makenna Justice, the owner of New York City's most elite private club, Mystik, has abruptly sold the business. Sources close to Ms. Justice said she is taking an extended vacation to St. Tropez, South of France. Could it be the ever-elusive Ms. Justice is finally off the market?*

This can't be true. There has never been any indication that she planned on selling the business, let alone take off to France with someone. I need to get to the club and see if I can figure out what is going on. I call it quits for the day, clean up, and head to the club to see if I can find out what the hell is going on.

I get on the ferry and pull up all her social media accounts—nothing. I log onto her computer again—nothing. I can't just go into the club and demand to see her. What am I going to do, hide in another doorway? Maybe I should go by her apartment to see if she really did leave. It's too late now and I'm already on the ferry.

Tomorrow, instead of going directly to my place, I'll go to hers.

There is a coffee shop across the street that gives me a direct line of site to her building. If that doesn't work, I know she has a brother. If I have to, I'll find him and beat it out of him. She's not getting away from me. I *will* have her. I've come *too* far to turn back now. I want to feel my fingers stroking her long neck. Her beautiful mane of flaming-red hair dancing around my cock, as her cherry red lips glide up and down. I close my eyes and will my cock to stop throbbing.

The boat docks. I get off, and head toward home. I was hoping Nicole wouldn't be home yet, but—no such luck. "Good evening, Nicole, how was work today?"

"I was asked to do a pro bono case on top of my already heavy caseload. Tell me again why we had to leave Chicago?"

I take a deep breath and rein in the urge to shut her up permanently. She is after all the perfect cover, she and the brat. "I'm sure now that you made junior partner, they want to see what you're made of. What type of case is it?" I pour myself a glass of wine and prepare to be bored, while I stroke her ever-growing ego.

"It's a murder case. They guy was a serial rapist and finally murdered his last victim."

Well, this just got interesting. "What do they want you to do?"

"It's his last appeal, and my boss wants me to make sure there are no mistakes." She takes a sip of her wine. "The firm is required to do a certain amount of pro bono cases per year to get a tax write off. Since I'm the only new junior partner in their criminal division, they tossed it to me."

"How much work do you think this is going to be? It is his last appeal, after all."

"Enough to keep me working late for the next couple of days."

"Does this mean we won't be going to the party tomorrow?" Oh, please say yes.

"No, we will still be going. I will have to meet you there. What happened with your potential client?"

"You know the way these old money clients can be. They want me jumping through hoops before they'll agree to anything." That should buy me some time away from home, especially when I get my hands on Makenna. "So, tell me more about your case. What would make the guy think he has a chance at an appeal?" Not that I plan on getting caught, however, one can never have too much information.

"He's claiming that he was discriminated against because he is white."

"Wait, hold up, that's a new one."

She pours us each more wine. "Not really, it's been used before but never in this context. He's claiming that since so many men of color are being locked up, the courts needed a scapegoat. He's forgetting he left his DNA in the stomach of one of the victims, and that's what nailed him for the murder. Science evolves and progresses over time. He left something of himself behind, and in the end, that's what bit him in the ass, not the color of his skin."

My mind instantly flashes to my first and the mistakes I made. Mistakes I will never make again. I will never forget her beautiful porcelain skin and flaming red hair. I've never seen anything like it, that is, until I met Makenna. Just the thought of her makes my cock throb. Maybe I can get Nicole to service me tonight. I put my glass down and reach for her, but she stops me.

"Not tonight, Mark, I have too much work to finish up."

This is why men go elsewhere to satisfy their needs. "I get that you're busy and you have deadlines, but I have needs. A simple blow job will suffice."

"I won't even dignify that with an answer." She picks up her papers and heads toward her office. Another night with just my hand, all the more reason I need to finish that room and find Makenna.

Makenna

A full day with just Andy and me and now I know why I live alone. I love him, but he is constantly up my ass. Stephen is working late, and we didn't hear from Fitz all day. My phone rings, snapping me out of my daze . . . Mom. "Hi, Mom, is everything okay?"

"No, it's not. Why did I have to find out from your brother that you have a new phone number?" she asks. I swear I'm going to kick Andy's ass.

"I was having a problem with my old phone number, lots of telemarketers calling me. How's Dad doing?" Maybe I can throw her off.

"He's fine, and don't change the subject, Makenna Marie. You can't lie to save your life. Why aren't you at work?" she continues her interrogation.

Shit, what the hell am I supposed to tell her? I race out of the room and slam into Andy. "Mom, hold on for a minute, I think my phone is beeping." I press disconnect.

"MJ, did you just hang up on Mom?!"

"What the hell am I supposed to tell her? She wants to know why I'm not at work and why I have a new phone number." Before he can answer, my phone rings again and it's her. "Sorry, Mom, new phone; I have no clue what I'm doing. I took a couple of days off to spend with Andy. I haven't spent much time with him and tomorrow we have a dinner party to go to for Stephen's work." Damn, I'm quick on my feet.

"Well, good, since you are with your brother, you can both come to Bingo with me. I know Stephen is working late tonight because *he* has the good sense to check in with me," she admonishes.

Crap. I smack Andy, and he begins to laugh.

"Okay, we will be by in a few to pick you up." I hang up and inform Andy we are going to Bingo. When we get there, she is outside talking to a man. I almost jump out of my skin until Mom introduces us to her bodyguard, Kevin.

"Mom, you're not supposed to socialize with him. He's here to do a job and you're distracting him."

"Nonsense, Kevin is doing a fine job. He even enjoyed Mass today. Although, I did have to explain to Father O'Connor that Kevin is Jewish," she adds. The look on Kevin's face is priceless. We all pile into my car and head over to Bingo. We get inside and Mom insists that Kevin has to play too. My brother is hysterically laughing and Mom is trying to match me up with Kevin! Finally, he saves me and informs her that he is married, his wife is pregnant with their first child, and she is due any day.

Mom takes Bingo very seriously, no talking until intermission. The minute intermission is called, there is a mad dash for the bathrooms. I race to keep up with her. "Mom, did you hear from Fitz today?"

"Of course, *he* checks in with me every day." Oh, the glaring look. *Thanks, Fitz, for throwing me under the bus.*

"Makenna, he is very busy on a new case, but he wanted to make sure we were safe. Is everything okay? Why are you staying at Andy's house? I'm only around the corner; you could come home and sleep in your old bed."

Now it begins, a peppering of questions, and I know I can't tell her much, but she is relentless. "Mom, please stop. I'm going home on Saturday. I just took a few days off to spend some time with my brother. I'll meet you back at the table; I need to make a phone call." And with that, I head out and try to call Fitz, but there is no service in here. I step outside and Lucas is by the curb. I call Fitz and he answers on the first ring.

"MJ, are you safe? Is everything okay?"

"Calm down. Yes, we are at Bingo. What is going on at the club? I hate not being there," I complain as I pick at a loose string on my jeans.

"Poor Kevin; Mass and Bingo all in one day. The club is very quiet, almost too quiet. I had Travis pull the file you had on your tech guy. He's clean and I'll leave him here. I don't want to raise any suspicions. Travis will still stay here and monitor everything from your office. Al is doing a sweep of the place every thirty minutes. Like I said, it's very quiet."

"Do you think I can come back to work?" Silence, I check to make sure the call didn't drop. "Fitz?"

"I'm here, MJ, please give me time," his plea is almost too much for me to take.

"I loved the pictures, thank you."

"You're welcome. You're going to the dinner party tomorrow night with Andy and Stephen." He's not asking; he's telling me I have no choice.

"Will you be able to come too?"

"I gotta go. I'll try to stop by tomorrow." Before I can say good-bye, I hear Travis calling him, and the phone disconnects. Just like that I'm alone—*again.*

Fitz

I hated hanging up on her, but I can't go there yet. I need to focus on right here and right now. The club is quiet except for some of the regulars that come in daily. I think it's more for the social inter-action. The regular bartender said it doesn't usually get busy until Friday night. I wanted to go to the dinner party with her, but I need

109

to be here. The sound of Travis yelling at me snaps me out of my thoughts. "What's the problem?"

"Let's go into MJ's office and talk." He's bouncing from foot to foot with excitement.

When I get in her office, I head right to the coffee bar. Something tells me I'm going to need it.

"I've been working on backtracking his movements to see if I can figure out exactly what he pulled from MJ's laptop and phone. Everything we do leaves a footprint, unless you permanently erase it. He's good, but I'm better. I copied everything from her laptop and dumped it into my system. I was able to wipe out the code he wrote. I haven't been able to track him yet, but I can see what he pulled from her computer. You might want to have a seat for this, Fitz."

I mentally pray this is not as bad as the grim look on Travis's face. I pull a chair next to his and take a deep breath. "Okay, what did you find?"

"First, he watched her for hours in her apartment. He made a video and embedded it in one of her computer files. I can't understand why he put it there. Did he want her to find it?"

God, this keeps getting worse. "Let me see it."

He seems apprehensive to let me watch it. "Before I do, I have to tell you it's very personal. Make sure you watch it to the very end. I'll step out, and when you're done, I have more." He steps out of the office, and I take a deep breath and click play.

There is nothing wrong with her giving herself pleasure. Knowing that someone was watching her without her knowledge makes my blood boil. There is no sound but when she finds her release, it's my name on her lips. I pause it; I have to gain control. I've wasted so much time and I'll never get that back. Remembering what Travis said, I click play.

The last frame is this sick fuck pounding his cock, coming, and then wiping it all over the screen! I throw my cup against the wall and it shatters into a million pieces. The crash sends Al and Travis barreling through the door. "Sorry, didn't mean to do that." It was that or break Travis's computer. He comes over and quickly closes the video.

"The second thing I want to show you is this, but please, Fitz, no throwing."

He brings up another video, and it's MJ in her bedroom applying body lotion. "Is it really necessary that I watch this?"

I reach for the mouse, but he grabs my hand. "Yes, watch when she gets to her right hip."

I see it, and my hand instantly touches mine. She's got the same tat as me, she never told me. "So she has a tattoo, millions of people have them, what's the big deal?"

"I know that. Hell, I have sleeves. But, remember the fake name the killer used? Lex Luther—Superman's archenemy. We need to find out why MJ has this tat; it could lead us to the killer." I hold my hand up, stopping him before he goes any further.

"I already know why she has it and it won't help."

Al leans up against the desk and squeezes my shoulder, trying to calm me down. "Fitz, maybe you're too close to all of this. Let me talk to MJ about the tat. She might feel more comfortable opening up to me. Besides, can you say one-hundred-percent you know why she got it?" she asks as if she doubts me. I stand up and unzip my jeans, pulling them down enough for her to see my tat. Her eyes grow wide and she bites her lip. "Yeah, I think it's safe to say I know why she got it."

I pull myself back together and go get another cup of coffee. "That doesn't change the profile this bastard made, calling himself Lex Luther," Travis pipes up. We both stare at him; he's right.

"You're right, it doesn't," I agree then turn my attention to my partner. "And Al, I know I'm close, but that changes nothing." I'm not turning this over to anyone. She gives me an understanding nod.

"I know you and Al probably thought of this, but could this possibly be part of a prior case you worked on or someone from MJ's past that knows about whatever it is between the two of you?"

"I thought of that the first time I saw the profile, but nothing comes to mind. You've been through MJ's social media accounts, so you know there are not a lot of pictures of me on there. I think there is only a couple from Andy's wedding. I've never wanted to put any of them in danger."

Al gets up and pours another cup of coffee. "I know you think it has nothing to do with you, but we can't rule anything out."

I know she's right, but my gut is telling me otherwise.

"Travis, the first video you showed me—the last scene—can you find that and roll from there, please?" Every time I'm in this damn office, I'm watching something that makes me sick.

The screen comes to life and the sick fuck's cock is in plain view. I want to cut it off and ram it down his throat. "I want you to try to isolate every object in the room. Now go to the last frame—*stop!*" I walk right up to the screen, my face inches from it.

"Fitz, what is it? All I see is a guy's right hand smearing his come all over the screen."

"That's where we differ. I see a wedding band on the guy's left hand and some sort of tattoo on his left arm. He's in a dress shirt and the cuff is rolled up enough to see the tat peaking out from under it. I see a tablet—not a computer, propped up on a bed. He somehow made a video of himself whacking off and added it to the end of the video. He wanted MJ to find this. We can't see MJ on his tablet because he has one of those privacy films over his screen, which acts as a mirror.

"We can't see him, but blow up that picture and see what is reflected on the screen. Look past the tablet on the upper left-hand corner of the screen, there is some sort of picture frame on a dresser. I want every item blown up so I can examine them. Try to get a clearer picture of the tat, it could mean something. Send both videos to my phone."

Travis gets to work on it right away, but Al is back at her whiteboard, scribbling away. "If he's so OCD, why did he smear the screen?" She writes it on her board, in red, with huge question marks.

"Who knows, maybe that's why he used a tablet and not his computer."

"Would any of your past convictions or open cases fit into anything involving this guy?" I'm about to answer where there's a knock on the door, and before I can see who it is, the manager, Bobby, walks right in. Al quickly flips the board around and Travis blacks out the screen.

"Sorry to interrupt, but there is a reporter here, and he is asking to speak to the new owners."

"Thank you, Bobby, please let him know I'll be right with him and next time, please wait for me to let you in," I'm assertive and I guess he's not used to that because he leaves with a puss on his face. Frankly, I don't give a fuck. No wonder everything of MJ's is compromised; she has an open door policy and no boundaries. Some things never change. I head out and find the guy waiting in the lounge. I take him to a more quiet area of the club. He introduces himself as Justin, a reporter from the Post. "Hello, Justin, I'm Mr. Rodriguez, one of the new owners. What can I do for you today?" I shake his hand and we have a seat. Both of us sizing each other up.

"Word on the street is this was a quick sale and everything is very hush-hush, why?"

"What does it matter to you? My partner and I purchased the business; everything went through the proper channels. Ms. Justice decided she wanted to travel. We were in the right place at the right time, nothing more." Why would this guy even care who owns this place?

"I find that odd since two months ago I interviewed her for a piece on Mystik and the woman behind the hottest club in New York City. Makenna never indicated that she wanted to sell, on the contrary, she talked about possibly branching out to another location."

Fuck, why didn't she tell me about the piece this guy did?

"I must have missed that article, Justin. You know, sometimes things just change. Who knows? For whatever reason, Ms. Justice decided not to expand. She took a rather lucrative deal and is headed off to France. I'm sure if you're that interested, you can try to contact her."

"The article came out last month, and it was a big hit. My editor wants me to do a follow up piece. I tried to contact her, but it goes straight to voice mail. I just find it odd."

"Why don't you leave me your card, and if I hear from Ms. Justice, I will pass it along to her," I offer. He gets up and thanks me before taking a quick look around and then he leaves.

I check the time, and right about now, I wish I had my bike here. I go back in the office and relay everything Justin told me to Travis and Al. "Travis can you access the *Post* database and pull that article for me? He said it was a month ago and all of this started around that time. Maybe there is a connection. Al can you and Travis close up? I need to go home and get my bike."

I start to head out the door, and Al grabs me. "Go easy on her. It could be a total coincidence that the article came out around the same time the killing started."

"It's actually dead out there. Why don't we close up early and you can drop me off. It will give me a chance to read the article."

We get the place closed up pretty quickly and head out. Al drives while I read the article. "MJ talks about the club but never really gives anything away about what type of club it is, only that it is a very elite, members only club. It's all pretty basic stuff, so why was this guy so hot to know why she sold?"

"Fitz, maybe he has a thing for her. He said her phone went to voicemail, which means she gave him her number. She's beautiful, young, and the owner of the top BDSM club in New York City. The only way he's not hitting on her is if he's gay," she hits me up with a dose of reality. "Do you want me to drop you at your house or Andy's?"

I put the paper back in the folder with the pictures Travis printed out for me. "Andy's house, please." She pulls up next to the officer I have watching the house and lets me out. I watch her pull away before I head up the steps. I could use my key, but it's late and I would like to think the alarm is on. I hit the bell and quickly get buzzed in.

Stephen's waiting at the top of the steps for me. "Is everything okay?"

"Yeah, I didn't want to set off the alarm. Where is MJ?" I'm trying not to sound pissed off, but the more I dwell on things, the more pissed I'm getting—at her and at myself. He hands me a bottle of water. "Maybe you should take a moment to gather your thoughts and try to calm down."

I know he's right, and I know I need to vent to someone. "Can we go out back for a chat?"

We head out back, and I reach in my pocket and pull out a dollar. I hand it to him and he smiles. "I'm invoking attorney-client privilege."

"Fitz, you know I would never betray a confidence."

"I know, but what I want to talk to you about is work related and I need your logical mind." I hand him the article. "Read this, please."

"Okay, I remember when she said she did this interview."

"The killings started when this article came out. It could be nothing, but I'm not sure. The reporter came by the club tonight looking for her. He had her cell phone number. Again, this could all be a coincidence. The killer watched her in her apartment and made videos. They are pretty sick. He spliced himself into one of them, beating off at the end and then smeared his come all over the screen shot of MJ."

"Well, it's apparent that she is the target. The question is: why?"

I throw my hands up in frustration. "Hell, don't you think I've asked myself that a million times? Al thinks I'm too close and, honestly, part of me agrees with her. The other part of me feels like I'm the only one who can save her. I'm finding it hard to be objective. I want to throw her on my bike, drive away, and never look back. What if I tell her how I really feel, and then it blows up in my face? They're all I have in this world. What would I do if that changed?"

"You're letting fear cripple you. I know in your mind that fear is very real, but everyone in this family loves you; you'll never lose any of us. I agree that you need to keep your head on straight right now, and that this might not be the best time to come clean with her. We will keep her isolated and safe while you concentrate on your job. You've got a cop stationed here and one on Mom and Dad. Andy is with her all day long so she is never alone."

"What about the videos? Should I tell her?" I know the answer, but I need to hear it from him.

"You know what I'm going to say. She needs to hear it, and it needs to come from you. If she finds out later or hears it from someone else, your ass is toast."

"I hate it when you're right. Give me back my dollar."

He's laughing as he heads inside. "Nope, easiest dollar I've ever made."

"Where is this dinner tomorrow? I think I want to add more security."

"It's called Daniel, it's in midtown. MJ and Andy will meet me there around eight. Are you coming?"

"No, I have to watch the club, and I'm not comfortable leaving

Al there alone. I might have Travis go as her date. He is our tech guy, and MJ has met him before."

He grabs my arm before I head down the hall to find her. "Go easy on her, she's in the first guest room."

When I get to her room, the light peers out from under the door. I knock, but there is no answer. I try the knob and it's locked. My chest instantly tightens, and I knock a little harder…*nothing*. Why the hell is the door locked? I'm about ready to kick the door in and Stephen grabs me.

"She probably didn't even realize she locked it. I venture to say she's probably fast asleep, I've got a key." He opens the door. MJ is asleep with all the lights on.

"I'll be okay, I promise. I won't even wake her." I wave good night and head inside, quickly closing the door behind me. She is a vision that I can't explain, I never could.

I've blocked my feelings for her for so long that I'm afraid if I let them rise to the surface, I might not be able to control them. I want to crawl into that bed and pull her into my arms. I know I can't; once I start, I won't be able to stop. There is no going back with her ever. I curl up in the chair next to the bed, and soon, I fall into a deep sleep.

CHAPTER TWELVE

Makenna

SUNSHINE FILLS THE ROOM. APPARENTLY, I forgot to close the blinds last night. I turn over and find Fitz asleep in the chair. He's got to be so uncomfortable. I get up and quietly head into the bathroom to shower. I wish he hadn't been at the club last night. Truth be told, I've never wanted him there. Unfortunately, life is not all sunshine and roses. Most days, it's lonely.

I'm almost thirty years old and the big excitement for me was going to Bingo with my mother and brother. Sometimes, I hate myself for loving him. My daydreams of him fill my head, making my skin flush. I quickly turn the hot water off and it instantly turns chilly. I finish up and head back to my room. He's still in the same position. I'll let him sleep a little bit longer before I wake him. I start to head out.

"Where are you going? We need to talk." I turn around at the sound of his raspy voice. The sad look on his face tears me up inside.

"What the hell happened? You look like you lost your puppy or something," I ask. He gets up out of the chair moaning and groaning. "It's a queen size bed; I wouldn't bite, you know."

He takes my hand and pulls me back toward the bed. "I know,

but I didn't trust myself," he barely whispers, but I know what I heard. My breath catches in my throat.

"What the hell happened? What are you afraid to tell me?" My stomach instantly knots, and I sit on the edge of the bed. He pulls the chair in front of me and sits down.

"Why didn't you tell me about the interview with the *Post*?"

My mind is racing, trying to remember what interview he's talking about. Finally, I remember the reporter who asked me out for coffee. "I really didn't think twice about it; I've done interviews in the past. It's all part of marketing. What's the big deal?"

"The article came out right around the time the murders started. The guy who interviewed you came by the club looking for you. Apparently, you gave him your cell number. Why would you do that?"

He can't be serious. Oh my God, he is. "I'm a single woman with no ties. He seemed nice enough and wanted to get together for coffee." I don't even remember his name; he was a momentary distraction and nothing more. "Fitz, what are you holding back? What are you afraid to tell me?" I'm trying to be strong and not that needy little girl, but the look on his face is grim.

"Travis found two videos on your computer. He had a whole technical term for how he did it, but bottom line: they were on there and they were a severe violation of your privacy."

My hands begin to tremble, and I fight to hold back the tears. "Tell me the truth, how bad?" I ask. He takes my hands in his, trying to stop the trembling.

"They were both in your bedroom. The first one, you must have just gotten out of the shower, and you were applying lotion. The second was more personal."

My lip is quivering as I try to get the words out. "Did you watch them?" He doesn't have to answer, his face tells it all. I lose the battle with my tears. He pulls me onto his lap and rocks me in the safety of his arms. My skin flushes a deep red—I'm totally mortified.

"MJ, you have nothing to be embarrassed about. You were in the privacy of your own home. Your expectation of privacy was violated. You did nothing wrong, please look at me," he pleads. I look up and he pulls off his shirt and begins wiping my tear stained face with it. "I can't reach the tissue box; my legs are numb."

I get up and grab a bunch of tissues and throw his shirt back at him. "So, after watching me in all my glory, did you at least learn anything?" It hits me that Travis saw it too and I feel my newfound courage begin to fail. I've been on display before, at my club but it was on my terms. *My* choice, not the choice of a deranged killer.

"Yeah, the guy is married and I'm looking into some other things I saw on the video."

Part of me wants to ask him to play them for me but then I feel the knot in my gut. "Maybe I should watch the v—"

"—No . Fucking. Way." He leaps out of the chair, his face inches from mine, shutting me down before I can even explain.

"I'm not a little girl anymore. Maybe you should stop treating me like one. Maybe I can shed some light on when the videos were taken. I know you want to protect me from all the ugliness but keeping me in the dark might not be the way to go here." I soften my voice and take a different approach with him. "I'm not ashamed of my body or what I've done. I'm pissed that I've been violated."

He closes his eyes and takes a deep breath… "Okay, but if it get's to be too much, stop it."

He pulls out his phone and his screen saver is the same prom picture. He unlocks his phone, pulls up the video, and hands it to me. "I'll step out and give you some privacy. Let me know when you're done."

I sink into the chair and hit play. The first one is after a shower and I'm putting on lotion. It dawns on me Fitz knows about my tattoo. I push that from my mind and focus on the video, trying to see when this was taken. This is my daily routine, so it's hard to tell, until I see the flowers on my dresser. The guy that interviewed me from the *Post* sent them to me. That, at least, establishes a timeline. I move on to the next video. I don't think I need to see myself with Fabio. Yeah, if I've got to use it, then he better have a sexy-as-hell name.

I'm sure Fitz realizes it's his name I call out, it always is. I freeze it and try to remember when this was. It's been about two weeks since Fabio came out to play, plus the flowers are gone. I press play and that's when this gets sick and twisted. I stop the video and get up to go find Fitz. When I open the door, he's leaning against the wall. I knew he wouldn't be far away.

"I've established a time line, maybe that will help you. In the shower video there were flowers on my dresser. I got those from the guy from the *Post*. The other video was about two weeks ago. The guy has a tat on his left arm that kind of looks like a rope in the shape of an infinity twist, but it is hard to make out on the phone. There also appears to be something in the middle of it but I can't make it out. His wedding band has some sort of design in the middle of it. Again, it's hard to tell what it is. Does this help you at all?"

I hand him his phone and he pulls me into his arms. "I'm in awe of you. You're so strong and brave. Yes, this does help me. Travis ran a check on the reporter last night and he's clean. I wanted to go to the dinner party tonight but I don't want to leave Al by herself, so Travis is going as your date."

"Is that really necessary? I'll be with Andy and Stephen, plus the extra security you put on us. Which by the way, Mom told Kevin he can sleep in your old room. I thought they were supposed to stay on the street?"

His jaw is ticking and I think I just got his friend in trouble. "Please tell me he didn't take her up on her offer?"

"I don't know for sure, but if he did, she probably made him pay with his Bingo winnings. Come on, you need a shower and I need coffee." As much as I hate for him to let me go, I know now is not the right time. I go downstairs to the kitchen and make coffee while he heads into the shower.

When I get into the kitchen, the smell of food cooking is wonderful, but, it also means Andy is nervous. He cooks when he's nervous, and if he's really upset, he bakes. I watch him from a distance, trying to gauge how upset he is. His meds help his tremors, but not all the time.

"I know you're there, MJ. Come in and sit down, coffee is ready." He sighs. I grab a cup and once again, I have to decide between ten different creamers.

"Fitz is in the shower. He is not going to the dinner tonight. Travis is going as my date. Did Stephen leave already?"

He refills his cup and sits next to me while we wait for Fitz to come down. "He ran out of here early this morning. You know Fitz takes longer than most women do, so spill." He takes a sip of his coffee. I don't know how much to tell him.

"Andy, quit trying to pump her for information." I never even heard him come in.

"Well, Stephen flew out of here this morning and he wouldn't tell me anything. Sit down, I made breakfast," he commands. Fitz quickly says grace and begins to devour his breakfast.

"While you're inhaling your omelet, let me fill you in on what I know about tonight. Stephen said he is having a car pick us up. He didn't think you wanted MJ to drive to the city or have us show up in a police car. Should we pick Travis up or will you have him meet us there?"

"I've already been in contact with the owner of the restaurant and security has been increased. Travis will meet you there, along with a female officer. You are to have an eye on one of them at all times. Hey, MJ, are you paying attention?" He nudges me and I almost spill my coffee.

"Yes, I'm paying attention, it's just a little bit overwhelming going from doing whatever the hell I want, when I want, to having a watch dog twenty-four seven. I do, however, have a question. If I'm supposed to be tooling around France, why would I be seen at a party?"

Fitz gets up and pours himself another cup of coffee. "I won't leave you alone in the house, not even with guards. The party is small and in a private room. There is an increase of security for the venue. The sale was only announced a few days ago, for all anyone knows, you could be leaving this weekend. I'm not squirreling you away and I'm not offering you up as bait, I'm having you live your life . . . carefully. I'll contact Stephen and have the driver for tonight replaced with Lucas. I'm going home to get Wanda and some extra clothes. I also need to talk to Mom about security. I didn't hire Kevin so she could take him to Bingo. I'm surprised she didn't try to match you up with him."

I shoot Andy the, *shut up before I smack you,* look.

"I have to go back to my place to get stuff for tonight." I get up and begin clearing the table. Andy cooked, I clean.

"I've got to get going, Andy make sure you hang with her all day. I've got my key; I'll be back later." He grabs his keys, and he's out the door.

"I, for one, have had enough of sitting in this house. I need to go to my place and get my stuff. And, while we're out, why don't we make a day of it?" I don't give him a chance to protest, I'm already pushing him out the door.

Fitz

I take the shortcut through the alley and find Kevin sitting on the stoop with Mom, having coffee. I rein in my temper and head over to them. "Hey, Mom, I need to talk to Kevin about work, can you give us a few, please."

"He's been very helpful, and he won at Bingo last night." That's her way of telling me to take it easy on him. She heads upstairs and when she is out of earshot, I lay into him.

"You are supposed to be keeping a watch on my family, not playing fucking Bingo!"

"Hold on, Fitz, I had no choice. I went with her to Mass and my Jewish grandmother is probably rolling over in her grave right now. That church is huge and has too many exits, so I went in with her. Then, when we went to bingo, Andy and Makenna were with us, so Lucas stayed outside and kept an eye on everything while I went inside. I had to look like I belonged there, I can't help it if I'm lucky at Bingo."

"How did she explain who you are?"

"She told everyone I was her nephew from Baltimore, and I was staying with her for a while."

"I'm a little shocked that she went along with all of this."

"She refused to lie to Father O'Connor. He made her say an extra Rosary."

"I won't be around much this weekend but I will check in with you." I head inside to get some of my stuff and check on Dad He was hurt in the line of duty and is homebound now by choice, but he can still make us all toe the line. They are my safe place, the only place I'm never judged, always accepted. They saved me when no one else would. If I ever have a child, they will be my guiding force. They made me a better person with their unconditional love.

I get my stuff, text Stephen and Lucas, letting them know about the changes for tonight. I need to get to the station and bring the captain up to speed. I also want to talk to Gail about the first murder in California. I'm sure the forensic department in LA did a great job, but another set of eyes can't hurt. I also want to show her the second video; maybe she will see something none of us have.

Mark

My mood today is dark, darker than usual. I've been sitting in this coffee shop for hours. I didn't want to miss her, but there has been so sign of her. Something is off. Every time I log into any of her social media accounts, it's like time stood still. She can't be gone, there was never any indication that she was selling or that she was involved with anyone. I'm giving her thirty minutes, and then I'm heading out to find her. I know she has a brother that also lives in Brooklyn. I pretend I'm watching some movie and when I look up, I see her heading towards the cafe with a guy. Not the same guy as the other day.

I quickly pull the brim of my baseball cap down lower and pop in my ear buds. The sound is off so I'm able to still hear everything. Her thick, long, red hair is in a beautiful side braid. The thought of my fist wrapped around it, while my cock is buried deep inside her, instantly makes me hard. The barista is chatting her up while the other guy is talking to another barista about the available pastries. He finally turns around and I recognize him from the pictures on one of her social media sites. I focus on her, and she tells the young man that she won't be around for a while, she is taking her brother on vacation.

The guy is joking around about his sister finally treating him to a trip. Hmm, so this is her brother, still not the guy on the bike. They take their stuff and head back across the street. So, she is leaving. Even more reason I need to step up my plan. I need to finish the room today and then go to that stupid party with Nicole. By tomorrow, I plan on making Makenna Justice mine—forever. I quickly gather up my stuff and head to my apartment.

CHAPTER THIRTEEN

Fitz

I GET TO THE PRECINCT and it's relatively quiet for a change. That is, until Captain Hart sees me. "Fitz, my office—now! " he bellows. I have yet to figure out why he always yells instead of talking like a normal person.

"Captain, before you go off on me, I'm here to update you before I have to head out." That shut him right up. I bring him up to speed on everything I know at this point, including the videos. Thankfully, he doesn't ask to see them.

He gets up and looks out his window to the street below. "Normally, Fitz, I would pull you off of this. You're too close—you know it and so do I. The thing is, you're the best at what you do. Exactly how you do it, I have no idea, but you have the ability to clear more of these types of cases than anyone else." He slaps the back of my shoulder. "Do you think putting the announcement in the paper might have scared him off?"

"No, I think, if anything, it has pushed his game plan up. We know he has MJ in his sights. He could have made a move on her already, but he didn't. She is the prize, although, I'm not sure when that happened. Sometimes a killer will get fixated upon one person

127

or one type of person. They kill over and over again, practicing until they get their prize. Sometimes they never go after the prize. Sometimes they keep it dangling in the distance as their motivator. If he knows she is leaving the country, it might make him do something foolish, make some sort of mistake. I've got a guard on her twenty-four seven. One of us is with her at all times and Captain, she is cooperating."

He sits down and takes a deep breath. "Do you think this guy knows about you? I mean, if he got into her phone and computer, then he must have at least seen pictures of you with her. I know your foster care records were sealed, but if he finds out who you are and that you're a cop, it could send him crawling back to wherever he came from."

"There's nothing I can do about that. Everything that happened to me, my father murdering my mother, is a matter of public record. I also put protection on Mom and Dad." I look at my watch and realize I've got to catch Gail before she heads out to lunch. "I need to get that video over to Gail and then meet Al at the club. I'll keep you posted."

"Fitz, please be careful, and if you need anything, call me." He gets real quiet and then quickly shoos me out of his office. He tries not to show that he's worried, but I've known him a long time. I know when he's worried.

I quickly forward the video over to Gail with a text to call me after she watches it. I know I'm grasping at straws, but maybe a fresh set of eyes might help. I check in with Al before I leave the station and she assures me everything is very quiet. I call MJ and it goes to voicemail. My heart leaps into my throat. I try again, no answer. I call Andy and he answers on the first ring. "Where the fuck is she?"

"Calm down, Fitz, we're at Mom's. MJ is in the basement."

I swear I'm wound up so tight, I'm about to snap. "Why the hell is she in the basement?"

"She went downstairs to get the fishing poles. We decided to hang out on the pier and fish for a few hours. We went to her place and got some of her stuff, but it was still early, so we figured we could get out of here for a bit. We wanted to go to Coney Island, but Lucas flipped out."

Sending her away is sounding better and better. "Please be careful and make sure Lucas stays close. I gotta run; my phone is beeping." Great, it's Gail.

"Hey, did you watch it?"

"Hello to you too, Fitz. Yes, pretty sick stuff. She must feel very violated. I'm not a computer person, but I will help you if I can. What do you want to know?"

"I needed another set of eyes, someone who is not personally attached to anyone in the case. When the video got to the part where he inserted himself into the frame, tell me what you saw?" I step outside and I'm instantly hit with that wave of August heat.

"From what I can tell, his penis is average size. He had no identifiable marks. He had a tattoo on his left arm. It looked to be some sort of infinity symbol made into a rope design. There was something in the middle of it, but I couldn't make out what it was. He's married and from what I could see of his nails and hands I would say well groomed. He has money and plenty of it judging by the dresser in the room. I think I know the company and I will send you over the link for their website. Does any of this help you?" Finally, some sort of lead, as slim as it is, it's still a lead.

"I want you to pull the file from the first case in LA. See if you can get anything from the evidence that they collected. Al thinks it was his first case, or, at least, the first one we know of. The first are usually the sloppiest. Let me know what you come up with. Thank you, Gail, and if you think of anything else, email me." I hang up, start up Wanda, and head to the 69th Street Pier. When we were kids, and MJ would get upset, she always went fishing off the pier.

It doesn't take me long to get there and, sure enough, Andy is sunning himself while MJ stares into the water. I stay back and watch her for a bit. Her beauty takes my breath away. She has never been a showy kind of girl. She's never needed all the trappings that go along with it. Family is everything to her. When Andy was first diagnosed, it nearly killed her. I know she's scared—hell—we all are, but she is trying to keep calm for his sake. I walk up behind her and laugh, she is the only girl I know who fishes with popcorn and always catches the biggest one.

"Hey, MJ, how many did you throw back so far?" She never keeps them.

"Six big ones, what are you doing here?"

"I wanted to check in with you before I head into the city."

She graces me with her million watt smile. "More like, checking up on me. We are fine, but if Andy doesn't put more sunscreen on, he will be a lobster by tonight. At least, I had the sense to wear a hat. Is there anything new on the case?"

I would love to be able to tell her we caught the bastard but right now all I can do is protect her. "When I have something, I promise, I will let you know. Now, where's my fishing pole?" I solicit a laugh from her and it is infectious.

"You might as well use Andy's; he's too busy reading trashy magazines." She nods her head to where he left it. I grab the pole, cast my line, and stare out at the waves. It's peaceful and tranquil and I miss this, it's been too long.

"What if you don't catch him? I can't stay hidden away forever."

"Give me a chance, please. I'm trying to put and end to all of this."

Her fingers tremble as she reaches up and tucks a strand of my hair behind my ear. "I know you are and I trust you. I promise I will do what you need me to. When I went home to pick up some more of my stuff, we stopped at the coffee house across the street. I let the barista know that I'm taking Andy on a vacation. We also spoke to the building super and told him the same story. I figured in case anyone inquires, they will, at least, get the same answers."

"That was good thinking." My phone beeps; it's a text from Gail, letting me know I need to check my email. "I gotta get going, I'll see you tonight. Make sure you stick together tonight." I pass Andy my fishing pole and yell at him to put more sunscreen on before he turns into a lobster.

I quickly check the email and it's more information on the dresser. I don't know that it will be useful but I will go over it with Al and Travis. I hop on Wanda and head into the city. This time of day I can be there in twenty minutes max. I pray she found some sort of clue that might help us.

Mark

I really like my new apartment, it's going to make the perfect hiding place. I put up the acoustic foam on the walls and then new drywall over it. Today, I was finally able to paint the room and it only took me two hours. It's amazing how much I can get done when I'm motivated. While I'm waiting for everything to dry, I look through the *Post* to see if there is anything else on Mystik or Makenna. Sure enough, there is another mention on Page Six. Nothing really new, just more mystery surrounding the sale and the so-called quick exit by Makenna Justice.

None of this makes sense to me. She was always at the club and now all of a sudden she sells it and makes plans to leave the country, why? Who was the guy on the Harley? She was way too comfortable with him for it to be a one night stand, or even a mild acquaintance.

The paint should be dry, and I need to get things finished up here. Obsessing about her is not going to get the job done. The new bed was delivered, along with a few chairs and a lamp. I look around and I think the place is finally ready for her. I need to get home and cleaned up for this stupid party tonight. I want to blow it off, but there would be no living with Nicole if I didn't show up. I take one last look around before I lock up and head towards home. The ferry is quiet this time of day and, before I know it, I find myself headed toward Mystik.

I know I shouldn't go by the club right now—it's a distraction—but I can't help myself. The thought of her instantly makes my cock throb. I casually walk past the alley, looking for her car. The only thing there is a small car and that Harley—*again*! I hang around for a little bit, but no one is coming out. I can't wait around any longer. If she really sold the club, then I will have to get her from her apartment, before she leaves the country. No matter what, she will be mine.

Fitz

Zipping through the city on Wanda gets me to the club in record time. I park by Al's car in the alley. She will be surprised that I actually drove myself in today. The liquor delivery shows up just as I'm heading in. "Hey, I'm Mr. Rodriguez, one of the new owners. Are you the regular delivery guy?" I inquire. He's eyeing me up and down. He seems apprehensive to answer.

"What happened to Ms. Justice? She didn't say she was selling the place," he finally pipes up. I hold open the loading door for him.

"Yeah, it was rather sudden. She decided she wanted to travel. So, how often do you make your deliveries here?"

"She usually gets her order in on Monday and I deliver on Friday. If you have a special request, you need to give me two weeks lead-time. Oh, and my name is Malcolm."

I know Al has vetted all the delivery people but sometimes it helps to make them feel comfortable. It gets them to open up more. "So, Malcolm, how long have you been delivering to Mystik?"

"This has been my route for two years now. Will you be making many changes?"

"Don't worry, we will be keeping everything the same. Not about to fix something that's not broken." That seems to satisfy his curiosity.

I head into the office and find Al and Travis talking with a woman that resembles MJ, so closely, I do a double take.

"Fitz, this is Olivia Holmes, an agent out of our DC office." Al gives a quick introduction. "Grab a cup of coffee and have a seat; I have a plan," she announces. I skip the coffee and have a seat. "Keep an open mind and hear me out. I pulled up all the stuff our killer has left on MJ's computer and I think we might be able to use his fixation on her to our advantage. Olivia's area of expertise is stalking crimes. I'll let her explain the plan." She shuffles her hand out to her to take over.

"Fitz, after looking over all the files, including the ones from LA and Chicago, it seems he was not seeking one type of victim. Everything about each victim was different. He only brought victim two and three here, not the first one. That would suggest he didn't see MJ until after his first victim.

"Back the timeline up and track MJ's movements from right after the first victim died. It seems like he found what he was searching for when he saw MJ. That fixation will cause him to make a mistake, they always do. I get that you announced the sale of this club to get her out of here and protect her, but that doesn't work to our advantage, it helps him." She leans forward in her seat. "I want to move into MJ's apartment and I'll hang out here, helping the new owners with the transition. Let him see that MJ is carrying on her life without a care in the world. He needs to feel comfortable enough to make a move on her. We don't want him to disappear or fixate on someone else," she finishes. I head over to the coffee bar, wishing I could have something stronger.

"So, I need to keep MJ totally hidden away while you assume her life. It sounds great except for two things. First, you are a close fit for her, but if he gets close enough, he will know you're not her. Second, how the hell am I going to keep her locked away while you put this plan in motion? MJ is the most obstinate woman on the face of the earth."

"We need to give him bait if we want to draw him out into the open and this is the best way. As far as MJ is concerned, maybe if we tell her everything we know she might be more apt to go along with the plan. I want Travis to set up her computer so he can see me in her apartment, but I will be careful not to let him see my face. I want to taunt him like he is taunting us."

"Okay, I'll go along with it. I don't see that we have a choice. Did you have any luck with the tat?"

"We were able to clean up the picture of his tat. It's a rope infinity sign with a small rose in the center of it. We couldn't do anything with the picture on the dresser due to the angle. The only thing that we could see from his reflection on the tablet is a guy in a dress shirt with the cuffs rolled up."

"Travis, have you gotten any further along with tracking the videos?"

"No, he's used some sort of program that I've never seen before; chances are, it's homemade. I did find another folder with more pictures. He labeled the folder 'Fun with Makenna'; it's sick, twisted, and there's no reason you need to see it."

My head is beginning to pound and all the coffee in the world won't help it.

"Fitz, I'm going to have Travis stay here with Olivia tonight, he's got to bring her up to speed on everything and then set her up in MJ's apartment." She looks at the time on her phone and rubs the back of her neck, a nervous habit of hers I picked up the first day we met.

"What's the problem, Al?"

"I was hoping to stop her from going to that party tonight and have you whisk her out of town, but she is already on her way. I'd rather have Olivia as bait and not worry about him getting his hands on MJ. At least Olivia is trained to protect herself."

I know she's right, we have very little to go on and this could be what flushes him out into the open. I close my eyes and rub my temples, trying to fight off my nagging headache.

"I've already tried talking her into going to a safe house and she won't leave Andy. The best I can hope for is to keep her locked up at his house until this is all over. I'll head over to the party and see if I can talk some sense into her, let me know if anything turns up."

I grab my keys and head out the door, grateful I have Wanda with me. I whip through traffic, hoping to get to the party before she shows up. Throwing her on the back of my bike and driving away is looking more realistic by the minute.

Makenna

I decide to wear my new form-fitting, cream, calf-length skirt with a matching sheer-lace midriff top. My skin is flushed from the sun today which makes my freckles pop. I have always loved shoes, it's really where I spend the most money. I pair my outfit with a beautiful Chanel high-heeled, nude sandal that is delicately embellished with jewels. I swipe my lips with some Dior blush gloss and take one last assessment in the mirror. If only he would notice… I can't go down that road.

"You look beautiful tonight." I nearly jump out of my skin. Andy is standing in the doorway, looking handsome in a suit, except for the fact that he is red as a lobster.

"Jesus, Andy, I told you to put more sunscreen on. Stephen better not blame me for this one."

We head downstairs and Lucas is waiting to take us. He introduces me to Julie. She will be shadowing me all night. Travis will be meeting us at the party. I don't know why I'm nervous; I've been to so many of these in the past.

The ride to midtown is not that long, but Andy is fidgeting more than usual. "Hey, what's the problem?"

"Besides being burnt like a lobster, I'm worried about you being out tonight. Honestly, I want to keep you locked in the house and never let you out. Why did all this happen to us?" his voice cracks and I feel a lump in my throat.

"I'm sorry, Andy. I never meant for this to come back on you. I was trying to find a way to be happy and somehow dull the pain." I'm determined not to cry, at least, not in front of him.

"Why didn't you ever tell him? Be honest, MJ, please."

I don't know how to explain it.

"Honestly, what if I told him and he walked away from all of us? What if knowing my feelings put a wedge between him and our family? We are all he has, the only people he's ever let into his heart. Mom and Dad would be destroyed if he wasn't part of their lives, we would all be. Having any part of him is better than none of him."

"This is no way to live. You're both going through the motions of life, nothing more. Imagine where I would be if I had succeeded in pushing Stephen away," he says. I widen my eyes at this. "Yeah, MJ, when I was diagnosed, I tried to end it with him, for his sake. I kept telling myself it was for the best . . . that Stephen deserved to have a life and not a burden.

"In the end, he made me realize that having a life and living life are two totally different things. Whether I have twenty years with him or a hundred, I will give it my all. You need to go balls to the wall with Fitz. If it doesn't work out, you will never have to say 'what if.' I know he doesn't believe it, but this family will never let him walk away. The past should speak for the future. Mom's had a grip on him since he was a kid, we all have."

I carefully kiss his very red face, "We're here, shelve it for tonight, please."

I've passed by this building a million times but I've never been inside. It is absolutely beautiful. We head inside and we are directed to the Bellecour Room, where Stephen is waiting for us. "Oh my God, Andy, what the hell?"

He turns toward me, and before he can blame me, I throw my hands in the air. "Hey, don't even think of putting this one on me. I gave him the sunscreen, and I kept telling him to re-apply it, but he was too busy reading smut."

He takes Andy's hand and shakes his head. "Yelling at you now will not change that my husband is as red as a lobster. Come on, let's mingle a little before dinner."

I've been to Stephen's company parties before, there are many familiar faces but also quite a few new ones. I take a glass of wine from a passing waiter; it's white, cold, and delicious. I turn around and bump into someone, spilling the remainder all over him.

"Oh, I'm so sorry," I gasp. One of the waiters quickly hands him a napkin.

"Don't worry about it, at least it's white and not red. I'm Mark Chambers, what brings you to the party tonight?"

"My brother-in-law, Stephen Cooper, is a senior partner at the firm, and you?"

"My wife, Nicole Chambers, is one of the new junior partners."

He steps closer, leaning in near my ear. "Quite frankly, I find these parties a total bore," he whispers.

Hating when someone invades my personal space, I take a step back. His hand is still holding onto my elbow. "I'm sure you will make it through the evening just fine." I excuse myself and try to make my way toward the bar. People are very friendly and introducing themselves. I look around and find Julie in the corner with Lucas, trying to mingle in with the guest, eyes always on me. Travis was supposed to meet me here, but I don't see him.

Something feels a little off but I'm not sure what. I make my way toward the bar when I feel a hand on my back. It's not a familiar touch and I nearly leap out of my skin. My whole body tenses up, and the look on my face must have alerted Julie and Lucas as they quickly make their way across the room. I turn around and it's Mr. Augusto, one of the firm's most senior partners. He's an old guy who I'm sure couldn't care less that he has a wife here somewhere.

"Hello, Makenna, how are you tonight?" Old bastard tries to undress me with his eyes. He even tried to get a membership to the club—*denied*. Julie and Lucas approach. I smile and nod, letting them know I'm fine.

"I'm well, Mr. Augusto, how are your wife and kids doing?" Dirty old man. He waves his hand as if he is dismissing them, which I'm sure in his mind he already has.

"They are fine, are you alone tonight?" He finally looks me in the eyes and not my girls.

"No, she's with me," Fitz says from behind me. He places his hands on my hips and pulls me back toward him. Pressing my back to his front makes my heart skip a beat. I catch my breath and quickly make introductions.

"You enjoy your evening, Makenna."

"I'll make sure she does," Fitz states. Augusto slinks back to wherever he came from.

I try to turn around but he has me glued to him. "MJ, how long do you have to stay here?"

"Where is Travis?"

He spins me around, "Why can't you just answer my question?"

He's wound so tight, I'm afraid he might explode. "We just got here and we haven't had dinner yet. Is something wrong?"

"I don't want you this exposed, besides there has been a change in plans. I will go over it all with you. Let's find Andy and Stephen."

We begin to make our way around the room when I spot them talking to a group of people. Something is making my skin prickle and Fitz's grip on my hip is getting tighter. We reach the group just as they announce dinner is served. Andy pulls Fitz and me aside. "Why are you here and not Travis?"

"He's working on something. MJ and I are not staying for dinner. We'll meet you at the house later."

"Fitz, I haven't eaten all day, and I've always wanted to try this place, can't we stay?" I give him my best puppy dogface.

"Hey, you might as well stay. You know when she puts that face on, we can never say no."

"Fine, but, MJ, I'm warning you, as soon as you're done eating, we leave."

We head to our table and Stephen introduces us to some of the new junior partners. There is quite a mix of different people among the new partners. Dinner conversation is light until dirty-old-man Augusto asks me how the club is doing. He's probably still pissed I denied his application. Fitz's squeezes my knee tightly.

"Mr. Augusto, you know I don't like to talk business, besides tonight is about the new partners, not about me." I give him my sugary *shut the fuck up and leave me alone* smile and Fitz loosens his grip. I quickly turn the conversation away from me and begin chatting up some of the new partners. The last thing I need right now are questions about my business. Mr. *I like to invade personal space*

Chambers is staring and I realize his wife is asking me something, but I have no clue what.

"Nicole, my sister and I went fishing today, and no doubt she is daydreaming about the big one that got away," Andy jumps to my rescue, thank God. Everyone laughs and I'm brought back to reality.

"Follow my lead," Fitz whispers into my ear.

He gets up and offers me his hand. "MJ, we have that other function to get to. If we leave now, we might make it in time for dessert. Andy, can you walk us out, please?" He glances over to him. I slip my hand in his and make my goodbyes, grateful to get the hell out of there. He pulls out his phone and calls Lucas, telling him that he and Julie need to stay here with Andy and Stephen.

When we finally get to the front door, he pulls Andy aside. "There has been a change of plans. If anyone asks you about the club or MJ, you say she's not leaving for a couple of months. She is going to assist the new owners with the transition. We've got to go. I'll meet you at home tonight and go over everything with you."

He grabs my hand and pulls me out the door. I stop dead in my tracks—oh. Hell. No! "No fucking way! I've got a damn skirt on. I'm not getting on that damn bike."

"Can't you just hike it up a bit?" One of those times when a guy is clueless how a woman pulls an entire outfit together.

"If you want the entire world to see why I have no panty lines, then, by all means, let me hike my skin-tight skirt up in the middle of midtown Manhattan and climb aboard your bike!"

He's glaring at me like this is entirely my fault. "Let's go, there are a bunch of retail stores on the corner that are still open. I'll get you something to wear."

I throw my hands up in defeat and start walking. "Why are you walking so fast? Are we in danger?"

"Why are you walking so slow? I need to get you out of sight as quickly as possible." His words make me freeze, my legs unable to move.

"Fitz, I have on high heels. What the hell happened that you want me out of sight?"

He scoops me up and carries me the rest of the way. Helmut Lang is still open and we quickly duck inside. I grab jeans, a jacket, sneakers and lets not forget the panties. He's quiet and for Fitz that's not good. I quickly change in the dressing room while he pays. He practically drags me out the door and we head back to Wanda, neither of us saying a word. I don't understand the sudden urgency, all I know is—the silence is deafening. He hands me my helmet, I climb on, and once again, we are speeding into the night with me hanging on for dear life.

CHAPTER FOURTEEN

Mark

THE SHOCK OF SEEING HER, smelling her, touching her as I leaned in and whispered into her ear almost made me forget where I was tonight. Her long, lean neck was so delicate, all could think of was wrapping my fingers around it. The smell of her lingers around me and I have to mentally talk my cock down from a full-blown erection. Being so close to her, inches from her beautiful face, only makes me want her more. I know it's her, the one I've been searching for my whole life. I want to take her and keep her forever. Of all the law firms in Manhattan, Nicole has to work with Makenna's brother-in-law.

He walked in and took total control of her. I've been able to possess women physically, but to have so much control with just a look or a whisper is amazing. He takes her hand and announces they have another engagement to get to. Stephen introduced him as Fitz, what kind of name is that? How does he fit in? He's the same guy from the other night outside the club. Nicole nudges my leg, snapping me out of my daydream.

"Are we that boring, Mark?" Her snide remark forces me to put on a fake smile, when really all I want to do is hunt down his sister and make her mine. I want to fuck her over and over again. Watch that beautiful face when it's blanketed with fear.

"I'm sorry, Andy, I was thinking how nice it would be to take my son fishing, like you take your sister."

"It's more like she takes me. How old is your son?" He smiles whenever he talks about her.

"My son is seven. We've haven't been in New York that long, so I'm not really sure where we would go."

"You can get all the information online, pick a place that's close to where you live. Where did you live before New York?"

"We lived in LA and then Chicago. Have you always lived here?" I know the answer but I need to take the focus off of me.

"Yes, my parents are from Ireland. They came here right after they were married. They settled in Brooklyn, and that's been home ever since. How do you like living in New York?"

"I'm getting used to it. I'm trying to find different things to occupy my time while Nicole is working. Mr. Augusto mentioned a club your sister owns, what type of club is it? It might be something to keep me busy."

"Actually, she sold the club, she's staying on to help the new owners with the transition. After that, she wants to travel," he offers. So, the sale is legit. At least she will be around for a little while, just enough for me to make her mine. He quickly dismisses all talk of the club and his sister, and then whispers something to Stephen. They begin to make their goodbyes. Nicole is so engrossed with sticking her tits in Mr. Augusto's face, she hardly notices but Mrs. Augusto does. Once Stephen and Andy leave, the Augusto's follow suit. The party begins to break up and we are finally out the door.

"Mark, why were you trying so hard to impress Stephen's husband? You should have focused your attention on Augusto. After all, he's the one with money and power." She's always so cut and dry.

"Well, if you must know, Mr. Augusto was fixated on Andy's

sister and the club she owns. I was trying to find out more information for you." The bitch will believe anything if I make it all about her.

"What kind of club is it? Maybe we should join it?"

"She just sold it, so it is of no use to you."

"Oh, I'm sorry I doubted you." She squeezes my arm and whispers "Let me make it up to you." Well, maybe my cock will actually get some service tonight. I quickly hail a cab before she changes her mind.

FITZ

Part of me wants to head upstate, but I know she will never agree to a safe house. We get to Andy's and head inside. "Do you want a something to eat?" I pull out the cold cuts and begin making a sandwich.

"No, we just got done eating. Besides, my stomach is in knots."

"That wasn't real food. Have a seat and let me bring you up to speed. Travis found another file on your computer. I haven't looked at it, but apparently it's filled with stuff this psycho wants to do to you. Al has called in another agent, Olivia, who really resembles you a lot. She will move into your place and will make it seem that you haven't left town." I finish making a sandwich and head over to the table. "The story is you will be assisting the new owners with the transition. When she is out in public, she will wear dark glasses and keep her exposure to a minimum. Just enough to be seen but not noticed. We are going to try to lure him out by using her as bait. I've instructed Andy on what to say if anyone should ask." I sit down and dig into my sandwich while I wait for the yelling to start.

"Why would you put someone in the crosshairs of a killer?

Don't even think of telling me it's her job!" Her face is flushed, and she slams her fist so hard on the table, she nearly knocks over my water.

"It is her job, MJ, this is what she is trained to do." I finish my sandwich and grab some more bottles of water.

"Come on, I'm tired. Let's try to get some rest, please."

"You're staying here?"

"Of course I am. I already checked in with Kevin and everything is quiet at Mom's. I'm jumping in the shower and then I'll be right in, *don't* lock me out." I quickly head down the hall, my heart racing at the thought of her alone. I need to calm down, the doors are locked, and the house alarm is set. A quick shower, I don't even wait for the water to get hot. I step out, and damn it she's sitting there, her eyes closed holding up a towel.

"Oh hell, MJ, at least you have the decency to close your eyes." I grab the towel and wrap it around my waist.

"I'm going to jump in the shower, are you done in here?"

"I am now." I gather up my stuff and head back into the bedroom. While she's in the shower, I throw on shorts and climb into my chair. A quick check in with Al and she confirms everything is very quiet. I shoot a text to Andy, letting him know we are home and everything is fine. She's finally back and holy hell, she is in a tank and boxers. She gets into bed and flips off the light. The moon still cast enough light into the room for me to see the outline of her beautiful body curled in bed.

"Fitz, get in the bed. I won't bite, you can't spend another night sleeping in that chair," she snaps lightly. My eyes dart from her to the bed and back again. She's right; I haven't slept in days. I'm an adult, not a teenager. I can sleep in the same bed with her. Maybe if I repeat it enough in my head, I will believe it. I climb into the bed, determined to get some sleep.

"Fitz, can I ask you a question?"

"One question, then go to sleep."

"Why are you so afraid of us . . . of you and me?"

I know I've held back, especially with her, but I'm not sure where to begin. "Go to sleep, MJ."

"You said I get one question, so answer it, and I will go to sleep." She tries to stifle her yawn, but it's not really working out.

"I'm afraid of another loss. A loss so great, I won't ever come back from it. Now, go to sleep."

She takes my hand and squeezes it tightly and then places it over her heart. "If you could feel what's in here you would know that my heart will always be home for you. I'll love you, no matter what," she confides. I listen to her breathing, and with my hand tightly in hers, we drift off to sleep.

Morning comes and I realize I slept without having any nightmares. When I open my eyes, I'm spooned up against her, my cock hard as stone, wedged between her beautiful ass cheeks. Oh Jesus, how the hell am I going to get out of this one? I try to slowly unpeel myself from her, but her grip gets tighter, my hand still pressed to her heart.

I try to tilt my head around her neck so I can see if she's sleeping. She begins to stir. Her lips part and a small moan escapes, sending a jolt from the tip of my cock down to my balls. She tilts her head ever so slightly, just enough for my lips to gently graze her neck.

I know I shouldn't, not now, but God, her sweet smell is all around me like the sweet smell of warm cinnamon buns with gooey icing. I know what I want, and I know what I need. I just don't know if it's what she needs. I've wanted her for so long, but it was always a dream, she was always my unobtainable dream. I press my lips to her ear and whisper her name. Her eyes flutter open at the touch of my lips. She pushes her ass back ever so slightly and giggles.

"I think you have a problem. Eventually, we will have to talk about it." She let's go of my hand and turns in my arms. Her gentle fingers tremble as she strokes my cheek.

I grasp her hand and bring her fingers to my lips, nip then kiss. "Yeah, I know, but give me a little more time, please. There is so much that needs to be said and so many changes that need to happen. If we go down this road, there is no going back—that's my biggest fear. I'm only a man, not the superman that you've put on a pedestal all these years. What if I fall? Think about that long and hard, babe. I need to get ready for work. *Don't* leave this house today!" I lift her chin and brush my lips across hers.

Her lips tremble at my touch. I climb out of bed and look back; she's trailing her fingers across her lips. My cock is so hard, even if I stuck it in a bucket of ice, there would be no relief. The only relief it craves is to be buried in her.

I head into the bathroom and turn the shower on, cold water—full blast. When I step inside, I turn and let the water pelt me, nothing. "*Fuck*...go down already, will you."

"How's that working out for you, Fitz?"

"Jesus Christ, Andy, why can't I ever take a shower in this house and expect some sort of privacy? Thanks, by the way; my cock just deflated." Bastard's laughing.

"Are you going to tell us what the hell that was about last night?"

I peek around the curtain, Stephen is leaning against the sink, and Andy is sitting on the edge of the tub with a towel. "Why don't we just have a party? Really, you might as well call Mom to come over, too." I shut the water off, and when I pull back the curtain, Andy throws me the towel.

"Al brought in another agent. Olivia looks a lot like MJ and she will assume MJ's life. I need you to tell anyone that might ask that MJ is helping the new owners with the transition. We are trying to flush him out. Hopefully, he makes a move on Olivia and not some

147

other victim."

"That guy at our table last night asked about the club. I think his name was Mark. Anyway, I told him what you wanted me to. He couldn't take his eyes off MJ, and his wife Nicole had her tits stuck in old man Augusto's face all night."

"Yeah, I noticed that too. What's the story with the two of them?"

"Mark and Nicole Chambers, they are married and have a son. They moved here three months ago from Chicago. I'm not sure what he does for a living; I didn't really pay much attention to what he was saying last night. Why, do you think he could be a suspect?"

The mention of Chicago makes the hair on the back of my neck stand at attention.

"At this point, everyone and anyone is a suspect to me. Stephen, send me everything you've got on him and his wife. I just have a feeling that the killer is closer than we think. Travis found another folder with all the things he wants to do to MJ. It's sick, twisted, and this is why I need to keep her locked away. I need to focus on him and what he is looking for, and I can't do that if I'm worried about her all the time."

While they take everything in, I finish getting ready. I know I need to be careful what I tell Andy, but he needs to know all the facts. No fucking around here. "Did you make coffee or were you too busy bugging me in the shower?"

"Wise ass, I made breakfast which is what I was coming in here to tell you. It's in the warming drawer. I'm going to check on MJ." Andy leaves while Stephen and I head into the kitchen.

"Fitz, tell me the truth, how bad is it?"

"Really bad, make sure you drill it into Andy that MJ does not leave this house. I gotta go. I want to check on Mom and Dad before I go." I grab my breakfast and head out the door.

Makenna

I'm replaying everything Fitz said over and over in my head. I can still feel his lips on mine. I know I've put him on a pedestal, how could I not? He said he's afraid. Well, damn it, what about me? I put my heart out there; it's raw and wide open. I look up and Andy is in the doorway. I never even heard him knock.

"Is he gone?"

"Yeah, you want to talk about it?" He tilts his head. I lift the covers and he climbs in.

"He said he's afraid, and if we go down this road, there's no going back. He thinks I've put him on a pedestal, and he's afraid he won't live up to what I've made him into. Do you think he's right?"

"Honestly, yeah, I do. Let's face it, MJ, you've turned to him whenever you've had a problem, and he's always gotten you out of every mess. Now, you are in a mess that might cost you your life. I know it's not your fault, but that doesn't matter to him.

"He has to save you, and he's not sure he can. He's scared, really fucking scared. I know he's holding back with me; I'm not an idiot. Right now, we need to follow all the rules. It's a matter of life and death. When all this is over, maybe you should ask him to explain to you why he has such a deep fear of great loss. Maybe if you knew the whole story, you would understand why *you* have the ability to push him over that fine line he walks every day."

Stephen comes in, hands me a cup of coffee, and climbs in bed with us. "MJ, you are not to leave this house today, no matter what happens. Do you understand?"

"Yes, Stephen, I get it. I'm a prisoner while a madman is running free. My life is now on hold . . . indefinitely."

"I'm leaving for work. I usually don't work on Saturday, but I have a trial starting Monday and I have some last minute details to finish up. Andy, the same rules apply to you—stay put!" He kisses him and quickly leaves.

"Well, any idea what we are supposed to do while we are holed up here all day?"

"I have some projects around here you can help me with. I promise it won't be so horrible hanging out with your brother all day."

"Do you think I did something to attract this lunatic?" I barely get the question out when he throws his arms around me and pulls me tightly against his chest.

"No! I don't care if you hung naked from the rafters. This man is sick and deranged. Who knows why he is attracted to you, but you did nothing but live your life. Now get up and let's get started." He lets go. I know he's right, but it's so creepy to think someone has been watching my every move without me knowing it. I shiver at the thought, get up, and head out to the kitchen for more coffee.

Mark

I know it's going to be a beautiful Saturday morning when I wake up with my cock in the bitch's mouth. I close my eyes and imagine it's *her* mouth. I want her to go deeper but she never does. Well, today is my day . . . it's all about me. I fist her hair and begin to move my hips. Slowly at first, but then I hit the back of her throat, and she tries to pull away. I place one hand around her throat and the other fists in her hair. It pushes me further. The fight, it ignites a fire in my balls to keep going. Her eyes begin to bulge as my fingers tighten around her delicate neck. I'm on the edge, teetering on that fine line.

I need more.

"Fight me, damn it!" I bark. She tries to push back, but I pull her hair—hard. I close my eyes and envision her red hair everywhere, fisted in my hands. That's all it takes to push me over that invisible line. I finally regain my composure and when I open my eyes, Nicole is glaring at me, her lips swollen and my handprints around her throat. Beautiful.

"Look at my neck, Mark. I told you to never leave marks!" She gets up and storms into the shower. She'll get over it. I need to get the hell out of here today and find Makenna. Only a few finishing touches and the apartment will be ready for her. I'm lost in my daydream when I realize Nicole is saying something to me.

"Are you even listening to me? What the hell is wrong with you? I'll have to work from home today thanks to the marks you left."

I want to tell her to fuck off, but that won't help me get out of here. "I'm sorry, I was so caught up in your beautiful, warm mouth that I lost all reason. Please, forgive me." You lazy ass bitch. "Besides, I thought you were off today, after all, it is Saturday." I hope I'm not going to get stuck with the kid.

"I'm still working on that death row case. It's not all cut and dry as I first thought it would be." She examines her neck again in the mirror.

Well, now this has piqued my interest. "Really, why? I mean you said he left his DNA in her stomach contents. Surely, that nails him to the cross." I'm intrigued by all of this. I've always made sure to pull out right before I come. I always brush their teeth before I leave them. Well, everyone except my first. Her beauty (something I haven't seen again until Makenna Justice stepped into my world) overwhelmed me.

"There was not enough semen for any more testing. The validity of the test can be called into question. If there is nothing else that can be tested, then I might be able to get it thrown out. The rest of the evidence is all circumstantial."

"Wow, so the guys entire case rests on one test. What do you think your chances are in getting this guy off?"

"Probably eighty percent in my favor. I'm preparing everything for the judge this weekend. I present it Tuesday morning. Mason is spending the weekend with his friend from camp. What are your plans?"

My world just got a whole lot brighter.

"I'm meeting with that client I've been trying to nail down. He invited us to join him at his home in the Hamptons this weekend. I wasn't sure what your plans were, so I didn't respond yet. With Mason gone, the house will be quiet and you can get everything done for Tuesday." I always have to make sure it's all about her.

"That's fine, go. I can get my presentation done while everyone is gone."

"Well, if you're sure you don't need me. Maybe, I'll get lucky and land this account." Hopefully, the only thing I'll be landing tonight is a beautiful redhead. I head into the shower. The sooner I get out of here, the sooner I can put my plan in motion.

Fitz

Mom and Dad are fine and, of course, Mom had a million questions. At least, I was able to get out of there unscathed. When I pull up at the club, Olivia is just getting out of MJ's car. I swear I had to look twice, the match is that close. Let's hope the killer thinks it's really her. I open the door for her and she heads right back to MJ's office. "How are you getting settled in at MJ's place?"

"Good, I made sure I was seen vaguely at the local establishments. Some people actually waved at me this morning."

Al and Travis are already waiting for us. I grab a cup of coffee and stare at Al's whiteboard. "Travis, do you have MJ's computer ready for Olivia to get her back online, so this guy still thinks he has access to her?"

Travis hands Olivia the laptop and a small bag. "It's all set to go. Never let him see your face and, Olivia, MJ has a tiny superman tat on her right hip. I went to see a friend of mine last night who has a shop in the village. He made up some very realistic ones for you to stick on your hip. Just don't get it too close to the camera."

"What do you want me to do while I'm here? If I mingle with the members, they will know that I'm not her."

I ignore her question as I'm studying my partner. Al isn't paying attention to anything but the board. Something must be bothering her about all of this. "Talk to me, Al, what's wrong?"

"I've been going over every case with Gail. The first victim in LA was the only redhead. Everyone else was either brunette or blonde. Now, he's fixated on MJ. Was he always after a redhead? Is she what he needs to go full circle? Is she the end all? He didn't brush the first victim's teeth. He did clean her apartment, and he did use a collar. The last victim is the only one whose neck he snapped. Why?"

"Write out the time line from the first victim till now; what do we have?"

She flips the board and starts at the beginning. "There is a three week gap between victim one and two. There is only one week between victim two and three. Then there is a three month gap before he surfaced in Chicago. There is a three week gap between the first victim in Chicago and the second one and then one week between number two and three. Again, there is a three month gap before he surfaced in New York. So, either he has moved on to another large city or he found what he is looking for: MJ."

"Al, I wish he'd left, but I doubt it. He wouldn't be so fixated on her. However, why only big cities? You checked his MO and the only hits we got were these three cities. What do they have that small town America doesn't have?" I feel like I'm missing something; it's swirling around the back of my head.

"All three are global cities. New York and Chicago have trading markets. Los Angeles has a huge entertainment industry. There are high-end law firms, not that other cities don't have them, but due to the entertainment industry and the large financial industry, they are more prevalent here. New York and Los Angeles are huge in media, not Chicago. What are you thinking, Fitz?"

"There has to be a reason he is in three of the top cities in the US. Chicago is a key. Eliminate everything that Chicago doesn't have in common with the other cities; what's left?"

She eliminates what Chicago doesn't have, and we are left with high-end law firms. "It's a nice thought but too broad, Fitz. Other states have large law firms. Why else would he pick these cities? Do you think he really is into the BDSM lifestyle or is it a ruse to throw us off? He puts the collars on afterward, why? Let's face it, you and I know there are a million ways to kill someone so why make it look like this?" She is drawing circles around BDSM. She's staring at the board seemingly lost in the giant puzzle.

"We're looking at this all wrong. Instead of comparing all the cities, and the victims, let's narrow it down more. Let's compare MJ and the first victim in LA. They are the only redheads. Let's start there and see where it leads us." Al clears the board while Travis puts the report for the first victim, Michelle, on the big screen.

"Start listing what they all have in common, no matter how small." It's amazing how much they actually do have in common. Two totally random strangers, yet they really are so much alike.

"Redheads, BDSM, both submissive, workout daily, same age, not flashy girls, aside from the hair color, the list is general and can fit any of the victims. A big difference was Michelle was a single parent."

"What about Michelle's work?"

"She was a waitress. Everyone at her job was questioned. They all said she was very well liked and never had any problems."

"Did Michelle belong to a BDSM club?"

"Yeah, it's a members only club in downtown LA. All of the members were looked into, but they also host private parties, film movies, and videos. I don't think they dug too deep until the third victim surfaced. By then, he was already gone."

"So, he is into the scene, but to what extent, we don't know. He's got to be banking on the fact that there is still a stigma associated with the lifestyle. He's hoping the cops don't give the investigations everything they should. He's hoping it will be swept under the rug. That will give him more freedom or so he thinks. Were all the other victims part of the BDSM community?" I grab another coffee, mentally thanking MJ for having an endless supply of the best coffee in New York.

"Only some of them were, but that's not to say that they weren't into it or new to it. We just don't have all that information."

I need to flush this bastard out. I can't sit back and wait for him to strike. I need to be the one to strike first. "I want to do an email blast and hit the *Post* for the evening edition with an announcement that Mystik is having a surprise masquerade party. It will be a soft grand re-opening for the new owners and a fair well party for MJ. Broadcast it across all social media sights too. We need to bring him to us and not sit around waiting for him to strike. We dangle Olivia and see if he takes the bait."

"When are we having this party?"

"Al, I'd love to do it tonight, but that won't give us enough time to announce it. I want to try to get the most people possible in the door. We will shoot for next Saturday. Olivia, are you okay with all of this?"

"Of course I am; it's my job. Are you sure it's enough time to get it all together?"

"Yeah, I need to make a call, I'll be back." I head outside to call her.

She picks up on the first ring. "Hey, what are you doing?"

"What the hell do you think I'm doing? I haven't left the house, and Andy has me sanding a dresser. Is something wrong, what happened?"

"Calm down, MJ, I have a few questions. I'm throwing a masquerade party next Saturday at the club. What do I need to know in order to pull this off?" I ask. She's quiet, and then I hear a heavy sigh. I know not being in control is hard for her.

"It's not that easy, Fitz. You can't just to decide to throw a party on a whim. There is a lot of planning, from the liquor order to the food. What theme will you have? There are the standard rules but are you going to have some new ones for the party only? Mystik is not an anything goes club, I don't allow certain things, but will you allow some of those things for this party?"

"I don't understand, can't you give me the express version?"

"Ugh, there is no express version for this, that's what I've been trying to explain to you from day one!"

"Stop yelling at me and calmly give me an example."

"Okay, will you allow knife play? It's not something that is allowed on a daily basis, but if there is a private party booked and it's requested then I might allow it. A special waiver has to be signed if something is being allowed that is not usually offered at the club. Insurance purposes, Fitz."

"Is there some sort of folder with all this information somewhere?"

"There is one on the computer. It should get you through all of this. It's labeled parties. There is also one labeled rules, you might want to familiarize yourself with that one, too."

She wants me to play by the rules. I've never done that before, why start now? "Do the owners of the different clubs have some sort of organization that they all belong to?"

"There is, but I don't belong to any of them. Since Mystik is private, I set the rules. I don't have to follow what the community wants. It's what I want and what I'll allow. However, safety always comes first."

"How did you come up with your rules?" I don't really want to know, but I need to know.

"In the beginning, I visited other clubs with a friend, and then when Andy purchased the place, I went by what I like and what I don't. Mystik is not an extreme type of club. I have different rooms set up for traditional types of role-play. The big room in the back, where the smaller bar is, I reserve for private parties.

The room in the front, that you've been in, is the main room that everyone gathers in. I would suggest, if you're going to pull this off, you open up both rooms. Have food catered and put it in the back room. Give away some sort of prizes to get as many people as possible into the club. Look, do you want me to come in and help?"

"No! So help me God, don't you dare leave that house. I'll get this all together." The last thing I need is her here.

"Calm down, Fitz, I would be safe with you."

I know she's right, it would be easier, but I can't take the chance. "No, stay put and if I need you to walk me through something, I'll let you know. Is there anywhere, other than the usual channels, that I should broadcast this party?"

"Do an email blast to all active and inactive members. Travis should be able to do it, no problem. Contact the reporter that did the story on the club, he can do a follow up on the sale and announce the party. Do you really think this is going to work?"

"I hope so. I've gotta go. Stay put and I'll let you know if I need you." I wait for her to respond. She's not hanging up, and she's not saying anything.

157

"MJ?"

"Fitzy, be careful, please."

I close my eyes and take a breath. All I want to do is take her in my arms and tell her everything I've held back for so many years. Letting my heart feel what my mind has held back for so long is driving me crazy. "I will, babe." It's barely a whisper before I hang up, leaving so much left unsaid. I head back inside with a long list of shit that I have to get done in order to pull this off. The only one left in the office is Travis. The girls left to get what they need for the party. Between the two of us, we get the email blast done and everything ordered. Now we wait to see if we can flush out a killer.

Mark

I finally got out of the house and away from Nicole. I need to get to my apartment so I can get everything ready for her. Saturday on the ferry is very quiet, and I pull up the video of her putting on her lotion. After being so close to her and smelling her sweet smell, I need to find out what kind it is. I want everything to be just like her bedroom.

I love how she hovers over her tat. When her fingers tremble, I can feel a jolt in my cock. I will take it slow with her, savoring every second. I pull up the club's website to see if there's anything new. Sure enough, they are having a masquerade party next Saturday. Perfect, I can use this to my advantage. A disguise that is actually required.

I need to figure out how I'm going to get her out of there unnoticed. I finally get to my apartment and pick up my landlord's *Post*, happy she's away all weekend. I quickly flip the pages and there is still no mention of me.

Maybe they really are clueless, although, I don't know how they could have missed the roses. I have no time to dwell on all of this. As far as I can tell, they have no idea that it's the work of one very talented man.

I need to get everything together for her and figure out what type of costume I will need. I decide to head out to the mall and get the supplies I need to make this room hers. I can also get my costume for the party. But before I do any of this, I need to get a car. I have a garage here to store it and it would help me transport her when the time comes.

After seeing how skittish she was last night, I will probably have to drug her to get her to leave with me. Once I have her in my grasp, she will see how much she wants me. Before long, she'll be begging me to fuck her over and over again. My cock begins to swell at the thought of her on her knees.

I look down at the bulge straining to escape its confines. I'm never going to make it through the day like this. My cock is so hard and pressing against my zipper to the point it's painful. I need relief. I take my jeans off and begin stroking myself slowly at first, root to tip. I lean back, close my eyes and imagine it's her delicate hand trembling as she slowly goes up and down.

Now two hands, one pumping and swirling around the head, while the other works my sac. Pressure tight and hard on my balls and then release. It's like a surge of electricity. My cock wants to explode, and every time I get to the edge, I squeeze my balls, cutting off the surge. I want to do the same thing to her delicate neck. Silence her breath and then feel it against the tip of my cock when it escapes in a giant rush.

Oh, God, that's all I need. I'm there, endlessly coming. I slowly work my way down before opening my eyes and back to the reality that I'm alone and I have a huge mess to clean up.

Makenna

Why the hell is he so afraid to let me in? I've only ever loved him and no matter what, I always will. I look up and Andy is standing in the doorway with a bloody towel wrapped around his hand. "What the hell happened?!"

"I thought I could...never mind what I thought, I might need stitches."

"Forget about what you thought; we can get you fixed up at Urgent Care. Lucas is out front, and I'm sure he can hit the lights and sirens to get us there quickly." I usher him out the door and Lucas jumps out of the car to help us. He pulls back the towel and decides we need a hospital not Urgent Care.

"Do you want me to call Stephen? "

He closes his eyes and his jaw is tight. "No, I'm sure he will never let me near another power tool again after this. Please let me keep what little bit of dignity I have," his voice trails off and my heart breaks for him. What short straw did he draw to be struck with this disease?

When we get to the hospital, Lucas flashes his badge and gets us through right away. They won't let me go back with him, so we sit and wait. Minutes seem like hours until the nurse finally comes out.

"Ms. Justice, you can go back now." She takes me to his cubicle. Andy is on the phone and slurring his words. No doubt pain meds are kicking in.

"Hey, what did the doctor say?"

"They are taking me in for surgery and Stephen wants to talk to you."

I grab the phone and mentally prepare myself for the verbal

thrashing I'm about to get. "Stephen, I'm sorry but he took it upon himself not to wait for me to get off the phone."

"Hey, I don't blame you at all, so calm down. This is the result of him not facing the fact that he is disabled and has limitations now. I'm on my way, stay put in that waiting room with Lucas. Call Fitz and let him know what's going on. I'll see you soon," he says then hangs up. The nurse informs me I have two minutes and then they are taking him into surgery.

He's out of it and looks so peaceful, no tremors. "I love you, Andy."

His eyes flutter open. "I'm sorry," he manages.

"Shh, stop apologizing. You did nothing wrong." I know he feels bad enough and doesn't need me making him feel worse. I give him a kiss before they take him into surgery and then head back to the waiting room with Lucas by my side to wait for Stephen. I need to let Fitz know where I am. I realize Lucas is talking to me. "I'm sorry, I wasn't paying attention."

"I said maybe you should call your parents and let them know what's going on. I can have Kevin bring them here."

Shit, my parents; I didn't even think about that.

"My dad is a shut-in, if Kevin brought her here then he would be alone. Maybe you should go get her."

"I value my life, MJ. Fitz would string me up. I'll call him and see what he wants to do."

"Don't. I'll call him. Better the news comes from me." I get up and head over to the window, trying to get a little privacy. He answers on the first ring.

"What's wrong?"

"I'm at the hospital. Andy had an accident, and he's in surgery now. Stephen is on his way, but I don't know what to do about Mom and Dad. Andy wouldn't want to drag Dad out for this. If Kevin brings Mom then Dad is alone."

"How bad is it?" His usually deep voice has gone up a few octaves.

"He was using some power tool, and he cut the flexor tendons and the palm of his hand. The surgeon is trying to repair it now."

"I will go get Mom. You stay glued to Lucas's side, no matter what. Do you understand me?"

"I'm not a child; yes, I understand."

"I'm sorry, I didn't want you out of the house at all. Put Lucas on the phone," he demands. I head back over to him and hand him the phone. After a whole lot of *yeses* and *of courses,* he hangs up.

"So, did he ream you a new one for letting me leave the house?"

His smile is warm and comforting. "I know you've known him a long time, but you know he's a bear on the outside . . . inside, he's got a heart of gold. I know to pick and choose my battles wisely. Letting him blow off steam is what's best for everyone."

Time slowly ticks by and the hospital coffee is equivalent to paint thinner. Pretty soon, the doors open and Stephen comes racing in. "Hey, MJ, have you heard anything yet?"

"No, the doctor said it would be at least two hours. I was on the phone and he just wouldn't wait."

He pulls me into a hug and assures me it was not my fault. "Do you think he will ever face the fact that he has limitations and they are not going away?"

"No, I honestly don't. If he does, then he gives up hope. I know you don't understand it, and trust me, it took a long time for me to finally get it. If he gives in and says 'I can't do this' then he is admitting there is no hope. When all is said and done, at the end of the day, all we really have is hope . . . hope for a cure."

We have a seat and now it's back to waiting. We don't have to wait long before Mom and Fitz come in. Mom is about ready to rip into me when Stephen pulls her into a hug.

"Mom, MJ can't baby him, so don't even think of blaming her

for any of this. You know how stubborn he is. When he comes out of surgery, no one is to yell at him and that includes you, Fitz."

"I'm going to kick his ass and you know it!"

"Fitzgerald, there will be none of that. I'm sure he feels bad enough. Besides, that is a job for his mother."

I pull Fitz aside while everyone is waiting for the doctor. I have a slew of questions, starting with what he told Dad. "What happened when you told Dad about Andy?"

"His physical therapist was there, so I played down what happened and assured him I would come and get him if anything changed."

"Did you get everything handled for the party?"

"Everyone is getting it together now. I made it a masquerade beach theme type of party. I've got a few other ideas I can run past everyone. The liquor and food is ordered and the email blast has gone out. Travis contacted the guy that interviewed you and we started advertising in the *Post* and the *Daily News*. Is there anything I've missed?"

"What about a DJ?"

"Travis is going to DJ, which will give him a reason to be out there with a computer setup."

He pulls me close and puts his hand in the back pocket of my jeans. He's got a tight grip and I know something is bothering him. "What's wrong? I mean besides the obvious."

"I don't like that you are out in the open. Even though we are all here, it doesn't make me feel good."

Suddenly, the surgeon comes out. He lets us know that he was able to reattach the flexor tendons and, after some physical therapy, he should make a full recovery. He will be in recovery for a couple of hours and then they will move him to a room. They want to keep him overnight, and if all goes well, he can go home tomorrow evening. My mother dishes out enough motherly guilt on the doctor that he lets her in to recovery with Stephen to see him.

"When Mom comes out, I'll take you both home. You're not going to get in to see him. Besides, he needs his rest," he adds. I know he's right.

"What about Lucas?"

"I want him to stay here with Andy and Stephen. I will stay with you." The thought hits me—I won't have to ride on that bike—and I smile.

"You want to share with me what you find so amusing?"

I lean in and whisper in his ear. "My panties are safe from Wanda tonight."

He gifts me with his beautiful smile. "Yeah, but are they safe from me?"

I believe my heart just skipped a beat. Before I can catch my breath, he is ushering Mom and me out the door.

CHAPTER 15

Mark

THE MORE TIME I SPEND in Brooklyn, the more I like the way they do business here. There are still people that rely solely on cash. Armed with a very-well-made, fake ID and a stack of cash, I head out to find a car. I have to make sure to keep it under ten thousand, so it's not reported. I don't want to deal with any large dealerships, only local mom and pop type of business. After a lot of searching, I'm now the proud owner of a silver car very similar to every other one around the neighborhood. I have a temporary paper plate and thirty days to get it registered. By then, it will be safely tucked inside the garage.

My new car doesn't have GPS, so I have to rely on my phone. I haven't driven a car in a very long time, but it's like getting back on a bike and before long, I feel comfortable driving around the local streets. When I finally find the mall, it's very crowed, which always works to my advantage. I blend in; just an average Joe, out for a Saturday shopping spree. The first thing I do, is pick up a car charger for my phone, since using the GPS kills the battery. Next, I pick up all of her favorite things. By the time I get back to my car, I have, at least, ten shopping bags filled with everything that will keep her comfortable for a very long time.

I head back to my apartment, but now I have to navigate the car down a long driveway and when I reach the end, there is a tight turn to get it into the garage. I'm sure after doing this a few more times it will be no big deal. Finally, everything is unloaded. I set up her bedroom to look just like her apartment.

Maybe I can get a glimpse of her tonight, a little reward for all my hard work. I fire up the laptop and sure enough, she is back at her apartment. Finally, a live feed of her, it's been too long. I pour myself a cold beer, sit back, and prepare to watch her, all night long. Oh, she's getting undressed. No doubt she'll go in the shower before dinner, she always does. Oh, Makenna, nice and slow, just for me. How sweet to have the time to sit and watch her live for a change. She's out of camera range but I can wait. I would wait a lifetime if it meant that I could get my hands on her.

I wonder if she is going to be at the club tonight. I would love to go but I can't take that chance. Only one more week and she will be mine. Finally, she's back in camera range. She has on boxers and a tank top. I would rather see her in something very sexy or nothing at all. I will fix that next week, Makenna. She walks over to the laptop and closes it. Just like that, my view is gone.

I decide to go for a run. I haven't gotten to the gym for a couple of days and I could use it. Near where I got my new car, I saw a great path that runs along the water. Getting out of the garage is a lot harder than getting in but after a few tries I'm on my way. I head to Shore Parkway Greenway Trail. It's dusk, the perfect time for a run. The trail runs along the water's edge. The long run affords me the time to think my plan through. One week. I have one week to get it all together for her. The room came out perfect, now I need to figure out how I'm going to get her out of that club.

Everything I've learned about her, so far, is family means everything to her, which was evident at that dinner party. I'll have to use that to my advantage. Maybe I can find out more about Stephen from Nicole? Seems the bitch might be useful after all.

Fitz

I finally drag Mom and MJ out of the hospital. I swear it seemed to take forever. I don't want her exposed for too long. We get Mom settled in and assure Dad that Andy will be fine. Kevin is happy to have his car back. Now I need to get MJ home. We finally get to Andy's and I lock everything up for the night. Stephen will spend the night with Andy, and Lucas is staying with them. It's just us and I know I can't wait any longer. I thought if I waited that I would be able to focus on the case. I can't focus on anything but her and not in a good way.

"Are you hungry? There's cold cuts, I can make sandwiches for us."

"Yeah, I'm starving." I grab two beers and begin pulling all the stuff out of the fridge. Trying to help, but she pushes me away.

Watching her makes me crazy. She puts the plates down and says grace and I silently thank God for saving Andy's hand. We eat in silence and I'm mentally preparing myself for what I want to say. Watching her tilt her beer bottle up to her lips makes my cock scream for mercy. She licks her lips and I'm done! I pull her chair around so fast her beer goes flying out of her hand. "We. Need. To. Talk. Now!"

"Have you lost your mind?"

"Actually, yes. I know I said we were going to wait till this case is over, but I can't let another day go by. Too much time has already been lost. I need to talk and you need to listen. I know I have to be honest with you about everything, and I can only hope that all is not lost. Look, you're my best friend's sister. I thought it wasn't cool to mess with your best friend's sister. I thought it would pass and I could move on. But I couldn't move on because I was living with you. Your parents became my parents. I became part of a loving family. I finally had the one thing that had eluded me for so long. Parents who genuinely loved me unconditionally." I take a deep breath and grasp both her hands. I need to explain to her why I am so closed off.

"Did Andy or Mom and Dad ever tell you why I came to live with them?"

"When I was younger, I asked Mom and she said it was God's plan. When I asked Andy, he said to ask you. I wanted to ask you, but I never knew how. I know it has something to do with your parents and the reason you don't like locked doors, but that's all I know. I figured when you were ready, you would tell me."

"I'm going to tell you my story, but I don't want your pity," I warn. Her face flushes, which is typical right before she yells at me.

"I would have compassion for you, for whatever you've been through, but never pity," she insists. I close my eyes for a second and gather all my strength so I can get through this story. She needs to hear it all. Not just what's in my head, but what's in my heart. Maybe letting her in might make the nightmares go away. I can only hope.

"Please, just listen. My father was a very abusive man. He would beat my mother endlessly, and he would beat me with either his bare hands, a belt, or whatever was around. The more he drank, the worse the beatings got. Your mom tried to get my mom to file charges against my dad but she was afraid. At the time, there were very little services for victims of domestic violence. One day my father came home very drunk, more so than usual. My mom knew it was bad and locked me inside the bathroom." Reliving this is making my heart race. I feel like it might leap right out of my chest. "Listening to my father beat my mother to death changed me.

I blame myself every day for not saving her. I laid on that cold, tile floor and I was able to see out the gap that was under the door. He kept pounding her head on the floor. All the while she begged him to spare me—not herself but me. Every time she begged him, he punched her harder.

"There was so much blood. I kept trying to get out of the bathroom to try to stop him, but the door wouldn't budge. I realized that she locked me in that bathroom to keep him away from me, to save me. My mother's unconditional love for me is what killed her.

"It was a holiday weekend, so there was no school. Tuesday, I never showed up for school. Andy and I were supposed to work on a project for the science fair and I never showed up. When your mom found out I missed school, she got worried and called your dad to come home. Your dad was the first officer on the scene. Later, he told me there was a padlock at the top of the door. That's how she had locked it from the outside. She hid the key in her bra." Taking a deep breath, I find the courage to tell her the rest.

"I listened to her die, MJ. I did nothing to stop him. The sounds haunt my dreams. For three days, I laid on the floor, calling her, begging her to move. She never did. You deserve someone better than me. You think I'm your hero? The truth is, I'm no one's hero. Her cries will be my nightmare for the rest of my life."

She pulls her hand from mine and strokes my cheek. "You were just a little boy, how could you be expected to save her from behind a locked door?"

"The policeman I am today knows that, but the boy that was trapped in that bathroom will always blame himself. You told me that you're in love with me, but how could you love someone like me? Someone who listened to his mom die and did nothing to stop it? I should have yelled louder and pounded on that door harder. I was crippled by fear. A fear that still cripples me today. I told you I'm a jaded man, no good for you."

"I see what you don't. I told you if you could see what my heart feels then maybe you would understand. I know how tender-hearted you are. You're loyal and faithful to a fault. I see what you try to hide behind those dark eyes. You don't give of yourself freely but when you do, it's for life. You've held back all this time because you fear you would lose us, but we love you unconditionally. You were only a boy, Fitzy, not the man you are today."

I lift her trembling hand to my lips and close my eyes. This is when I need to get out of my own way. "I love you, MJ, and I always will. I've never given my heart to anyone. I want you. Hell, I've always wanted you, but I don't share. I never want you to step foot in that club again. I get that you did what you had to do to cope. We all have a past, and I'm no saint. But, I will never share you with anyone. That scene you showed me will never happen again. I will love you and worship you with everything I've got stashed in my heart for you and only you. I want it all and I want it with you. But after what I've told you, if you don't want me, I will understand."

She leans in and presses her lips to mine. They are so tender. I pull back and look at her beautiful face. I take a deep breath and wait for her answer.

"I love and want you, Fitzy. Nothing has changed for me. It never will. I think you need to understand some things. This club, and the whole Dom/sub thing, fulfilled something I was missing at the time. You asked me why and all week I have really thought about that. I think I need balance and I don't have that in my life. Honestly, I don't know how anyone finds that balance. I'm strong and I don't put up with anyone's bullshit. When Andy got sick, I had no choice but to become stronger. That has kind of made me unapproachable. What I've found in a Dom is someone that nurtures. I can let my guard down and let myself feel. But, the most important part for me was always the aftercare. It's that loving and caring that I've come to realize I need most of all. You want me to give up the club and walk away from the lifestyle; I don't have a problem with any of that. But, I also know what I want and I'm not going to settle. I need to know that I can stand by your side as an equal but that you will always catch me when I fall."

I think I finally get it.

"MJ, you know I would give my life for you. I will never make you feel less than me. In my world, you have and always will come first. I do, however, have a confession to make and then I swear you know everything." I take a deep breath and blurt it out. "I flattened all the tires on your prom date's car."

She begins to laugh uncontrollably. "I already knew that. Come on, did you really think I would believe that all four of his tires just happen to go flat at the same time? What I am surprised about is how you were able to keep the secret all these years. Everyone knows never to tell you a secret."

"How the hell did you find out and why didn't you call me out on it?"

"Oh please, Andy is worse than you at keeping secrets. I didn't call you out on it because I knew you and Andy hated Joseph or as Andy always called him 'no neck Joe.' I figured you had your reasons. Now might be a good time to explain."

I'm about to try to dig myself out of this mess when my phone rings. "Travis, what's up?" I motion to her that I'll be back and head into the living room to take the call.

"The bastard logged onto MJ's computer. I still can't trace him, but at least we know he didn't skip town. Unfortunately, he's still here and fixed on her." Good and bad news, double edged like the blade of a knife.

"If Olivia can keep him on longer would you be able to trace him?"

"I told you he's scrambling the signal."

"Yeah, I know what you told me but I also know you. What

have you got, Travis?" I've worked with him in the past and I know he's always trying something that's not government sanctioned.

"I've been working on a string of code that could break the scramble. I'm not guaranteeing anything and it's, by far, a long shot. Fitz, it's by no means legal. I also think we should set up additional security at MJ's apartment. I know it's a secure building, but I don't think we should take any chances. Better safe than sorry. Al and I are just closing the club and I've already let Olivia know that I'm on my way over to set up additional security. How's Andy doing?"

"Thank God the doctor was able to save his hand. How close are you to being able to use this code that you've developed?"

"I can hang out with Olivia tonight and keep her computer on for longer periods of time. If I see him log on then I will try it. There are no guarantees but something is better than nothing. I'll keep you posted. Tell MJ to hang in there."

I hang up the phone and try to put everything but her out of my mind. She deserves to have my total focus. When I turn around, she's standing in the doorway juggling four movies, two beers and a bowl of popcorn. I quickly grab the movies and put one in the DVD player while she gets comfortable. At least it's an *Avengers* movie and not a chick flick.

"You know, MJ, when I finally found the courage to tell you everything, this is not how I envisioned this night going."

"Yeah, me neither, but I need it to be like this right now. I don't want to rush it and I want it to last. I want and deserve all your focus. I'm just glad we got everything out in the open."

We curl up together on the couch and watch the movie. I'm content, which is something I never dreamed possible. I always thought I would remain on the sidelines but now I know, I have a shot at having it all. Everything hinges on catching a killer and I won't rest until I do.

Mark

The long run did nothing to quench my thirst for her. The more I think about Makenna the stronger my desire becomes. I need relief and my hand isn't cutting it. I have one more night alone here and then I have to head back to reality, living in purgatory with the bitch. With the kid out of the house for another night, maybe if I head home now, I can smooth talk Nicole into some role-play tonight. Something is better than nothing at this point. Before I pack up, I do an inventory to make sure I didn't miss anything. I want it perfect for her. After all, I plan on keeping her for more than one night.

It's been hours since she's been on line. I open my laptop and log into her computer. It's a live again—hell yeah—twice in one day. What are the odds since she's been so quiet ever since the sale was announced? She's moving about her living room, but there is someone else in the room. That's new, all the times I've watched her she's always been alone. I can't see who the guy is; he's sitting in front of the computer with a beer in his hand. Makenna straddles his lap, her back to the screen. All I can see is her beautiful red hair and his hands working their way up her back. He fists her shirt and pulls it off, her bare back is golden. My cock starts to twitch at the sight of her. Who is this guy? It's not that guy Fitz from dinner the other night; this guy's arms are covered in tats. The picture on the screen freezes and my connection is lost. What the Fuck?! My computer powers down, kicking in my fail-safe mechanism. Someone is trying to track me, has to be. When I tapped into Makenna's world, I wrote the program to automatically shut down my computer if someone was trying to track me.

That means someone has found my hidden files of her and they are aware that I can see her. That has to be why she was so quiet all week. They can't know much, only the bread crumb trail I left for her. Maybe she found one of the videos and hired someone to clean up her computer. Why would she do that? I know she would love to see the video I made of the two of us climaxing together.

There was nothing in the newspapers or online about the killings being the work of one man. They can't possibly link me to Mystik. Both times I was there, I used an alias. I made sure to avoid the cameras and once I took a girl there, I killed her afterward. Dead women tell no tales. I'm being paranoid. They can't possibly know who I am and where I am. If they did, they would have been all over me Friday night at the party. Just to be safe, I'll toss the computer. I won't take the chance of turning it back on, besides I always keep everything on an external hard drive. I close everything up and take another look around to make sure I didn't forget anything before I head to the ferry.

It's a Saturday night, and the ferry is practically empty. When I'm half way between Brooklyn and Manhattan, I toss my laptop overboard. Thankful that there is no one around to see. Now I need to come up with a story for Nicole on why I came home a day early and why I need to get a new laptop. I have to keep my prize in sight. Next weekend, I will make her mine, but for now, I'm not opposed to groveling to Nicole. I can see the big picture, the end game.

I get home and find her in the living room with a stack of papers next to her. Her headset is on and there's an empty bottle of wine on the floor. Well, I know what she's been doing. When she finally notices me, she lets out a yelp and pulls off her headset.

"Are you trying to give me a heart attack? I thought you were staying in the Hamptons?" Now's my put up or shut up moment.

"I was but, honestly, I was bored and I missed you." That should buy me some brownie points.

"Did you land the account?" All she cares about is money. Might as well make her night.

"Yes, but I will still have to kiss his ass for a couple of weeks. He will slowly filter his investments my way. Once he feels comfortable with me, I'm sure he will transfer it all. Did you finish putting together your presentation for the judge on Tuesday?" I always have to make it about her.

"Yes, I finished it up earlier. I was looking for a summer vacation home for us. The heat in this city is unbearable."

"I agree. I'm going to shower, how about you join me?" She gets up and wraps her arms around my waist.

"I'm all for having some fun tonight, Mark, but don't leave any marks." She gives my lips a peck. Oh, now this is intriguing. The shower can wait. We head into the bedroom, and I quickly pull out some of my toys before she changes her mind.

"I promise I won't leave any marks, at least where anyone can see them. I'll walk you through every step, making sure you're comfortable. First, I need to put your beautiful, thick, golden hair into a ponytail."

She turns around and as I gather her hair, I close my eyes and envision Makenna's thick red hair. The thought sends a jolt directly to my cock. With her back toward me, I begin to intricately tie her hands and arms using a French Bowline Knot behind her back.

"Are the ropes comfortable? I'm using the soft nylon rope you like so there won't be any marks." She has to feel like I really give a shit about her. We dabble in the lifestyle, but by no means are we fully immersed in it. She's never been to a club. Hell, I've only recently gone myself. Only because of her . . . Makenna.

"Hmm, yes it's fine, Sir." Finally, she's getting into her role. Knowing her place is half the battle. She knows in this position, she is my sub. I'll take care of her needs, her wants and desires. No matter how much she tries to turn the tables, it never works. I'm in charge in this relationship and I always will be. She loves all things anal and tonight I'll make it all about her. First, however, my cock needs some pleasing.

"Drop to your knees."

She quickly complies and I continue to get things ready for her. My heart races at the thought that this could be Makenna, bound and mine. I make another circle around her, admiring my handy work and when I stop in front of her, I place the tip of my cock on her lips. "Open," I command. She keeps her eyes cast downward as her lips part. Slowly, I gently push my cock into her mouth. I don't want to come just yet, so I keep my movement's slow and the pace gentle. When I hit the back of her throat, her eyes open wide and she looks up. "That just earned you a spanking." Realizing her mistake, she quickly cast her eyes downward again assuming the proper position. The night is young and I don't want this to end, besides I need to make this all about Nicole. If I do that, it will guarantee me full access to her in the future. I pull out and sit in the chair. Instructing her to drape herself over my lap. This is the position she loves, knowing her ass is fully exposed to me.

She begins to wiggle which earns her eight alternating smacks. Not hard but enough to sting. I trail my fingertips gently up and down her spine. In my mind, it is Makenna with her freckled skin, flushing at my touch. But it's not Makenna, *smack, smack.* Over and over again until her ass becomes a beautiful crimson. I reach for the extra thick lube and warm it up with my fingers. After all, I'm not a monster. Slowly stroking and pressing my fingers over her rosebud until it flowers open for me. In and out, slow at first and then a little faster. She wiggles which earns her a few more smacks followed up with her favorite butt plug. Holding the jeweled end, I gently twist it.

"Stand up and head toward the bed."

She stumbles to her feet, fighting to keep the plug in place. I don't wait for her to get to the bed; I lift her and place her on her knees in the middle of the bed. The sight before me is beautiful, her hands still tied behind her with her ass high in the air. The jewel from the plug is winking at me. I twist it a few more times before I pull it out and replace it with my cock. Oh, she is so ready for me. I pull her hips back to meet my thrust.

"Tell me what you want!" I smack her ass a few more times, harder than I usually do. That does the trick.

"I'm begging you, fuck me harder, *please?*" Begging. I love begging, whether it's for me to make her come or to spare their life. It's the push I need and I'm coming. I reach my hand around and one quick swipe over her clit and her orgasm hits. It's so powerful that her insides constrict around my cock, milking me dry. I quickly untie her and massage her shoulders.

"See no visible marks. Did you enjoy that?"

She rolls over and winces. "How red is my ass?"

"Not bad, nothing that a cool shower and some soothing cream can't fix. Come on, let me take care of you." I always make sure to give her the best aftercare, after all that will ensure she will let me go a little further every time.

After a cool shower, we get into bed and I gently apply cream to her ass. My handprints are still visible and every time my fingers glide over them it causes my cock to jolt.

"Mark, let's do something together tomorrow, just the two of us. It's been so long and, since we got to New York, we've never had alone time."

"I have to go pick up a new laptop tomorrow, but after that we can do something. What would you like to do?"

"What happened to your old one?"

"I was on my client's yacht yesterday and while I was showing him some graphs on my return ratios one of his grandkids knocked into me and it went overboard. He offered to replace it but how would that look?" I'm impressed with how I can come up with this shit on the fly.

"How about while I'm out getting my replacement, you look up the different museums and figure out which one you would like to go to. It would be great, just us, wandering around for hours." As long as it's something she wants to do, I know I'm golden. She hums in agreement as I stroke her back until she's asleep. I just have to keep reminding myself only one more week till I make Makenna mine. Slowly, I slip out of bed, making sure not to disturb her and head into the kitchen. I put together a quick egg sandwich and a cup of coffee.

My days and nights are consumed with Makenna Justice. I have to try to stay more focused. How the hell did anyone find the code in her computer? I knew she would eventually find the files, but I thought they would intrigue her. I mean, for Christ's sake, she owns a fucking sex club. She can't possibly be offended, that is, unless she doesn't like to be watched.

Come to think of it, every time I've been at the club she has never done a public scene. I need to get back into her computer and poke around. I won't do it from any place I can get caught, but I have an idea that just might work. Tomorrow, before I go buy a new computer, I'll stop at an Internet café and access her computer. Maybe Monday after work, I'll go by her apartment and see if I can find out who this new guy is. The thought of anyone touching her but me makes my blood boil. I've got a plan and I need to stick with it. Tomorrow, I'll find out more but I need to get back inside before Nicole finds me missing.

Chapter Sixteen

Fitz

WHY IS IT ALWAYS HARDEST to sleep late when you don't have to get up? It's Sunday and I want nothing more than to spend a lazy day with MJ wrapped in my arms. That's not going to happen. Instead, it's morning and I'm alone on the sofa. By the smell of things, MJ is, apparently, making breakfast. I hate to cook and do just enough to get by. Mainly Mom and Andy make sure I'm well fed, but MJ likes to cook.

It smells wonderful as I take the time to stand in the doorway and watch her work. She's got her headset on and she's singing. She loves to sing, even though she can't, and it's beautiful. The barriers in my mind are finally coming down. The walls around my heart crumble. I can't wait; I've waited too long already. I walk in, spin her around, and kiss her. Gently at first, but as my tongue explores her warm mouth, I know there's no holding back. When I lift her up, she wraps her legs around my waist, takes one of her ear buds out and pops it in my ear. Lee Brice is singing "Always The Only One", the words swirling around us like the fire in my gut. I want more, need more, and gotta have so much more. She reaches over me and shuts off the stove. Glad someone has her wits, right now. I know only one thing. I need her in so many ways. I pull back and search her eyes; they have all my answers.

With her still draped around me like the American flag, I head into the bedroom and kick the door closed behind me. I toss aside her iPod as she pulls my shirt off. She traces her tongue around one of my nipples and it pebbles to her touch. When she wraps her lips around it, I feel a jolt. Slowly, she takes it between her teeth and pulls gently at first, but then a little harder. She grates it between her teeth and then trails kisses across my chest to my other nipple. I look down and it's like it has a mind of it's own, pebbling at the anticipation of her sweet tongue rolling around it.

"Dear God, MJ, I—my cock and balls are having a tango party in my jeans right now and you need to address this." All I get is a hum as she sucks harder. She unwraps her legs from around my waist and slowly slides down my body. Kissing and nipping her way down my abs. I'm looking down at her and she's on her knees. There's no going back, no matter what happens now, I can never go back and, fuck me, I don't want to. She quickly undoes my jeans and exposes my tat. Her lips tremble when they touch it.

"You'll always be my hero, Fitzy."

I close my eyes and pray I always will be. She pulls my jeans all the way down and gasps. She's seen me in the buff but never like this and never this close. Her lips part and when she places the tip of my cock on her lips, my heart skips a beat. She's got one hand on my ass and another wrapped around the base of my cock. Slowly guiding me in and out.

"Babe, please, if you don't stop now, there's no going back." I try to pull out but she pushes me deeper. Swirling her tongue around as she goes so deep. When I bump the back of her throat, I know if I don't stop her, this will all end too quickly. I pull back and stop her. "Not like this. I need more, so much more. We only have one chance for a first and I want it to last."

"Don't toy with me, Fitz. I need all of you."

I lift her up and kiss her swollen lips as I attempt to step out of my jeans. "I'm not babe, but we do have a problem. I don't have any condoms here."

She grabs her bag off the floor and pulls out a long strand of condoms. "Good lord, woman, there has to be at least a dozen. I know you think I'm Superman but not even he can go that many times!"

Her skin flushes that beautiful crimson. "I wanted to be prepared for anything."

I take them and toss them on the nightstand. "Not yet, right now I need to explore every inch of you." I make quick work of her clothes and lay her down on the bed. Slowly, I kiss her neck. It's long and has faint freckles around the base. "I want to kiss every one of your freckles."

"We might be here for a while then, I have them everywhere."

"I want to play connect the dots with my tongue." I work my way slowly down to her nipples. They're a deep pink, and when I swirl my tongue around them, she arches her back. She wants more but I'm in control. I work my way slowly down her right side to her hip. My lips hover over her tiny tat. "Hmm, it's so tiny and so beautiful."

"I got it so that a part of you will always be with me."

I kiss it and make my way to the left side. Her skin is so soft and flushes to my touch. Every inch of her is sheer perfection. Her body telling me everything I need to know. Like a good book or a fine wine, waiting for me to indulge on. I work my way down to her sweet spot and gently kiss the sides, the top, all around but never dead center and it's making her wild.

"Please, Fitz, don't tease me. I need more, *please*."

My tongue swipes up and swirls around her nub, which makes her gasp. I use my tongue to enter her then back out and around her little ball of nerves. Followed by a gentle tug of her nub with my teeth. It's all about her; I want to hit her sweet spot over and over again. I need her to scream for me and it doesn't take long. My name, on her lips, begging me is like a siren's song. I'm not ready for this to end. I leave a trail of endless kisses over every one of her freckles. When I reach her lips, she kisses me tenderly at first, but then there is an undeniable urgency.

I grab one of the condoms and smile when I see she got extra-large. As I slowly roll it on, I take a moment to catch my breath. I need this to last and I want to rock her world. I lift her legs over my shoulders, lean down and rest my forehead on hers, slowly entering her. "Only one chance for a first, our first, babe."

Slowly, I begin to move. Our bodies are one, a perfect connection. She takes my hand, kisses it, and places it on her heart. "See what I'm feeling, Fitzy."

My God, I can feel her heart racing toward the finish line. I grab her hand and place it on my heart. "I'm right there with you, babe." I don't want this to end, it can't. I slow down trying to prolong the inevitable, but there is no slowing down.

"Fitzy, please, I need you. Please don't hold back."

She arches her back and her whole body turns a beautiful shade of crimson. I rock my hips in an upward motion and hit her G-spot over and over again.

"Fitz, I'm coming, I can't, oh God, again! Yes!"

As I take both her hands in mine, I finally let myself go and it feels like all the years of holding back have come flying to the surface. It's an intimacy so deep and so pure that I know I will never be the same.

"Oh God, MJ, I love you." I've laid myself bare to her. It's like she's healed me from the inside out. "I think I finally understand what you've been trying to show me, what's in your heart."

I pull out and make quick work of getting rid of the condom.

I hate those things but that's a conversation for another day. Right now, I want to hold her and love her all over again.

She curls into my side and her delicate fingers are drawing the outline of my tat.

"Fitz, when exactly did you get this? I mean, I know you've had it a long time, but when?"

"The night of your prom. That was the first time you ever called me Superman. I really felt like your hero that night, even though I did let all the air out of No-Neck Joe's tires."

"I know we both wasted so much time, but let's not dwell on the past and what if's. Let's move forward and see where this leads us."

I lift her fingers to my lips and take a little nip. "Right now, babe, the only place this is leading us to is round two. We've got a lot of condoms to use up."

Her giggle is infectious as she climbs on top of me. "What I have in mind, right now, doesn't need a condom. Oh, and for the record, Fitz, I've always used a condom, I'm clean and on the pill. What about you?"

Her lips are all over me, my chest, abs, oh God . . . down the happy trail. She takes my cock in her mouth, it's warm, and she's swirling her tongue around the head. Focus, Fitz, she's asking you something. "I've always used a condom, from day one. I just had my yearly work physical and I'm clean."

My cock does the throat bump as her fingers press that sensitive spot just under my sac, "*Fuck!*" I lose any control I thought I had. I don't even get a chance to warn her. With my hands fisted in her hair, I'm coming.

I'm trying to catch my breath as she is kissing her way up my body. Before I can put the pieces of my brain back together, my phone rings. "MJ, pants, phone, need to answer." Fuck she's pulling my nipples between her teeth. I reach down and grab my phone out of my pants; it's Travis.

"Hey, Travis, what's going on?" She's flicking one of my nipples with her tongue and my cock is responding. Hell, maybe I really am Superman.

"Fitz, are you okay? Have you been running? What the hell was I thinking, we all know you don't run. The bastard logged on to MJ's computer again. I used my program, and I traced it to an Internet café on the west side. Al was at Mystik and raced over there but he was gone." I leap up, nearly knocking MJ to the floor.

"Fuck, did Al pull all videos from the place and the surrounding area? Do you think he's used this place before or do you think he knows that we know?"

"The place has no working videos. Al pulled the credit card information and we know it's the same guy: Lex Luther. The city has a camera on the corner but it's facing Broadway. I'm pulling footage anyway, just in case we see a familiar face."

"What about any of the surrounding businesses?" I look over at MJ and she's already dressed and motioning me that she's going to make coffee.

"Nothing viable. Al spoke to the manager at the shop, but he was busy playing video games and could only remember the guy is white. He did say that the guy cleaned the entire area before he left. I'm not sure if he knows that we are on to him or if he's been using cafés all along. I will tell you, to do the programing and streaming that he has done, he would need a great connection and not the shit you find at these places. Al did confiscate the computer and I'm on my way to Mystik now to see if I can pull anything off of it."

"Didn't the manager find it odd that the guy cleaned before he left?"

"It's New York, Fitz, you know nothing is odd around here."

"Where is Olivia?"

"She is going to stay at MJ's place. She wants to show herself around the neighborhood."

"Are you sure she should be alone?"

"Fitz, she's an agent, trained to protect herself. She knows what she's doing. I put a camera outside her front door and added an alarm system. I'll call you later and let you know what I find out. Tell MJ to hang in there."

I know he's right, but I have a bad feeling about this. I throw on my jeans and head into the kitchen for some coffee. I pour a cup and when I look in the fridge I see at least ten different creamers.

"Is he serious with all this shit?"

"You know him, I'm surprised there's only ten. What did Travis find out?"

"The guy tapped into your computer again, this time from an Internet café. Still no leads on the guy. Olivia is staying at your place trying to be seen around the neighborhood."

"Is she safe?" It's like she can read my mind.

"I hope so. I have an uneasy feeling, but I need to stop thinking of her as you. She is a trained agent, capable of taking care of herself." Before she can answer, I hear the front door, Andy and Stephen are home.

Andy looks better than I expected and Stephen looks tired. "Hey, did you guys eat anything? MJ's cooking lunch," I offer. She gives me her classic *what the fuck* look and I try not to laugh.

"Apparently, I'm making lunch and Fitz is helping me." Before I can protest, she pulls a knife out of the butcher block and glances down at my crotch. My hands instantly protect my jewels and Andy is laughing.

"The doctor said I could take a shower as long as I don't get my hand wet. Stephen is going to help me with that while you two sort out lunch. Good luck, Fitz."

"Are you really expecting me to cook? You know if it wasn't for Mom and Andy, I would starve."

She pulls her phone out of her back pocket. "Mom, Andy is

home and there's nothing in this house to cook. Okay, I'll let Fitz know."

"Let me know what?"

"You're to stay away from the stove. She said she will be over in a little bit. Is it safe that Dad is home alone? I know he can take care of himself, but still I worry."

"He's the last person I would worry about, for Christ's sake he sleeps with a .357 under his pillow. I put Kevin on Mom because she is always out and about." I kiss her and I swear she taste like warm cinnamon buns with gooey icing.

"Umm, excuse me." Stephen clears his throat. I was so lost in warm buns I never heard him come in. "I'm glad everything is working out for you two, but we need to talk. Andy needs to follow up with a specialist and will probably need to have physical therapy. MJ, will you be able to take him or do I need to hire a nurse? Is it even safe for them to leave the house? It's Sunday and if I need to make some arrangements, I need to know."

"Get the follow up appointment for the doctor scheduled. I'll make sure he gets to the appointment. Have the therapist come to the house. I don't want MJ out of the house. I'm sorry, but until we catch this guy, I need you to stay put." I give her a stern look. MJ is squeezing my hand and I know she's pissed, hell, I would be too.

"Mom should be here soon with the food. I'm going to check on my brother." She leaves and Stephen puts his hand out.

"Give me a dollar, Fitz."

I reach in my pocket and pull out a ten. "This is all I have."

"That will do. Let's go out back while you fill me in on the case."

The afternoon sun is warm, but it feels good. I'm happy that I have Stephen to bounce things off of and I know he has to keep it confidential. "The guy is tapping into MJ's computer. Travis used a program he designed to trace the guy's online movements. I feel like a carrot is being dangled and I can't grasp it. Olivia is assuming MJ's

186

life, which has me worried. I know she's trained and all, but this guy is sick."

"I take it that the program Travis created is not legal?"

"Glad I paid you the ten bucks. No, it's not, but I'm desperate. We also set up a masquerade party for Saturday night. Maybe that will flush him out."

"What about you and MJ?"

"I took a chance and told her everything, including the fact that I love her. I always have and always will. Nothing will ever change that."

"Well, thank fuck you finally got your head out of your ass. She loves you and would do anything for you. I hope you see that."

The door swings open and Mom is here. I swear she's like a whirlwind wherever she goes.

"Let's go, boys, it's time to eat. My son needs his nourishment. Lord knows that hospital food was not edible. Stephen, I made your favorite: roasted chicken." Just like that, the consultation is over.

CHAPTER SEVENTEEN

Mark

NICOLE WANTED TO TWEAK A few more things on her case before she presented it on Tuesday, which was good for me. I left her to her work, and I found an Internet café that was open today on the west side. I decided to go there first, before I went to buy a new computer. The kid that was managing the place was more interested in playing video games than anything that I might be doing.

The connection was shitty, but I was able to connect to her computer. She had it open and the same guy was still at her apartment. I wish I could hear what he's saying and doing that makes her want to be with him. The thought of anyone fucking her but me makes me see red.

I don't want to be on here too long, just in case someone is really trying to track me. I make sure to wipe down the computer and the entire area with the bleach wipes I brought with me. After all, I don't need to make a stupid mistake.

I head out, but it's still too early to go to buy the computer. Two doors down, there is a coffee shop. I grab a coffee, pastry, the *Post* and sit in the corner window seat. I'm not there ten minutes when

I see, at least, six cars with flashing lights pull up to the Internet café. I pull the brim of my hat down low and continue to watch out the window. It doesn't take long for them to leave the café with a computer.

I wasn't being paranoid; they are looking for me, or, at least, the person that hacked her computer. They can't possibly link me to the killings, or to Mystik. The few times I was at the club, I used an alias. Even if they found the videos of Makenna, it's still nothing more than stalking. There is nothing tying me to the murders. I'm mentally going over each kill and the clean up to see if I possibly made a mistake. I notice an officer walking toward the coffee shop. He walks in and asks to speak to the manager.

While he waits he looks around the shop. When the manager comes over, he inquires if they have any working video cameras. She informs him they don't and he quickly leaves. Fuck, I can't get caught, not when I'm so close to having her. I need to up my game. I'm not waiting till Saturday, I can't wait that long. I finish my coffee and formulate my plan. I'm coming for you, Makenna, and no one will stop me.

First things first, on my way home, I stop at the computer store and get a whole new setup. When I finally get back home, Nicole is livid, which is never good for me.

"Where the hell have you been? You said you were going to get a new computer and come right back. That was hours ago, Mark." Times like these, I want to snap her neck.

"I'm sorry but the first store didn't have what I needed and when I got to the second store, there was something going on in one of the buildings and the area was closed off. I really thought I would be back here sooner."

"Well, I don't feel like going to the museum anymore. Why don't we get something to eat? I haven't eaten all day. When we get back, you can work on your new computer."

"Of course, that would be great. I'm starved. While I freshen up, figure out where you want to go." I head into the bathroom and grab one of her sleeping pills. That, mixed with enough of her favorite champagne, should knock her out for the night. I need peace and quiet to work on my plan. I shove it in my pocket and head out. Let's hope this works.

I get into the living room and she's still talking away. "I heard about a place in Tribeca that's supposed to be wonderful. I made reservations while you were getting cleaned up."

"Great, I know how you hate to wait. What time is Mason coming home?"

"He called earlier to let me know he's spending the night at his friend's house and he's going straight to camp from there. We have the house all to ourselves…again."

We head out to the restaurant and now I know for sure that I have to knock her out tonight. I just have to wait for the right moment.

We don't have to wait long at the restaurant and the constant flow of champagne works wonders. When she finally shuts up and goes to the ladies room I slip the pill into her coffee. I'm so proud I was able to pull it off. Nicole tries to stifle a yawn, and I know she won't last too much longer, so I quickly settle our bill. Between the champagne and the pill, I barely get her home before she passes out. Finally, I get her tucked into bed and get started on my new computer.

The first thing I need to do is send my boss an email, thanking him for his condolences and letting him know that my grandfather's affairs were more complicated than originally thought and I would need additional time off. I have unused vacation days, he can pull from there. With that settled I check my other email account and find one from my landlord.

She fell while visiting her son and broke her hip. She will be staying with him indefinitely. Her son will be by next week to pick up her mail and if I need anything, let him know. She thanks me for watching the place and taking care of everything for her. She should only know. Her misfortune is my good luck. Now I don't have to worry about her seeing anything. Oh, and an email requesting a review of the tranquilizer dart gun I purchased. That will have to wait until I use it on Makenna. After that, I'd be more than happy to help sell your product. Finally, I log into Nicole's work account and I'm able to find Stephen's home address. Since he's married to Makenna's brother, now I know another place I can probably find her. Next, I check my offshore account, and everything seems to be fine. I opened this account ten years ago and began to slowly siphon funds off of my client's accounts. No one is the wiser and if I want to leave the country with her, I have more than enough funds to do so.

It's three a.m. and finally, everything is loaded. I check my gym bag one more time. Since Mystik is closed on Mondays, I'll head directly to Makenna's place and put my plan in motion. I crawl into bed and Nicole is still passed out. Only a few more hours and Makenna will finally be mine. "Hmm, life really is beautiful."

Morning comes and Nicole is up before the alarm. "You're up early."

"I don't even remember going to sleep last night. What the hell happened?"

"You were so exhausted yesterday, no doubt from all the hard work you've been doing. You were falling asleep on the way home from the restaurant last night. When we made it upstairs, I put you to bed and let you get some much needed rest."

"Thank you, that was very sweet of you. I need to get ready, but I'll make it up to you tonight." She seems content with my bullshit.

"Oh, don't worry about it. Besides, I'm working late tonight. I have a meeting with my client again. You know I really want him to trust me and give me all of his business. Unfortunately, to do that, I have to kiss some ass along the way."

She gets up, gets ready, and quickly heads out the door.

I have the place to myself, but I don't want to deter from my daily routine. After all, that's how mistakes are made. I put on my best power suit, check myself in the mirror, and head out the door. Just another business executive headed out to work.

By the time I get to my apartment, I'm ready to rip this suit off. The heat is already unbearable. I decide to head to Makenna's apartment first to see if she is there. If not, then I'll head to her brother's house. One way or another, today I'm making her mine. I make a couple of passes around the block to make sure no one is watching. Alternate side of the street parking makes it almost impossible to find a spot. Who ever thought this shit up should be shot. It ends at eleven and if I have to wait, I will.

Fourth time is a charm; finally, someone leaves and I pull in. I put a hat on, pulling the brim low, and then head into the parking garage to check if her car is here. I feel my heart skip a beat when I see it in her spot. I'm about to find a place to hide when I hear the elevator chime. I squat down and wedge myself between the hood of the car and the wall. The sound of footsteps coming toward me gets louder, and I pull the tranquilizer gun from my waistband.

When she hits the remote to unlock her door, I take my chance and fire. I've only practiced shooting this thing in my apartment with pillows, but I'm still able to hit her in her thigh. I need to act fast, so no one will see me. When I jump up to grab her, her hat and sunglasses come off. I'm looking at the woman and, if I didn't know every inch of Makenna's body, I would swear it was her. *It's not her!*

Who the fuck is she and what the hell am I supposed to do with her? I can't leave her here, what if someone is watching us? *Fuck!* I quickly get her into the car and drive out of the garage with my hat pulled down low. Once we get out to the street, I have to circle around the block to get to my car. The last thing I want to be doing is driving her BMW. Lucky for me, alternate parking is just about over. I pull up next to my car and quickly get her in to the back seat. I park her car and take my bleach wipes and wipe down all traces that I was ever here.

When I get back in my car, I take a moment to look around. It's that off time between breakfast and lunch, so the streets are not that busy. If the cops were watching, they would have been on me already. I look back at the girl in my back seat, still amazed how much she resembles Makenna. Whoever she is, she will be knocked out for a couple of hours. I slowly pull out and head toward my apartment. Once I have her secured and restrained, I can figure out who she is and where the hell Makenna is.

It's been two hours, and she hasn't moved. Maybe the tranquilizer was too much for her. Pacing is not going to make her wake up any sooner. Watching her sleep, I realize how much she looks like Makenna. They have to be on to me, first the computer trace and now this. It has to be a trap, and I walked right into it. *Fuck!* I can't panic, that's how mistakes are made. And, if they've gotten this far, then I've made some mistakes.

However, if they knew who I was, they would have arrested me already. They're fishing, setting the bait for me to take. Well, fuck that, I'll get rid of her and move on. Oh, who the fuck am I kidding?—it's all about Makenna. Ever since Michelle, I've been looking for my perfect fit. None of them have ever fit. None, that is, until I laid eyes on her.

Being so close to her on Friday re-lit a fire deep inside of me. I haven't felt that spark in years. Her sweet smell, her fire-red hair, and her beautiful smile. I've worked so hard to have her and the only thing I've got to show for it is an imposter and a hard-on that is, yet again, requiring my hand for relief.

Fitz

Last night's dinner was great and at least MJ and I didn't let Mom in on anything going on between us. She would have been all over me, like a fly on shit. MJ's probably in the shower. I'll head in there and surprise her. I can't wait to catch this bastard and finally have the chance to give her my all. Jesus, I thought I took a hot shower; she's got the entire bathroom filled with steam. I quickly step out of my boxers and pull the curtain back. I've got one foot in the tub and one foot out when I realize my mistake. "Holy fuck, Stephen, what the fuck are you doing here?"

"I probably could ask you the same thing. I believe I'm taking a shower—alone, or at least I thought I was alone. Now if you don't mind, I'd like to finish."

"Why aren't you in work already?"

"Well, if you must know, I decided to take Andy myself for his follow up. Look, Fitz, can we talk about this when I'm done?"

"Where's MJ?"

"Somewhere in the house, Fitz, goodbye!"

"Yeah, yeah, I get it." I throw on my boxers and head out the door. Pissed that I missed her in the shower. I find her in the kitchen having coffee with Andy. Both of them are laughing.

"Hey, thought you were in the shower."

"Apparently, you found out the hard way that I wasn't."

I grab a cup of coffee. "Why do you have so many fucking creamers and what time is your appointment?" I'm grumpy, no doubt because I really wanted alone time with MJ.

"I like variety and my appointment is in an hour. What is the plan for today?"

"I'll stay here till you get back, then I need to meet with Al. Did you get your therapy sessions set up?" I ask as I sit down.

"They won't do that till after my appointment. I'll keep you posted."

Stephen comes in and before I can apologize for bursting in on him, he's ushering Andy out the door.

"You know, MJ, I could really use that shower." She gets up and straddles my lap.

"Really?" She fists her hands in my hair and tugs. Damn, she's so beautiful. When she skims her lips along my jaw, I feel my cock twitch at her command. Is this what its like to feel so consumed by someone that a simple touch makes you lose all reason? I lift her up, my hands firmly under her ass. I don't want to fuck her; I want to make love to her. I get it, I think. I finally know the difference.

"I wanted to hold you up against that wall and fuck you till you were screaming my name, but then I realized what I really want is to make love to you."

With her hands still in my hair, she kisses me hard. "We can have both, I want both. I need both."

Who am I to deny her? Slowly, I let her slide down, and I slip out of my boxers. "I'm all yours, babe."

She kisses me and I wish I could bottle that sweet taste. She's got her shorts off and never missing a beat I lift her back up. I've never gone bareback, never wanted to; it wasn't worth it, not until now. "Are you sure?" God, I hope she says yes.

"More than anything, make me feel all of you." I tilt her back not ready to take her yet. Her nipples are like a treat, designed just for me. Slowly, I work my way down her neck, first a nip followed by a kiss. I feast on her like I haven't had a meal in weeks. Slowly pulling first one and then the other nipple lightly between my teeth.

"I can't wait, please." She's grinding her hips against my rock-hard cock for some sort of relief, and I smile, knowing I'm the only one who can give it to her. I lift her higher and slowly rub my cock back and forth. When I begin to enter her, she sinks her teeth into my shoulder. I stop before I'm all the way in, fighting myself for control.

"Look at me—*now!*"

When she looks into my eyes, I slowly sink all the way in and stop. "Fuck yeah, just like that. Un-fucking-real, if you're okay, I'm gonna move now." With her hands still fisted in my hair, I kiss her and begin to move. Slow at first, until she kicks her heels into my ass wanting more. I'm pounding into her until she lets go of my hair and I stop.

"Please, don't stop!"

"Not until your hands are back in my hair, pulling—*hard.*"

She grabs it and pulls hard. "Hell yeah, just like that, babe."

The harder she pulls, the harder I pound into her. Everything in me is racing towards the finish line, but not without her. When she finally screams my name over and over again, I let lose with all I've got. My legs begin to shake and I drop to my knees, still buried deep inside of her. "I don't think I'll ever be able to look at that wall again."

I reach around and grab my boxers and her shorts and attempt to get up off my knees.

"What are you doing?"

"Taking you into the shower, I need more of you. This was nowhere near enough. I have years to make up for." I start heading in. Her giggle is infectious and I'm rock hard again.

"Maybe I'll buy you a cape and you can wear it the next time we make love."

"Ha! Now *that* would be a sight." I turn on the water and step in, not waiting for it to warm up and she takes one of my nipples and twists it.

"Hey now." She unwraps her legs from around my waist and I

let her slowly slide down my body. She takes a washcloth and puts some gel on it. The smell is wonderful, and I'm back to dreaming about her and gooey cinnamon buns as she washes me. When she works her way down, my cock is about ready to burst. She's on her knees with my cock between her lips. Good things really do come to those who wait.

The deeper she goes, the more my balls dance with excitement. I'm trying to mentally slow down. My heart is racing and I'm trying to catch my breath. I really believe, in my clueless mind, that I can slow down the tidal wave that is threatening to consume me. But then she does the throat bump—that's it for me. I'm coming and good lord, I don't want it to stop. When I hit the back of her throat again, I reach out to grab on to something. I end up with the shower curtain. It comes tumbling down nearly taking me with it. My fucking legs are quivering as she kisses her way up my body. She hums, "Mmm, I want more."

"Dear God, I'm only human!"

She hands me the washcloths and laughs. "I guess you're going shopping today for a new shower curtain."

Finally, finding the presence of mind, I turn the showerhead so at least the water is not all over the bathroom floor. "It's all your fault, that's my story and I'm sticking to it." We finish up, but not before she let's me worship her body and bring her to a place of sheer ecstasy. When I head into the bedroom to get dressed, I check my phone. I've got three missed calls. Fuck, it's Travis.

"Hey, what's up?"

"Have you heard from Olivia today? I tried calling and there's no answer. I checked the phone finder app on her phone and it shows that she is still at MJ's. I'm worried that she's not answering."

"Did you check the GPS on her car to make sure it's still there?"

"Yeah, it's still there. It's not like her not to answer the phone."

"I can be there in ten minutes. I'll call you back." I'm throwing on my clothes as she walks in the door.

"I have to run to your place. Do. Not. Leave. This. House. Lucas is outside, Andy and Stephen should be back soon. Promise me, MJ."

"I promise. What's going on?"

"I'm not sure. I'll call you." I kiss her head and run out the door, racing through the alley to get my bike.

Every minute that ticks by feels like an hour. When I finally pull up to MJ's building, I see her car parked on the side street, not in the garage. Now, I know there's a problem. The car is unlocked and empty except for her cell phone and bag on the floor. I pop the trunk and hold my breath, praying I don't find her in there. Nothing.

Thanking the good Lord, I race upstairs, hoping she's in there, but my gut tells me she won't be. She's not here and nothing is disturbed. I call in the crime scene unit and I'm about to call Travis when I see him and Al come rushing in.

"She's gone. Her car is parked on the street and it was unlocked. He left behind her cell phone and her bag. CSU should be here any minute. Nothing in here was disturbed. Pull footage from the garage and let's see if we can see anything." Travis is staring into nothing and Al is barking out orders.

"Travis, don't lose it now, she needs you to keep it together. Pull the footage now!" This is not like him, but that seems to do the trick. He snaps out of it, pulls out his laptop, and gets to work.

I feel like I'm missing something that's right in front of me. It's there but I can't focus in on what. It finally hits me—alternate side of the street parking. "Travis, pull the footage from 10:30 am forward and pull all footage from cameras in the street. We need to get footage from all the buildings in the area. Alternate was up at 11 am and there was only one other car parked near hers. That means it had to happen after eleven or she would have gotten a ticket."

While Travis is furiously typing away, Al pulls me aside. "It could have happened earlier and maybe she just didn't get a ticket, have you thought about that?"

"Al, this neighborhood is the absolute worst when it comes to alternate. They would kill their own mother for a spot. Hell, in the winter, they shovel out what they consider 'their' spot and put chairs so no one will park in it. I've gotten a ticket for parking five minutes before the time was up and I was sitting in MJ's car. I even tried flashing my shield, and she gave me the ticket and warned me I should have known better. I'm telling you, he had to have gotten her between 10:30 and 11:00."

Travis jumps up. "Got it, 10:45 am. He was in the garage, the video is grainy, but it looks like he shot her with something. There's no flash like a regular gun. You can't see his face, he has a hat pulled down low and dark glasses."

"Run it again in slow motion. It's a tranquilizer gun." Al's already on the phone to CSU, advising them to dust the front bumper, hood, and the underside to the door handle for prints.

"Al, you're with me. We need to talk to all the surrounding businesses and see if anyone saw anything. Hopefully, someone has some footage we can use."

Travis stops me before we head out. "Fitz, do you think she's dead? God, why did I leave her alone?"

"Hey, you couldn't have known and like you told me, she's a trained agent. Once he saw it wasn't MJ, he could have killed her on the spot, but he didn't. Let's just focus on finding her. The best way to do that is find some footage that can help us. The street her car is parked on is a one way, so he would have to come up to the corner and then turn either right or left on to the avenue. The main avenue has cameras in both directions, so pull footage from 10:00 to 11:30. Run the plates on every car that has gone up or down the avenue at that time. I'll check with you in an hour." Al and I head downstairs to see what we can find. Why the hell did he take her? He had to have seen it wasn't MJ. Why take her?

"Let's split up, you go up one side and I'll hit the other. Text me if you get anything." This is a tight community and if anyone saw anything, they would have reported it. First place I hit is the dry cleaners. I know they have cameras that are actually working; I helped install them. Mr. Chen didn't see anything, but he pulls up the footage from this morning for me to watch.

I'm watching the same silver car go around the block four times. Looking at the time stamp and its 10:20 am, after the fourth time, nothing. Did he find a spot, did he give up, or am I grasping at straws. Then it's 11:07 and MJ's car comes around the block. At 11:15 the silver car comes around the block again. After that, absolutely nothing. Only someone who's dealt with alternate side of the street parking their whole life can understand the frustration. With Mr. Chen's help, I email the footage to Travis, instructing him to put a BOLO out on the silver car and try to get a better shot of the temporary paper plate. If it's not our guy, maybe he saw something. In the mean time, I head out and hit every business on the avenue.

Chapter Eighteen

Mark

I'M SITTING IN A CHAIR by her bed and she hasn't moved. I know she's not dead, but I thought she would have been awake by now. The first thing I did was check her tat, and it's a fake. The more I think about everything, the more I realize I have no choice but to get Makenna before Saturday. This party at the club is a ruse to get to me. Finally, she begins to stir and her eyes flutter open. "About time you decided to join the party. Who are you?"

She lifts her arm and looks at the metal handcuff that's attached to a long chain which is bolted to the floor. I modified the cuff so Makenna would be comfortable when she was restrained. "You have enough chain to go to the bathroom, nothing more. The room is soundproof, and the landlord is away for the summer. Now, who are you?"

She lifts the covers and gasp when she realizes she's only left with her panties. "I'm only going to ask you this one more time. Who are you?"

"My name is Olivia, I'm in town visiting my cousin. Please let me go, I promise I won't tell anyone anything."

"Why do you have a fake tat? Why do you carry a gun, are you

201

a cop?" They look enough alike that I could believe they are cousins but the tat, the gun, I don't think so.

"My cousin has one, and I was thinking of getting the same one. My boyfriend has lots of them and last night I decided to test it out on him. I have a permit to carry the gun for protection. Please, just let me go."

"I know the laws for concealed to carry permits in New York City. You're a cop, so don't even try to bullshit me."

I go into the kitchen and get her a bottle of water. When I come back she's sitting up trying to wiggle out of her restraint. I toss her the bottle. "Don't bother, you'll never get out. I'll be back."

I leave and lock the door from the outside with a deadbolt. I need to figure out if she's telling me the truth or if I'm paranoid. I fire up my computer and begin my research, starting with her brother. Thanks to Nicole, I have his address and a Bio on Stephen. Their parents are still alive and they live in the same area in Brooklyn. It's amazing how much information can be pulled off of the web, especially when systems are so easy to hack into. Apparently, he was in the hospital and was released yesterday.

There is no mention of any cousins; there are only some distant relatives in Ireland. I've already tried to find out about the guy she was with at the party. He was introduced as Fitz, what kind of name is that? I tried different variations on the name but without the last name, it's hard. I looked through all her pictures on her social media accounts. I found only one picture with him and that was from her brother's wedding. Even on there, he's only mentioned as Fitz. He's a waste of my time, but I can tap into Stephen's personal information.

He's an only child, originally from Boston. Ivy League schools, the whole pompous bullshit. I didn't like him before and I like him even less now. Nothing helpful except it proves Olivia is not Makenna's cousin, and now I'm stuck with her. I could snap her neck but there's no fun in that. I want to feel my hands around her neck and watch her eyes beg me for mercy. That split second when she realizes it's not a game, well, at least, not for her.

My cock is pressing against the zipper of my jeans. Oh, what a thrill it would be, almost like having her. Almost like a warm up for the main event, but not in Makenna's room. Control, Mark, it's all about control. Maybe I'll keep her just in case I need some sort of leverage. In the meantime, I need to feed her and find Makenna. I'm not taking a chance and waiting for the party. It's a setup that I won't walk into. I need to lure her out of wherever she is hiding and I have a feeling she's with her brother, especially since he just got out of the hospital.

I put together a sandwich and take it in to Olivia. Stupid bitch is still trying to figure out how to get out of the restraint. They never learn, but, at least, that will keep her busy while I concentrate on putting together my plan. Everything rests with the brother. From what I could see, she is very close with him. He's the key to lure her out of wherever the hell she's hiding. *Get to the brother . . . get to her.* Tapping into the hospital records, I'm able to pull up his medical history.

He has Parkinson's which accounts for the tremors I saw. He injured his hand and had surgery to repair the damage. All the medical jargon means nothing to me. Finally, I find the notes on his release papers. Follow up with a specialist and start physical therapy. Well, the doctors aren't going to start PT until it's healed, so how the hell am I going to get to him?

Before anything, I need to check out where her parents and brother live. Then I'll be able to figure out how to lure her out. The online map says it's a thirty-minute drive. Brooklyn is a lot bigger than I realized. I better check on Olivia before I go, and give her another bottle of water. When I open the door, I find her on the floor, trying to loosen the bolts from the metal plate that's holding the restraint in place.

"I told you, you're wasting your time. Here's more water, I'll be back later." With that, I lock the door and leave. I don't have time to waste on this nonsense.

Thirty minutes without traffic, unfortunately there always seems to be traffic. I've driven all over California and Chicago, but I've never seen anything like this. People are triple parked like they own the road. It's a one way, so I have to go around the block. I'm going slowly so I don't miss the house. Between the pot holes and the traffic, I don't have a choice but to go slow. When I get closer to the house, I can see a fire hydrant out front and a car parked in front of it. There's someone sitting in the car reading. With my hat pulled down and dark sunglasses on, there's no way he can see who I am. I'm only able to catch a quick glimpse but he seems familiar. When I get to the corner, I turn left and then left again and I'm on their parent's block. When I get to the right house, there's an older lady climbing the steps with a guy following behind her, carrying her groceries. The woman has to be Makenna's mother; she has the same red hair. Slowly, I cruise by and, when I get to the corner, I go left and then left again. I cruise by Andy's house one more time, and it hits me . . . cops.

It's August and the guy helping the mother has a sports jacket on. The other guy is parked in front of a hydrant for no apparent reason. My mind is racing in all different directions. Maybe having Olivia can work to my advantage. If I can send them on a chase to rescue her, maybe I can distract them and get to Makenna. What I can't do is panic. That will surely get me caught, and that's not an option. I head back to my place to stash my car and form a plan.

Makenna

No matter how many times I look at my phone and will it to ring, it won't. Andy's not back yet and Fitz hasn't checked in. Hell, even my mother's not home. I've got cabin fever and I'm not allowed outside. I've done nothing wrong, yet, I'm the one locked up. Travis has banned me from any social media until they catch this nut. The only thing keeping my sanity is reliving the events from the last twenty-four hours.

He said he was afraid that I put him so high up on a pedestal that he couldn't live up to it. Hell, even I feared he might be right, but he wasn't. My heart is racing just remembering it all. I pray I'm as much to him as he is to me. So much time wasted, time that we can never get back. Living within the confines of fear's four walls and letting it dominate everything we did or didn't do is so sad. Well, not anymore—not this girl. I'm determined to grab that brass ring and I'm determined to have it all. I hear the key in the door and a flurry of activity, which can only mean one thing: Andy's home.

"Hey, Stephen, what happened at the doctor?"

"I've got to get to work. I'll let Andy fill you in." He quickly kisses him goodbye and runs out the door.

"Sit down and fill me in. I'm making an iced coffee, do you want one?"

"Of course I do. The doctor was very nice and said the surgeon did a wonderful job. I can't start physical therapy until the stitches are out. Normally, he wouldn't have me back until it's time to take out the stitches but because of the Parkinson's and all of my meds, he wants to check me sooner. So, I go back this Friday, and then, if everything is okay, he'll take the stitches on Thursday."

"Out of the plethora of creamers, which one do you want?"

"Surprise me. So, what's going on with Fitz?" He holds his good hand up to stop me. "Don't even think of telling me about the sex. There are some things that your brother doesn't want or need to know."

"You're an ass. I wasn't going to tell you about it, although, he does owe you a new shower curtain. Let's go sit out back, I've been cooped up in this house all day." We head outside. It's warm but there is a nice breeze.

"He told me everything about his mom and dad, which explains why he's afraid of rocking the boat. He can't take another great loss and for him, we're all he's got. Dad's treated us all the same, but Mom is very over protective when it comes to Fitz and now I understand why. There is something I need to talk to you about—*Mystik*. When all this is over, I want to sell it. You can have all the money; I don't want any of it. Just cover Mom and Dad's mortgage until I can find a job. I appreciate everything you did for me. I know why you did it but I think it's time to move on." I wait for a response but he's not saying anything and now I'm worried.

"How long have you known? I mean, why I did it."

"From the beginning, Andy. I know you thought that I was led down a path that I didn't want to go, but, the truth is, I willingly went down that road. No one led me anyplace I didn't want to go. You never asked me why I became consumed by the lifestyle, why?"

"I felt that was personal, but now that we are talking about it, can I ask why you did go into that lifestyle?"

"Fitz asked the same thing. I spent all week really thinking about that. I think it satisfied a need at the time. I've been so much for everyone but not for me. Having a Dom took away my need to fix everyone and to nurture everyone. The Dom took care of me in a very loving and caring way. He fixed me when I needed fixing. I'm hoping that I can find that balance with Fitz. Does that make sense?"

"Yeah, I think I finally get it. We can sell the club and we will find a way to cover everything. I want you to be happy, that's all I've *ever* wanted for you. Do you have any idea what you want to do?"

"I don't want to own a business. I was thinking of going back to school. I looked into it and I only need twelve more credits for my degree. I was thinking of going into marketing."

"Well, you've always been a bossy little thing, I'm sure you'll have no problem convincing people to buy shit they really don't need. Are you going to keep your place? You can move in here, I would love to have you around more."

"I haven't thought that far in advance. I do know I can't stay at Fitz's since he lives downstairs from Mom and Dad."

"Yeah, I didn't even think about that. Oh, and great job curtailing it last night at dinner. Mom would have been giving you both the third degree."

My phone rings and it's Fitz. "Hey, what's going on?" I answer.

"Is Andy back?"

"Yes, we're out back having an iced coffee. Are you going to tell me what's going on?"

"Put the phone on speaker," he says. I hit the button and Andy lets him know he can hear him.

"Olivia has been kidnapped, he got her from your parking garage. It looks like he drugged her. He hasn't contacted anyone, and he hasn't been online. He knows she's not you and he still took her."

"Is there anything we can do to help?"

"Yeah, Andy, I need to know that you're both safely tucked away. Please, don't leave the house for any reason. I'll touch base again later. MJ, take me off speaker." Andy gets up and heads inside, no doubt to give us some privacy.

"Hey, I'm here; Andy went back inside. How is Travis holding up?"

"How is it I'm always the last to know? He's trying to keep it together. We have a small lead that we're following up on. I need you to promise me you're going to stay put, please."

"When you're in the zone, everything else around you falls away. I already promised you I wouldn't leave. Promise me you will be careful."

"I will, how is Andy?"

"He'll be okay. Are you coming back here tonight?"

"I'm not sure, I'll try." He gets very quiet.

"I love you, be safe."

"Me too." It's barely a whisper, and he hangs up.

Mark

When I pull up to my place, I'm happy that I have the garage because this alternate parking is a fucking joke. The first thing I do is check on Olivia. She didn't eat but at least she drank her water. Stupid girl is still trying to get out of her restraint. If nothing else, she is persistent. "I told you there's no way to get out. Are you ready to tell me the truth? I know you're not a cousin, so, who are you?"

"Please, I don't know what you want from me."

"The truth, God damn it! That's what I want." Maybe I need to fuck it out of her. As I step closer, her eyes grow wider. Yeah, baby, fear me; that will guarantee me some answers. I take few steps closer and unbutton my jeans.

"Please don't."

"Tell me the truth and I'll leave you alone." Another few steps and she's out of the bed with her back up against the wall. "What's it gonna be?" As I get closer, pull off my shirt and toss it aside. Her eyes are filled with fear as she follows my every move.

"I told you my name is Olivia and I'm visiting my cousin. I don't know what else you think I can tell you."

When I'm close enough, I reach for her and she tries to round kick me. She's good, but that was expected and a waste of time. I quickly block her kick, reach in, and try to backhand her across the face. She blocks my hit. Her actions tell me everything I need to know. I quickly grab her hands at the wrist and hold them above her head. With my hips firmly pressing hers into the wall, she is pinned. My face only inches from hers. "Don't waste your time, I'm a fourth degree black belt. So, you're a cop, and not a very good one, considering the position you're in."

"I'm not a cop. What's it going to take for you to believe me?"

"You can't convince me otherwise, so don't waste your time. Now, what is the plan? Do the cops really think I don't know that this masquerade party is really to try to trap me?"

"I'm telling you, I have no idea what the hell you're talking about."

I push myself off her. "Fine, have it your way." I'll leave her alone all night and maybe by the morning, she'll realize talking to me is in her best interest. Besides, I need to get home before Nicole pitches a fit. She has to present her appeal to the Judge in the morning, and I'm sure she will be a royal bitch tonight. The less I rattle her, the better off I am.

Fitz

I've been up and down the avenue and spoken to anyone and everyone. How could no one see a thing? So many businesses have fake cameras, it's ridiculous. Travis and Al have already gone back to the station to wait for the results from CSU. Before I head over, I shoot a text to Stephen, reminding him to send me the info on that couple from the party on Friday night. The cool breeze and setting sun makes me want to ride forever, but unfortunately, tonight that's not an option. I'm not in the door two minutes and of course my captain is bellowing my name.

"Fitz, how the fuck did this happen?"

"You know as much as I do. I'm hoping CSU has something we can go on. I need to get with Al and Travis. I promise I'll keep you posted." At least that seems to satisfy him. I find Al in front of her whiteboard and Travis fixated on his computer screen.

"Hey, did anyone come up with anything?"

"The best video is the one you got from Mr. Chen. I also found the footage on the City's street camera. It shows the same car going around the block four times and then nothing. Then MJ's car comes around the block once. After that, the silver car comes to the corner, makes the right, but then he goes straight up the avenue. I pulled footage along the way; we lost him when he turned off of the avenue. I searched the area where he turned off, but it's like he vanished in thin air."

"What is around that area?" I ask Travis. He's staring at his screen like he's willing it for more answers.

"It's all residential. I tried to pull a close-up to see if we can get a look at him but it's so grainy."

"Al, did CSU come back with anything?" I'm praying he left something of himself behind.

"He wiped down the car. I even had them check under the door handle and the seat adjuster—nothing."

My phone pings with a text message from Stephen to check my email.

"I need you to check something for me. Friday night at the party, there was a couple there, and the guy rubbed me the wrong way. Stephen just sent me all the info he has on the couple. I'll forward it to you. It's probably nothing, but my gut is telling me to check it."

"At this point, we have nothing, so I'll run with anything you've got."

"What about the paper plate on the silver car? Can you make out what kind of car it is?"

"Well, since the Patriot Act, any car paid for with cash that's ten thousand or above must be reported to the IRS. Nothing showed up for that. I pulled the numbers from the plate and it's a 2009 Honda Civic. The car was purchased from a lot in Brooklyn for $9,500. The guy paid cash, his ID was a fake, and the address he gave is in the middle of the East river. I have a sketch artist going over to the lot in the morning and maybe something will come of that. In the meantime, I'll pull whatever I can find on that couple from the party."

"Well, at least we know our guy has a car and we know what kind. It's more than we had before. Let's try to keep positive."

While he works on his project, I want to go over everything for the party with Al. "Are we all ready for the party?"

"Everything is ready, and the response has been huge. Maybe we'll get lucky and it will draw him out."

"Has he logged onto MJ's computer since he took Olivia?"

"No, do you think he will?"

"Maybe. What if we leave a message for him on her computer?"

"What, like taunting him so that he makes a mistake?"

"Yeah, exactly. Travis what do you think, is it something you can set up?"

"Yeah, it might work, but what do you want to say? Oh, and this couple is squeaky clean. The only thing in common is that they lived in the same city at the same time as the murders. Do you want me to dig deeper?"

"No, not unless you see some reason to, otherwise, let's concentrate on leaving a message on MJ's computer for him. How about something like: you screwed up, now what? Nothing long, just to the point." It's a long shot, but I've got to try something.

"I'm going, if anything comes up, call me. Otherwise, I'll meet you at the club tomorrow."

Something is gnawing on my brain. I'm missing something, but what, I don't know. Maybe a long ride will clear the fog. I make sure I stop and pick up a shower curtain, which I know I'm never going to hear the end of. When I finally pull up to Andy's house, I still have no clue what I'm missing. Lucas informs me it's been quiet all day.

"I'm here for the night, you can go. I'll see you in the morning."

When I open the door, she's standing right there. "Jesus, are you trying to give me a heart attack?"

"I heard Wanda, what happened?"

"Nothing new, we might have a lead on the car, but that's it. Did you eat?" I need to get my mind off of this for a bit and maybe it will come back to me.

"Yeah, come on, I'll fix you a plate."

"Where's Andy?"

"Sleeping, his pain meds have knocked him for a loop." She turns and I follow her. Having her to come home to and just doing the simple things with her is sheer heaven. I realize I haven't eaten all day and I'm starving. I say a quick grace and a prayer for Olivia's safe return. When I look up from my now empty plate, she's staring at me like I have three heads.

"What?"

"I just figured out why Mom is always forcing food on you whenever she sees you. You didn't eat all day, did you? Don't bother answering, I already know. You want more or dessert?"

"What I'm planning for dessert is not in that fridge." Her face flushes and her lips slightly part. I lean in and swipe my tongue lightly over her lips and she moans. A moan that resonates clear down to my balls. I put my dish in the sink, take her hand, and pull her into my arms. "Dance with me."

"There's no music."

That's when I place her hand on my heart. "Listen to the music in here." With her hand on my heart I pull her close, rest my lips on her forehead and begin to sway. "I use to love to dance. When I was a young boy, I would dance with my mom. She would dance me around the kitchen. The day she died, I stopped dancing. I've never wanted to dance again, until now." The feel of her hips swaying to the beat of my heart makes me believe there really can be a happily ever after. Something that I never believed was in the cards for me.

"I need a shower, want to join me?"

"You need to set up the shower curtain first." Her giggle is infectious, it makes my skin prickle. She grabs it off of the counter. "I'll start setting it up while you go lock up your gun." She knows I never leave it lying around. She heads into the bathroom and I quickly head into the bedroom. When I walk into the room, I'm staring at my lock box on the dresser and it hits me like a brick between my eyes.

Fuck me, I knew there was something. I quickly get Travis on the line. "Hey, something's been bugging me, and I couldn't remember what the hell it was until now. You remember the video of the guy beating off while he was watching MJ? Remember there was a dresser in the background, and Gail said it was a high-end designer. She sent me over the website. I forwarded the email to you. Contact the company and show them a picture of the dresser. See if they will give you the purchase records for anyone who purchased the dresser in the last 3 years. Focus mainly on either Cali or Chicago. If that doesn't pan out, then branch out to New York. If they give you a hard time, then get a warrant. I know it's a long shot but something is better than nothing. Has he logged on the MJ's computer?"

"No, nothing. I'll get on this now. I'll pull the company records and find the owner. I know it's after hours but time is our enemy and I'll do whatever I have to."

"I hear you, keep me posted."

When I hang up, I find MJ standing in the doorway. "Is there any news on Olivia?"

"Nothing, babe, I had a thought and wanted to run it past Travis. I promise, the minute I hear anything, I'll let you know." I sigh. A tear escapes and she quickly tries to wipe it away. "Hey, talk to me; why are you crying?"

"It's because of me she's missing. Before you tell me otherwise, you yourself said she looks a lot like me. It should have been me, not her and poor Travis. I don't think I'll ever be able to look at him again," her voice shakes. I pull her into my arms and let her cry. As much as I can't bear to see her cry, I know she needs this.

When I look up, Stephen is heading down the hallway, he stops and sticks his head in. "Is everything okay here?"

"Olivia was kidnapped today."

"Oh my God. MJ, you know it's not your fault. You can't blame yourself for the actions of a madman." Stephen can zero in on exactly what the real problem is, that's why he's such a kick ass attorney.

"My mind understands it, but my heart, well that's another s-story."

"Come here." He pulls her into a big hug. "You have a huge heart, but Olivia was doing her job, the same way Fitz goes out there every day and does his job. Even though it scares us and we hate it, at the end of the day, we have to accept their choices and support them."

"I know, but it doesn't make it any easier. How's Andy doing?"

"The pain meds make his stomach upset. I just wanted to get him some crackers and applesauce. If you hear anything more about Olivia, please let me know."

Andy is so lucky to have someone as special as Stephen.

"Come on, I really need that shower. Did you get the curtain up?"

"Yeah, come on, I'll join you."

214

Olivia

There has to be a way out of this room. I can't be trapped here like a mouse. I've already torn apart the bathroom. There's nothing of use in there, not even a window. The walls have all been sound proofed; when I tap on them, the sound is like a thump. My family owns a construction business, and I've gone on many job sites with them. I've seen my brothers make something out of nothing, there has to be something here I can use.

"Think, Livy, think of your FBI training." Oh crap, now I'm talking to myself. It's only one handcuff that he somehow welded to this long-ass, heavy chain. If I stand a chance to get out of here, I need to eat to keep my strength up. I'm picking at the sandwich he left when I realize it has mayonnaise on it. Carefully, I scrape it off and work it around my wrist. It's still too tight for me to slide my wrist out. I need something to make a shim. First, I have to get the grease off of my fingers. I grab a towel from the bathroom and stare at the room. He positioned the bed so that I can't get near the window and the bed itself is bolted to the floor. Shit, I'm trapped, really fucking trapped. No, I'm not giving up. The toilet!

Quickly I pull the lid off and look at the guts. Yes! Attached to the arm that goes up and down is a metal clip with a long chain. In less than a minute, I've got the cuff off. Now, how the hell am I going to get out of this room? The door is bolted shut from the outside, so that's not an option. The only window in the room is nailed shut and there are metal bars on the outside. The window faces the back yard and I can't see any of the neighbors. I don't think escaping, just yet, is going to be an option. What I need to do is have some sort of weapon to use on him when he comes in

215

the door. I've got a plan, which is more than I had when I started. Now, I have to wait.

CHAPTER NINETEEN

Fitz

IT'S VERY EARLY; THE ALARM still hasn't gone off. MJ is fast asleep, her warm body wrapped around me. This is very new for me. I've never taken a woman to my place. Mom and Dad are upstairs, and I would never disrespect them. I've never stayed overnight at a woman's house. I've never wanted to until now. This can't be comfortable for her, especially since I'm extremely hard right now. I shift a little to see if she will slide off, but she moans and holds on tighter. Oh fuck, that's not good. Her eyes flutter open and she tilts her head up. Her beautiful emerald eyes are sparkling at me, which makes my cock twitch. "Hi, beautiful."

She moans and swirls her tongue around my nipple. It stands at attention to the constant touch of her warm tongue. "I think my other nipple might be feeling neglected."

"Really? Well, we wouldn't want to show favoritism, now would we?" She works her magic on my other one. When she releases it I quickly flip her over.

"My turn to have my way with you." I lavish attention on each nipple. A swirl of my tongue followed by a gentle tug with my teeth. She's trying to lift her hips but I've got her pinned down. Slowly, I

217

kiss my way down to her tat. I swipe my tongue over it followed by a gentle kiss. I keep kissing her all the way to her sweet spot.

When I roll my thumb over her nub, she fists my hair and pulls. God I love it, the taste of her is so surreal, and it makes me want even more. I'm not letting up; my tongue and fingers act like a man who hasn't eaten in years. She let's go of my hair and I instantly stop. She quickly grabs it and yanks it. She's coming and crying out my name. I slow down and let her catch her breath before I get on my knees and enter her. When I'm all the way in, I cocoon her with my body. I'm mentally gaining control so this is not over in the blink of an eye. I take a deep breath and flip us over. "Ride me hard, babe."

She takes my hands and puts them on her nipples. "Only if you play with them—hard."

"Oh, hell yeah," I agree. She lifts up and when she comes back down, I lift my hips up, slamming into her while I'm rolling her nipples between my fingers. I feel that pull in my balls and I know I'm so fucking close. I feel her legs begin to tremble right before she cries out. So fucking beautiful to watch right before I come endlessly. She collapses on top of me and I can't help laughing.

"Well, I wasn't expecting laughter that's for sure. What the hell is so funny?"

"I was thinking this is exactly how I started out this morning with you draped around me like a flag. I could get use to this." The alarm on my phone begins to blare. *I don't think so.* I quickly hit the snooze. "I want more of you." I tilt my hips and then roll us over so now I'm on top. "Nice and gentle this time."

I'm kissing those tender lips and the sweet taste drives me insane. How the hell is that even possible that they always taste so good? She hooks her heels under my ass and pushes upward. With my lips locked onto hers, we both find our release, long and slow. "Wow, so beautiful. Hang on to me, tight." I manage to get us out of the bed without breaking my neck. "Grab the sheet and wrap it around us."

"You know you can put me down and I can walk."

"Yeah, but this is fun. Plus, I want to keep the connection as long as possible." We get into the bathroom and quickly climb into the shower.

"Why the hell don't you ever wait for the water to get warm?"

"Well, this way, I wake up quicker. I have a question." She slides down, planting her feet firmly in the tub. Her head is back, and the water is cascading down her back. I look down at my cock and he's coming back to life. Maybe I really am Superman.

"Hello, Fitz, what's your question?"

"Oh, yeah, sorry; I got distracted. Is it true that in one love-making session where there are multiple orgasms that the last one is the most intense?" Her eyes are wide and I lift her chin to close her mouth.

"Can I ask where you heard about this?"

I pull the curtain back and point to the magazine on the floor. "If you don't want me to know these things, then you shouldn't leave them lying around."

"Okay, well everyone is different. Let me ask you, was the first one different than the last one?"

I take the washcloth and start washing her. "They are different, but I'm not sure if it's because of the different positions or if it changes after each orgasm?"

"I think they change and each one is great in a different way. I guess we will have to experiment some more."

"Sounds like a plan. Now finish up, I'll meet you in the kitchen." I know I must have a goofy look on my face but, for once in my life, I'm happy and I want to enjoy it. When I finish up, I head into the kitchen and everyone is already up. The heart of this house has been and will always be the kitchen. Even with Andy being sick, that never changed.

"Morning, everyone, what's the plan for today?"

"The plan is: my husband is being a pig-headed ass. He had a fever all night and I want to take him back to the doctor, but nope, he thinks I'm over reacting." Oh boy Stephen is pissed.

"How high is it? Did you at least call the doctor?" He is pig-headed, but he's also my best friend and I will always go balls to the wall for him.

"It's not that high and I promise, if it goes up, I'll call the doctor. Now, can we drop it, please?"

"I gotta go. Keep me posted. I'll check in later." I take MJ's hand, and she walks me to the door.

"You know what I'm gonna say, but humor me. Don't leave the house and keep me posted on him." I eye her to make sure she gets it. She kisses me and there's that taste again. God, how does she do it? Stephen rushes past us and out the door to catch his ride into the city. "Hey, call the doctor, because you know Andy won't and I'll check in later," I add. When she is back inside, I hop on Wanda and head to the precinct.

Mark

Nicole was a complete bitch all night and again this morning. I know she has been the perfect cover for me, but once I get my hands on Makenna, I won't need her anymore. I sure don't want the kid. Hell, I never wanted him to start with. After getting trapped by the bitch, I made sure to get fixed. She used me to set up the perfect family to further her career. The well-rounded woman, who needed to show that she can have it all.

Appearances, like the mirrors in a funhouse, skew what the world sees. Now, I use her like she used me. But, if I have Makenna,

I won't need anything else. Nicole is leaving early today which is even better for me. I grab a couple of Nicole's sleeping pills in case I need to drug Olivia, better to be prepared for anything. The nanny's got the brat, and I'm out the door. As far as anyone is concerned, I'm the perfect businessman heading out to work.

By the time I get to my apartment, the rest of the world is already at work. I'm going after her today. I'm not waiting around, giving them any more opportunities to find me. I quickly change into the nondescript looking jeans and t-shirt with a hat and dark glasses. I put together another sandwich for Olivia, grab one of the water bottles and dissolve a sleeping pill in it. That should keep her quiet for a few hours.

When I open the door, I don't see her, but the chain is stretched into the bathroom. I step into the room and she comes out from behind the door with the lid to the toilet and she swings it hard. Instinct kicks in and I throw my arm out to block it, which knocks it to the floor. I kick her in the stomach, and I hear the crack of what's got to be at least one of her ribs. She falls to the floor with the air knocked out of her and she's curled in a ball. The lid has shattered all over the floor. My arm is swelling; no doubt it's either deeply bruised or possibly broken.

"Are you happy now? How the fuck did you get out of the cuff?" When I pull the chain out from the bathroom I see the cuff is still attached. I have no idea how she did it but I fasten it on her wrist again and make sure I make it even tighter. I would love to snap her fucking neck right now, but I might need her. I have to keep all my options open. I pick up all the pieces of the lid and the sandwich, but I leave her the water.

Taking a closer look at my arm, I don't think it's broken only badly bruised. I need to head to Andy's house, that's where I know I'll find her. I'm not waiting any longer. My backpack has the tranquilizer gun, Olivia's handgun, rope, cuffs, and duct tape. "I'm coming for you, Makenna."

Makenna

When I go look for Andy, I find him curled up on the sofa, wrapped in a blanket. "How high is it and don't think of blowing me off."

"It was 99° but I feel like it's going up and my head is pounding."

"You might have an infection. I'm calling the doctor and don't even think of arguing with me," I snap. He hands me his phone and has already pulled up the doctor's information. The front desk puts me right through to the nurse. Knowing Andy's on so much medication for his Parkinson's, she wants me to bring him in as soon as I can. I let her know I can have him there at 11:30.

I send a text to Fitz and Stephen, letting them both know what's going on and then help Andy get dressed. I throw on my favorite jeans and one of Fitz's t-shirts. Even though it's huge on me, it makes me feel like I'm enveloped in his arms. I'm helping Andy into the car when I hear that familiar ring tone. "Hey, I know I told you I wouldn't leave the house but I have to get him to the doctor."

"You go directly to the doctor and text me when you get there. You never lose sight of Lucas and you text me when you're leaving the doctor and again when you get home."

"Yes, got it."

"Be safe, MJ."

"We will, you do the same." I hang up. Right now, I'm more concerned about Andy than anything else. We get in the car and I feel the hair on my neck stand up. Thankfully, the doctor's office is not that far away. Hopefully, we can get in and out quickly.

Mark

Even though it's still morning, it takes me forever with traffic to get to her brother's house. I find a spot and wait. I can see the same car parked at the hydrant again. If he has the window open, I can walk by and probably take him out quickly with the tranquilizer gun. I'm about to get out when I see her and Andy coming out of the house. Shit, I can't make my grab right now. I'll have to follow them, making sure I stay two cars behind. With the way traffic crawls, there's no way of losing them. Even though we never leave Brooklyn, every minute that passes feels like an hour. Finally, they pull up to a medical building, pull around back, and park. Now, I have to wait. While they go inside, I pull in to look around for a potential hiding place. I have to be able to get rid of the cop. Andy won't be able to stop me, and if I have to, I'll get rid of him, too.

Fitz

Travis got in touch with the owner of the company, turns out it's a very nice lady who was more than happy to give us everything we asked for. Unfortunately, it is one of their most popular dressers. Travis is doing something on his computer and he has his headset on. That's usually his "do not disturb" sign.

"Al, did he figure out a way to narrow all of this down?"

"Yeah, he's creating an algorithm that will read all the data and somehow do what we need it to do. I don't understand it, but I'm praying we can find her alive. You keep checking your phone, are

223

you waiting for a call?"

"MJ had to take Andy back to the doctor. She's suppose to text me when they are leaving the doctor's office."

"Do you think we have any chance with all of this information to actually catch him?"

"They caught Son of Sam with a parking ticket. There's no such thing as a perfect crime. No matter what happens, I'll never give up looking for him."

Travis gets up and pulls out his ear buds. "I got it! It can't be coincidence you yourself said, there's no such thing. That couple that you asked me to look into last night purchased the same dresser when they lived in California. They paid cash, but the delivery went to Nicole Chambers in California. I dug further into his background. He's a commodities trader with a Masters' Degree in Computer Programming. He started trading in California and has all the standard licenses. He is originally from Wisconsin and has an older sister, Dawn Spenser. She is married with four kids, still living in Wisconsin. Both parents are deceased."

"Where is he now?"

"He should be at work, hold on let me contact his company." I keep checking my phone and still nothing from her.

"Human resources at his company said there was a death in his family and he has taken paid time off. Fitz, he could be anywhere."

"Pull everything you can find on him, and the wife. He has a kid that he talked about at the party. Find out where the kid is and find any household staff that works for them or might have worked for them. See if he's had any connection to any of the victims. I'll call Stephen and find out exactly where Nicole is now."

I look at the time and hope Stephen's not in court. "Augusto, Cooper, and Donaldson, how may I direct your call?"

"I need to speak to Stephen Cooper, please."

"I'm sorry, he's in a meeting. Can I take a message?"

"Ma'am it's an emergency, interrupt him now, tell him it's Fitz."

"Oh, I'm sorry, sir, I'll put you through right away." Apparently, she has strict orders to put me through, no matter what.

"Hey, are you alone?"

"No, but I can be if you need me too."

"Just answer yes or no. Can you tell me where Nicole Chambers is right now?"

"Yes."

"Is she in the room with you?"

"No, only my paralegal. What's the problem?"

"Where is she?"

"At the federal court house on Pearl Street, arguing an appeal. It just started and should be at least an hour, does that help?"

"I haven't heard from MJ or Andy yet, have you?"

"Andy checked in and said the doctor had an emergency and is running late. Fitz, you're scaring me."

"I don't know anything yet, but stay near the phone and if you hear from them, let me know right away. We're headed to the court house now." I quickly hang up and Travis has already pulled up the information on the kid.

"What did you find out?"

"Apparently, they only have one nanny, Phyllis Martinez. She started with them when Mason was born. She is originally from the Dominican Republic and she is legal. The kid is in a special school for gifted children. When school is not in session he goes to a soccer camp, which is where he's at now.

"Okay, Al, you go to the camp and get the kid and the nanny. Travis and I will go to the courthouse and get Nicole. We'll meet you at their apartment." I race into the captain's office to fill him in on what's going on. He tosses me his keys. "Fitz, be careful. Remember, you just want to talk to her. We need to find out where this bastard is hiding Olivia."

Lights and sirens get us to Pearl Street in less than twenty minutes, although Travis's nail marks are permanently in the captain's dashboard. We find the courtroom but court is still in session. It's against the law to go in and pull her out. So, now, we wait. Minutes tick away like hours. I'm willing my phone to ring, but still nothing from MJ. I try to call her and Andy but it goes right to voice mail.

Finally, she steps out of the courtroom. "Hello, Nicole, I'm Detective Fitzgerald Rodriguez and this is Officer Travis Knox."

"Yes, I remember you. You were at the dinner party Friday evening, a friend of Stephen Cooper's, I believe. How can I help you?"

"Ma'am where is your husband?" My understanding from Stephen is that she is a very good attorney, so I need to tread lightly here.

"At work. Why, is there a problem?"

"He might have information on a case we are working on. He's not at work. Is there anyplace else we might find him?"

"I know he's been working with a new client. He's been trying to get everything from the client moved over. He mentioned the client was in the Hamptons, but he should still be at work. I can try calling him for you." Oh hell no, the last thing I need is for him to be tipped off. Something tells me she's clueless and he's been spinning a web of lies and deceit.

"I'd rather you not. If you wouldn't mind coming with us, we have some additional questions we would like to discuss with you."

"I'm not going anywhere with you unless you tell me exactly what is going on?" She digs her heels in and squares her shoulders. She's a small woman, putting on a suit of armor to go into battle, except this is a battle with me and she has no chance of winning.

"We are investigating a kidnapping. Your husband was seen in the area and we just want to find out if he saw anything. We can go back to your home and discuss this further or we can go to the precinct. Time is of the essence, and I would like to think that you would want to do anything you can to help save a life." I lay it on thick and sweet for her.

"Of course, I will do anything I can to help, but I need to check in with my office and let them know what's going on." While she's checking in with work, I try MJ and Andy again—still nothing. A text comes through from Al; she has the kid and the nanny and they are headed to the apartment. CSU will be meeting us there.

When she finishes up her call, we head out. While I drive, Travis tries to make idle chit chat, no doubt trying to make her relax a little.

We arrive right after Al. She quickly introduces us to Mason and his nanny, Phyllis Martinez. The kid barely looks up from his tablet.

"Who gave you the right to pull my son from camp?"

"We needed to talk to Ms. Martinez and I'm sure you wouldn't want your son left alone at the camp." Al looks at me and raises her eyes with skepticism. What can I say, I'm blessed with the gift of bullshit.

Giving her a chance to digest the bullshit, I begin to walk around, taking in the surroundings. Everything is high-end, which is what I expected, since they spent a stupid amount of money on a dresser. "Do you have a computer?"

"Of course, Mark and I both have laptops."

"We'll need to see both laptops and any other electronic devices, including your phones."

"You said you wanted to talk to Mark, that he might have been a witness to a kidnapping. What does our personal electronics have to do with any of this? I'm not answering any of your questions until you tell me what you're looking for." She crosses her arms and glares at me like she did at the courthouse. Her lawyer persona is back on.

"I don't think you want to have this conversation with your son in the room. I told you earlier we are trying to find your husband

227

for some routine questions." I can't get a read on her yet. Part of me wants to think she wouldn't be a part of all of this, especially with the kid in the house, but fuck, stranger things have happened.

"Look, I know you're bullshitting me, so tell me everything or this interview, or whatever the hell it is, stops now." She waves her hand to emphasize her point, which makes me want to spin her around and slap the fucking cuffs on her.

"Do you want me to arrest you in front of your kid?" I ask. She looks between her son and me and throws her hands up in defeat.

"Fine, Mark takes his laptop to work with him, although he just got a new one on Sunday. Mine is in the office, last door on the right." She reaches into her bag and hands Travis her phone. "Do you need Mason's cell too?" Travis takes both phones and races down the hall while I keep Nicole busy.

"Why did he get a new laptop?"

"He was at his client's home in the Hamptons this weekend and it was damaged. What does any of this have to do with Mark witnessing a kidnaping?" Before I can answer, Travis comes racing down the hall.

"Fitz, can I see you for a minute." I follow him down the hall into the master bedroom. It's the room in the video. If there was any doubt, there's none now. "When CSU gets here, have them tear this place apart. In the meantime, get started on her computer. Did you find his tablet? Remember, he had a tablet in that video."

"No, do you think it's the kid's? That would be pretty sick if it is." I have to remember we're not talking about a normal guy.

"Confiscate it along with anything else you find." When I head back into the dining room, Nicole is sitting at the table talking with Al. Maybe she can get some sort of information from her. I decide to talk to the nanny. Maybe she heard or saw something without realizing it. She's in the kitchen, putting together something for the kid to eat.

"Hi, Ms. Martinez, I'm Detective Rodriguez, but you can all me Fitz. Do you mind if I chat with you for a bit?" I have a way with the older ladies. They either want to feed me or match me up with their daughters.

"You can call me Phyllis. I don't know anything about Mr. and Mrs. Chambers' personal business. I only take care of Mason." She's been with them all these years; she knows. She's either been instructed to keep quite or turns a blind eye. Either way, she's got to know more about them.

"I can tell you do a wonderful job with him. I bet they are very busy with their careers, as most people nowadays are."

She puts some fruit and cheese on a plate in front of me. "I'll be right back. I need to give Mason his snack." Yeah, they all want to feed me.

When she comes back, I get up and pull out the chair for her. Her smile is warm as she sits and takes my hand. "Your mother raised a gentleman. A good mother tries to teach her son to respect a woman and treat her the way they would treat their own mother. I try to teach Mason, since no one is ever around for him. Mrs. Chambers works very long hours and Mr. Chambers wants nothing to do with him. He's a good boy, extremely smart."

"Can we talk a little bit about Mr. Chambers? Have you ever seen anything or heard him on the phone talking about another house or apartment? Some place he might like to go to be alone."

"No, but one morning while Mr. Chambers was in the shower, Mason picked up his dad's tablet instead of his own. I quickly put it back so Mr. Chambers wouldn't find out, otherwise, he would have gotten in trouble. Mr. Chambers doesn't want anyone touching any of his things." She genuinely cares about the kid, and by the way her hands are trembling, I sense she is afraid of what could have happened.

"Phyllis, you know you're not in any trouble, we just need to

229

find Mr. Chambers and talk to him. Did you see something on the tablet that day?"

She hesitates but only for a second. "Yes, he had a map open of Brooklyn and the section called Dumbo was highlighted. I thought it was funny that there was a place named after the movie. That's all I saw, I quickly closed it and got Mason the correct tablet before Mr. Chambers found out."

"Phyllis, thank you very much. You've been very helpful. If you think of anything else, please let me know." I give her my card. *At least* we can narrow down the area he might be in.

"Oh, Phyllis, one more thing. How many cell phones does Mr. Chambers have?"

"Two, but I'm only allowed to call him on one of them."

"Do you have both numbers?"

"No, sorry. Like I said, I'm only allowed to call him on one of them. Mrs. Chambers might have it."

"Thank you, Phyllis." I give her a nod. She goes back inside to take care of the kid. I check my phone and still nothing. Al is sitting at the dining room table, talking to Nicole about children. No doubt trying to keep her comfortable and the information flowing. I, on the other hand, am a bull in a china shop. I don't have the time or the patience to coddle her.

I slam my hand on the table a little harder than I anticipated. "Nicole, why does your husband have two phones?"

"One is his work phone, the other is his personal phone."

"Didn't it seem odd to you that a commodity broker carries two phones? You can't be that fucking clueless. What are the numbers?"

"I don't have the business phone number, I never call it."

"Who pays the bill Nicole? Is it part of your plan or does he have a separate plan?"

"I pay the bills but that phone is not on our plan. I think his work pays for it. I don't have the number. Like I told you, I never call it."

"Your world is coming down around you like a house of cards. You need to tell us everything you know before it's too late."

"Everything I know about what? None of this makes any sense. It sounds to me like you suspect Mark of something. What could he have possibly done to warrant the attention of the FBI and the police?"

"Like I said, right now, I just need to talk to him."

"I know my rights, and I think, at this point, either charge me with a crime or get out. If you need me for any further questioning then you can contact my attorney," she states sternly. She's right. I have nothing to charge her with. Everything is circumstantial and none of it really points towards her.

Travis pulls me aside and hands me her laptop and her phone. "There's nothing on either one of them that links to Mark or anything he's done. I did, however, copy everything on to my thumb drive. I want to cross-reference the contacts and all the documents I did find, just in case. I also pulled everything off the kids phone and tablet."

I hand her back everything. "We'll be in touch." When we get out onto the street, I let everyone know what Phyllis told me about Dumbo. "Hell, if we have to do a door-to-door search, we will." We're about to leave when my phone rings. Kenny Chesney's "Always Gonna Be You" starts playing. Finally, MJ is calling.

Makenna

We get to the doctors office without any problems. The parking lot is in the back of the building and I keep looking around every corner for the boogie man. I swear all of this is making me paranoid. I follow orders and when we get inside, I send a text that we arrived safely.

The nurse finally comes out to get us. At the same time Andy's phone rings, it's Mom. "MJ, can you please deal with her." Before I can answer, he shoves the phone in my face.

"Mom, I'm at the doctor with Andy, it's just another follow up but they are calling us back now."

"What's wrong? I should come there right now."

The last thing any of us need is my mom to come down here now. "No, there's no need for you to come here. I promise I'll have him call you back as soon as we're done." When I hang up, I flip it to silent and quickly stick it in my back pocket, trying to avoid the nurses glaring looks. I reach down and grab my bag off the floor while apologizing profusely to the nurse and quickly rush to follow them back. The nurse brings us into a room, checks his vitals, and then leaves us to wait for the doctor.

I hate waiting in a doctor's office. They have all this horrible shit on the walls that I swear makes me feel like I have everything they are trying to warn against. Finally, the doctor comes in. I've never met him and he's a lot younger than I thought. "Hello, Andy, I'm Dr. Watts, I believe you met my partner yesterday."

"Yes, this is my sister, Makenna."

"So, you're temperature is holding right around one hundred degrees. Let me have a look at the wound." He begins to unwrap the bandage, and I look away. Not something I need to see.

"Well, you'll be happy to know that there are no visible signs of infection, such as redness or swelling. I think the fever is coming from the tetanus shot you were given. The nurse will give you instructions to follow. Get some rest and we will see you back here on Friday."

At least it's nothing bad; in a couple of days it should pass. Armed with all of our instructions, we finally head out. Andy's been through so much and this is the last thing he needs. "I know you didn't want to get this checked out, but better safe than sorry. Let's go home, I'll text everyone and then I can make you something light to eat."

We head out to the late afternoon heat. Lucas is in front of us as we head around back into the parking lot. All of a sudden, he grabs his neck and falls to his knees. He's moaning, and he pulls something out of his neck. It's some sort of dart. "Run, MJ."

I'm trying to lift him, but he's too heavy. "Andy, grab one side and help me, try to lift him." Everything is happening so fast, yet, it seems like it's in slow motion.

"Let him go or I'll shoot your brother." When I turn my head, I see a man in dark glasses and a hat pulled down low with a gun pointed towards Andy's head. He let's go of Lucas and tries to pull me behind him, trying to shield me from a madman. "Andy, stop!"

"Listen to your sister if you ever want to see her again."

"Let her go, please. I'll do whatever you need me to."

"You're right. You *will* do whatever I need you to do. Step aside and let go of her. Don't make this any harder than it needs to be. Ma-ken-na, I have no problem shooting him." When he says my name slow and low, I remember the voice from the party Friday night. He's the space invader with the wife shoving her tits in Mr. Augusto's face. He says it in such a sick and taunting way. "Andy, I'll be okay, just step aside and let me go." I step away from Andy.

"You got what you wanted, now let him go." He turns the gun on me and I hear Andy gasp.

"Drop your bag and come with me now, Makenna."

I do as instructed, yet he still turns the gun and shoots Lucas in the back. "So you know I mean business." He quickly pulls me toward his car and pushes me into the passenger seat. He climbs in, starts the car, and shoves his gun into my ribs. I look back as we drive away and watch Andy fade from my sight. I close my eyes and say a silent prayer that my last memory won't be of the fear in my brother's eyes.

Fitz

"Hey, are you home? What did the doctor say?" I can barely hear anything over the blaring sirens. He's yelling my name and I realize it's Andy, not MJ.

"Fitz, can you hear me? He got her and shot Lucas. It's that guy from the party the other night. I'm in the ambulance with Lucas; they are taking him to New York Methodist. Fitz, find her!" he yells. The blood is pounding so loud in my ears I can hardly hear him.

"I'm on my way." Everything seems like its in slow motion. "Lucas has been shot and Mark's got MJ. We have to get to the hospital." I jump in the captain's car. Al and Travis barely make it in before I take off. How could he have gotten his hands on her? Where the fuck was Lucas? I make a thirty-minute trip in twelve minutes. When I pull up to the emergency entrance, I find Andy sitting outside. He appears to be in a daze.

"Fitz, he's in surgery. He got her. I tried to protect her and then he threatened to shoot me, that's when she went with him." He's shaking so badly, and I don't know if it's from the fever, Parkinson's, or shock.

"Hey, let's go sit inside and tell me everything from the beginning." He needs to calm down so he can give us all the details. What might seem like nothing to him could be a clue to finding her. Al checks on Lucas and he's still in surgery. She sits next to Andy and takes his hand. She is a nurturer, and it comes out whenever she deals with people one on one. She's able to keep them calm and talking.

234

"Andy, I know right now your mind is racing to try to help us find MJ, but what would really help is if you could try to relax and let me ask you some questions. I promise I will fight tooth and nail to get her home safely. Let's start at the beginning, you came out of the house and got into Lucas's car and drove to the doctor's office without any problems. Where did Lucas park the car?"

"In the lot behind the building. There were only a few cars in the lot. We walked around the building and into the office."

"Do you know what kind of car Mark had?" Before Andy got sick he worked as a master mechanic and could tell you anything you ever wanted to know about cars.

"Yes, a 2009 silver Honda Civic. I used to work on cars. In 2009, Honda changed the wheels on the Civic."

"You're doing great, Andy. Now walk me through what happened next."

"We walked in and checked in with the front desk. They handed me a clipboard and wanted more paperwork filled out. MJ told them we were just there yesterday, but they didn't care. They also informed us that the doctor was running late. We sat down and MJ pulled up my medical information on my phone. I keep it all in there, it makes life easier.

"I was just finishing up when the nurse called us back. Mom called and MJ told her she would call when we were done. The doctor said my fever is a side effect from the Tetanus shot. He gave us some information and sent us on our way. We stepped outside with Lucas in front of us. When we turned the corner, he grabbed his neck and fell to his knees. He pulled out a dart and yelled for us to run. MJ grabbed one arm, and I grabbed the other. We were trying to get him to safety, and that's when the guy said, 'Let him go, or I'll shoot your brother.'"

He takes a deep breath and Al squeezes his arm. "You're doing great, Andy, go on."

"I turned and saw him with a gun pointed at me. I let go of Lucas and tried to pull MJ behind me, trying to shield her. She yelled at me to stop and the guy told me to listen to my sister. He told her to drop her bag and go with him. She did as she was told and when he grabbed her arm, he pointed the gun down at Lucas and fired. Then he shoved the gun in MJ's side and they walked toward the car, got in, and drove away. I ran inside the building and the doctor came out to help Lucas. The ambulance came, and here I am. Please find her, please."

"When he pulled out on to the avenue, did he go right or left?"

"He turned right."

"Travis, see if there are cameras in the lot or just outside and start looking for the car. Also update the BOLO with everything we've got, including that he's armed with, at least, two hostages. Google the quickest route from the lot to Dumbo, he's only had his car a short time, plus, he's new to the city. Look for any cameras along the way." I have to stay calm and focused; thinking with my heart will get her killed. Every minute that he has her is a minute I'll never get back. Hart comes in with Lucas's parents, followed by at least a dozen other officers.

"Captain, any news on Lucas?"

"He's still in surgery. The bastard shot him with a tranquilizer dart and then shot him in the back while he was down."

I pull him aside; Travis doesn't need to hear this. "Now that he's got MJ, I'm not sure how much time Olivia has. Let's face it, he's got his prize, so why does he need her now?"

"Let's try to stay positive. When I heard what happened, I had the wife brought in for additional questioning. She wasn't too happy about it and threatened to sue the city. Blah, blah, blah, like I haven't heard that shit before." I'm glad Hart is here, but I know he's worried. He's not yelling, for a change.

"Let's go back and see if Travis has come up with anything."

236

Before I walk away, he grabs my arm. "I promise you we will find them."

"Yeah, I just pray it will be in time."

CHAPTER TWENTY

Makenna

I'M CURLED INTO MY SEAT with my body wedged as close to the door as I can possibly get. He drives a few blocks away, pulls out his phone, and tosses it out the window. He pulls out a second phone and I hear those famous words "Calculating route". He hits mute right before it gives the address. This asshole doesn't even know how to get to wherever the hell he's taking me. I begin to laugh, which I usually do whenever I'm nervous. He turns towards me and pulls off his glasses.

"Mind telling me what you find so amusing?"

"You've got to be the stupidest serial killer on the face of the earth. I mean, *really?* You kidnap someone and then you have to Google where the fuck you're going. Not too bright on your part."

In an instant, his hand is around my throat and my laughter instantly ceases.

"I wouldn't be laughing, if I were you. Especially, at the man who gets to decide if you live or die." He releases his grip, slides his fingers down my neck and over my breasts. His touch makes my skin crawl. I feel bile rising in my throat.

"Message received, where are you taking me?"

238

He doesn't answer me. The phone is in the door rest so I can't look at the screen. I look around and try to remain calm, taking in everything around me. The Manhattan Bridge comes into view and I know we're in the Dumbo area of Brooklyn. He pulls up to a house that sits just on the outskirts of the neighborhood. A long driveway curves around the back of the house where there's a garage and a small cottage. It takes him a couple of tries to get the car into the garage. Once he has the car stashed, he orders me to get out and head into the cottage. I stop and look around to see if anyone can see me. Every window and blind is closed. When we get inside, everything is very neat and organized.

"Where is Olivia? Don't even try to deny that you took her." He walks up to a door and unlocks the padlock. He pushes the door open and I see her curled up in a ball on the floor. "What the hell did you do to her?"

When I attempt to push past him he grabs my arm stopping me. "Not yet."

I'm trying so hard not to show fear, but I feel the sweat bead up and run down my chest. "Please, why are you doing this? Let her go, she hasn't done anything." He ignores my plea and drags me back to the closet by the front door. He pulls out a large plastic container. It's filled with chains and handcuffs and God only knows what else. You would not find this stuff at a sex shop. One look and even I can tell they are the real deal.

"Let's go." He picks out the stuff that he wants and pushes me into the bedroom. Olivia is not moving, and I'm not even sure if she's still alive. He's got a chain bolted to the floor with a cuff at the end that's attached to her wrist. On the other side of the bed, there's another metal plate bolted to the floor. He sets up the chain and attaches it to my wrist. He squeezes it so tight, I let out a yelp. "Is that really necessary?"

"I can't have you trying to escape. The room is soundproof so don't waste your time trying to yell. The landlord is away for the summer. I'll be back, Ma-ken-na." The way he says my name makes me sick. He leaves and I hear the bolt. Is this what Fitz felt that day? The fear of being trapped is overwhelming. I can't fall into self-pity or fear; I need to survive. First, I need to make sure Olivia's okay and then I need to figure out a way out of here.

"Olivia, can you hear me? Are you okay?"

She moans and her eyes slightly open. "I think I have, at least, one broken rib. Don't drink the water, this last bottle he left for me was drugged." She's tries to move and cries out in pain. I'm staring at her; I can't believe how much we look like each other.

"Let me help you get into the bed and then we can try to figure a way out. Put all your weight on me and let me lift you," I instruct. Somehow, I manage it and slide her into the bed.

"Listen to me. Under the bed is a metal type of shim I made. You need to get it so I can get the cuff off you." She's curled up into a ball again. I'm on my hands and knees trying to see under the bed, but I can't see shit, besides the fact I have no idea what the hell I'm even looking for. There is not a lot of room between the bed and the floor. I see something, but I can't reach it. I try to lie as flat as I can and shimmy under the bed. The frame hits my ass and I hear a thump.

That's when I remember what's in my pocket. After whacking my head, trying to get out from under the bed, I pull the phone from my back pocket. My hands are trembling so badly, and then I realize I don't know Andy's password. I look at Olivia and begin to cry. "It's my brother's phone, and I don't know his password." I sit on the edge of the bed staring at the phone.

"Make sure it's on silent. Try some different combinations, like birthdays or something that is important to him. If you hear that lock, slide it under the bed."

I'm trying to think of everything and anything but my mind

is blank. Fear is consuming me, but I can't let it. The phone rings and it's my phone number on the screen. I quickly hit answer; It's got to be Fitz calling. My hands are shaking. And then, I hear the lock. Before I can react, Olivia grabs the phone and slides it under the bed. The door opens, and he walks into the room carrying a TV tray with food. "You need to eat and make sure you drink or you'll get sick."

"I'm not hungry, besides why do you care?"

He puts it on the end of the bed and then puts his hands around my throat. Literately, lifting me off the bed. "Get it through your sweet, little head. You are mine forever, Ma-ken-na. If you want to keep Olivia alive, you will eat. I'll be back." With his hands still around my neck he leans in, his face inches from mine. He tries to kiss me and I spit in his face.

"You're a pathetic excuse for a man," I am barely able to growl out the words.

"When you fight me, it makes my cock even harder for you, Ma-ken-na." He grabs my hand and tries to put in on his cock. I know I shouldn't fight him. In some sick, perverse way, it probably makes him want me even more, but I can't help it. The thought of him this close is twisting my insides. I'm kicking, spitting, and try-ing to scratch his eyes out. Anything I can to fight him off. He's too quick for me, and pushes me down. I fall on top of Olivia and she cries out in pain.

"Eat your food, I'll be back." He leaves and I hear the lock. Round one goes to me but how much longer can I keep him off me? I silently pray that Fitz finds me. If I ever needed him to be my Superman, it's now.

When I reach under the bed and find the phone it says 'low bat-tery'. The damn thing is going to die and probably taking me along with it. "Find me, Fitz, we're on the outskirts of Dumbo."

"Olivia, I can't hear him, and it says 'low battery' what should we do? It's only beeping."

She grabs the phone. "Fitz, if you can hear this, I'm disconnecting the call to save the battery. Have Travis track the phone." She hits end and slides it under the bed. The only thing we can do now is wait.

Mark

I need to always be in control and I almost lost it in there. She fights like an alley cat; all that did was make me want to throw her down and fuck her hard. Harder than she's probably ever been fucked in her life. Olivia has become a problem for me, one that needs to be addressed. I thought I could keep her for some sort of leverage, but Makenna will see her as a weakness for me.

Maybe she thinks I didn't kill her because I have a heart. She'll soon learn I have a heart . . . a dark, cold heart. I've been prepping for this day from the moment I met her. I thought I could keep her here and go on with my everyday life, but after today, I know that's not possible.

By now, every cop in the city is probably looking for me. I let my emotions slip when I shot that cop. That won't happen again. We're going to have to lie low until the next big thing happens. This is New York; it shouldn't be that difficult to create some sort of panic. Maybe I can use something in the news to divert the attention off of me. When I pull up the website for the *Post*, the lead story is the shooting of police officer Lucas O'Brien and the kidnapping of Makenna Justice. There is a grainy picture of me in the car. I'm glad I have the car stashed in the garage, but I will have to find a different set of wheels to get us out of town. First things first, I need to get rid of Olivia.

Fitz

The waiting room is filling up with fellow officers donating blood. Stephen comes in and Andy loses it. Personally, I don't know how he's kept it together for this long. It seems like an eternity before the doctor comes out to talk to us. Lucas made it through surgery and if the bullet had been one inch to the left, it would have severed his spine. He said Andy's quick thinking probably saved Lucas's life.

Travis finds some video and we are watching the feed bounce from one camera to the next, when I hear her ring tone. Andy has her phone and passes it to Stephen. "It's Mom and I can't handle her right now. Please, Stephen."

Every fucking hair on my head stands on end and the skin all over my body prickles. I grab MJ's bag from behind Andy's chair and dump the contents out on to the floor. "Andy, where's your phone?"

"Oh my God, MJ had it. I thought she put it in her bag. When everything happened I just grabbed the first phone I could find and called you."

I grab the phone and quickly dial Andy's phone. What I hear next cuts me like a knife in my heart. It sounds like she's trying to fight him off her. I hear a door slam and then MJ is on the line, but she can't hear me. Then Olivia says she's disconnecting the call to save the battery.

"Travis how quick can you track Andy's phone?" Before he can answer, Stephen hands me his phone.

"Andy and I have iPhones. We have an app that finds friends. If she has the phone, and it's on, the app will show you, within a few feet, where she is."

I'm running out the door with half the NYPD following. I'm

driving like a bat out of hell while Travis is yelling which way to go. All the while, I'm praying, harder than I've ever prayed in my entire lifetime. Hell, even as an altar boy, I've never done this much praying. "Dear God, keep her safe."

We've got to be within a one-mile radius on the outskirts of Dumbo. "Travis, how close are we?"

"It looks like we are within two blocks."

"Kill the lights and sirens and let the others know to do the same. I don't want to spook him."

"Fitz, it's says that we're within a block." I grab the radio and order both ends of the street and the alleyways to be blocked off. When we get out, we start a door-to-door search. It's late summer, so it's still somewhat light out. It's a very mixed area, with lots of apartment houses. On the outskirts is where there are some older homes. Every door is a dead end, and the car is nowhere to be seen. "Talk to me, Travis, what are you seeing?"

"It says we are right on top of the signal." We are in front of a one-story house with all the lights out. A long driveway wraps around the back of the house. We make our way quietly down the driveway. When we make the turn around toward the back of the house, I see a garage and a small cottage. It's a tiny cottage with only one visible window with bars and a door. Curtains are drawn and I can't see in.

Unlike the main house, the lights are on. Al goes up to the front door, takes the back of her flashlight, and is about to knock when I stop her. Something in my gut is telling me not to. I hold my hand up and whisper. "Hold up, Al, I've got a bad feeling about this. Let me look around."

I work my way around the cottage to see if there is another way in or out, there's no other door, but another window has bars on it. There's a small separation in the drapes, only a slight crack, but I can make out a bed and that's when I see them.

He's got Olivia, and he's pulling her out of the bed while MJ is trying to pull her back. Oh fuck, he's escalating, and there's no time to wait. I race around front, draw my gun, and yell to hit the door with the battering ram. My whole world is rushing past me, yet, everything seems like slow motion. MJ's screams make me run faster than I've ever run in my lifetime. Until I get into the doorway of the bedroom, and I freeze. He's got his arm wrapped around Olivia's throat and the barrel of a gun on her temple. He's literately got her lifted off the ground. Her body is his shield, *fucking coward*.

"Let her go, Mark, it's over."

He slowly rubs the barrel down her cheek, and then up again. Constantly taunting her. She's trying to pull at his arm for some air. There are at least a dozen cops behind me, trained to take the shot but they have to have a clear one or Olivia is dead.

"I don't think so. It seems to me that I have the upper hand here. I could snap her neck with one hand and shoot Makenna before you even get in the door." He's cutting off Olivia's air supply, and she's clawing at his arm. The more she fights him, the tighter he squeezes his arm around her neck.

There's a split second when you see a person's mind flip from having hope to knowing there is no hope. It's in that second that I see his eyes go dark, and I know. The curtain just came down for him.

He knows there's no way out for him. He wants the one thing he's been fighting for all along—MJ. Everything he has done, leading up to this point, he's done for her. In his sick mind, he probably thinks if he can't have her in this life, he can take her with him in his death. He turns the gun toward MJ and in the same instant, Olivia swings her leg back and hits him in the knee.

Her quick thinking throws his balance off just enough for me to make my move. I take a running leap, propelling myself between MJ and the shot that rings out. I might not run like an Olympic gold medalist, but even under extreme pressure, I am a deadeye shot. I nail him, blowing off the right side of his head, but not before his bullet burns into my hip.

In an instant, MJ is all over me. She kisses, yells, and smacks me all at the same time!

"Hey, are you okay? Did he hurt you?"

"Me?! Fitz, he shot you! What the hell would possess you to dive in front of a madman with a gun?" I look down and my jeans are soaked with blood. This is the first time I've ever been shot; *that fucker burns.*

"I told you I would give my last breath to save you, babe." The EMT's are on me in an instant, cutting away my jeans to get to the wound. I look down, "Shit, that fucker's bullet hit me right in my tat!" I squeeze her hand tightly, "Don't worry, MJ, I'll get another one, I promise. Is Olivia okay?"

"The EMT's are with her now, she appears to be okay."

The EMT's examine my wound and they don't see an exit. The damn thing won't stop bleeding. They are trying to apply pressure as I'm fading in and out of consciousness. The last thing I remember, as they are loading me into the ambulance, is hearing her tell me she loves me.

Makenna

The ride to the hospital seems to take forever and Fitz is rushed into surgery. The shock finally hits me and my body begins to uncontrollably shake. Captain Hart pulls me into a big bear hug. "Makenna, you know he is tough as nails. He will survive, if for nothing else, just to piss me off on a daily basis," his voice is soothing. I know he's right; Fitz is tough.

All I can do now is sit down and wait. I look down at my shirt, Fitz's shirt . . . covered in Fitz's blood and I let my tears fall. I silently pray that he fights like he's always fought. The only way he knows how: hard. "How's Lucas?"

"He made it. You should be very proud of your brother. Andy's quick thinking saved his life."

It's comforting having him here, but right now, I really want my family. Every minute seems like a lifetime. I'm staring at the clock on the wall, watching the seconds tick away, yet I don't know how much time has passed. The doors open and Andy comes in with Stephen, Mom, and even Dad. My dad is retired NYPD. He got shot in the back on the job. He's been in a wheelchair for twenty years. He's a shut in—his choice—only leaving the house for doctor visits. Andy is crying and pulls me into a one-handed bear hug.

"MJ, I'm sorry I couldn't stop him."

"Andy, I can't breathe."

He pulls back and finally notices my shirt.

"Oh dear God." My mom gasps when she sees my shirt, thinking the blood is mine. Then she realizes it's Fitz's and Stephen grabs her and helps her to the chair. "Makenna Marie, why can't my children live nice quite lives?" she asks with great worry in her voice. I don't have a clue what to tell her.

I lean over to Captain Hart. "I think you can handle this one." I'm praying that Fitz can feel all the love in this room.

My dad quickly looks away and pushes himself off to the side. I get up, following him over toward the windows and sit next to him. "Daddy, I'm in love with Fitz."

"You're not telling me anything that I didn't already know."

"You knew? Since when?"

"Makenna, you've only had eyes for him from the first day your brother brought him home. Other boys have come and gone, but I knew none of them meant anything." His hand pushes at the air in front of him, emphasizing the dismissal of those other boys. My dad knew all along that I was in love with Fitz. I thought I hid it so well. Apparently, the only one I was really able to hide it from was Fitzy himself.

"Daddy, I finally got up the courage and told him."

"I know, he told me." He takes my hand and rubs his thumb over my knuckles.

"Wait, he what? When? Why?"

"Calm down, Makenna. I called him the other day about the officer he has taking your mother to church and bingo. I might not leave the house much, but I'm not out of the loop. When he didn't call me right back, I called a friend, and he told me what was going on. I left Fitz a message that I knew everything that was going on and he needed to come and see me right away. When he came by to check on us, he sat down and told me everything. He's been in love with you for a very long time. He let himself be ruled by fear. I'm going to tell you the same thing I told him. I love you both and nothing will ever change that."

"Daddy, I can't lose him."

"You won't, trust me." I rest my head on his shoulder and gain my strength from him. Finally, the doctor comes out, and I push Dad over to talk to him.

"How's my boy?"

"I was able to stop the bleeding and remove the bullet. He's strong and healthy and should make a full recovery. His biggest problem will be figuring out what to do about his tattoo." He looks at my shirt. "Would you like me see if the nurse can find you some scrubs?"

"Thank you, but I'll be fine. When can we see him?"

"After recovery, he will be moved to a private room. I know everyone wants to see him, but keep it to immediate family only, and keep it short," he instructs. My mom keeps thanking him and telling him she will keep him in her prayers.

With the news that Fitz is going to be okay, the waiting room begins to thin out. I haven't seen Olivia since everything went down. I check at the nurse's station, and they said she should be released soon. I walk around the room, not sure what to do with myself. Stephen comes over and silently slips his hand in mine. "He's going to be okay, we all will."

"Stephen, I never want to step foot in that club again. I want to close that part of my life for good. I know Andy has big medical bills, but maybe we can figure something out. I'll help anyway I can, just don't ask me to go back there."

"Don't worry, Andy and I already talked about selling the club. I've put some feelers out and let's see what happens. He said you want to go back to school. I think that's a great idea."

"I don't want to go back to my apartment. The thought that he was watching me there just makes me sick."

"You can stay in your room by us for as long as you want. We can even convert the basement into an apartment for you. One day at a time, MJ."

"My brother is very lucky to have you, we all are."

"The road we travel goes both ways. I'm very lucky to have all of you in my life. I've never been part of a close family like this one. Even though some of the moments can be crazy, I wouldn't change a thing."

Finally, Travis comes out, pushing Olivia in a wheelchair. I feel a rush of relief wash over me. She put herself in the sights of a madman just to protect me. I know it's her job, but I'm still grateful that anyone would run into the face of danger to protect someone they don't even know. I quickly introduce her and Travis to Stephen.

"Olivia, I can never thank you enough for everything you did to help me."

"Nonsense, you saved my life. You didn't back down from him.

Thank you. Oh, and just out of curiosity, did you ever find out your brother's password?"

"Oh my God, I forgot all about that. Stephen, I kept trying to figure out Andy's password, so I could call for help. Thankfully, Fitz called before the battery totally died."

"You never would have guessed it. It's the date we first met, but at least I had that app on the phone to find friends. Without it, you both wouldn't be here."

Al comes over and gives me a hug. "MJ, I'm going to take Olivia and Travis home, tell Fitz I'll be by tomorrow morning."

It's only the family left and we are back to waiting when the nurse comes to get us. We are advised that only one visitor at a time can go in. They make an exception and let my Mom and Dad go in together. When they come out, Andy goes in and Stephen sneaks in too. This family has never followed the rules, why start now?

They don't stay long; they know I need to be in there with him. "I'm going to spend the night, you guys make sure Mom and Dad get home okay. I'll call you in the morning."

They leave and I finally head in. My big, strong Superman looks so pale. I force myself to be strong for him. I have to be his rock, like he's always been mine. I sit next to the bed, take his hand, and place it on my heart. "This will always be home for you, Fitzy."

The nurse comes in to change his IV bag and informs me that visiting hours are over. "Please, I can't leave him. I promise I won't bother him. I'll just sit here and be very quiet."

He grips my hand tighter. "She stays or I'm out of here, the choice is yours, ma'am," his voice is deep and barely a whisper, but there is no mistaking the power behind it. She rolls her eyes and walks out the entire time threatening to call security.

"You're finally awake."

He tries to move and winces. "Fuck me, my hip hurts."

"The doctor was able to remove the bullet and stop the bleeding. He did say you're going to have to figure out something else to do with your tat." I can't help giggling.

"I still can't believe that bastard shot me right in my tat. I mean what were the odds of that happening? I've had it for so long, now what?"

"Is that all you're worried about?"

"No, how is Olivia?"

"She has two broken ribs, but she'll be okay. He didn't do anything to either of us. He didn't want her and the one time he tried with me, I fought him off. After that, he never had the chance."

"It makes me sick that he even got that close to you."

"Let's put it in the past, I don't want to waste any more time—especially on him."

"How's Andy doing?"

"He blames himself that he wasn't able to stop Mark from taking me and shooting Lucas. It's ridiculous for him to feel that way but I can't ignore his feelings. Hopefully, Stephen can make him understand there was nothing he could have done. Captain Hart said Andy was responsible for saving Lucas's life so maybe he can focus on that."

"I'll talk to him about it when I get out of here." He closes his eyes as I run my fingers through his hair and he moans. "Please stay."

"Always, now stop fighting the pain meds and get some sleep." I don't have to wait long for him to fall back to sleep. I keep a tight grip on his hand and try to get some rest too.

FITZ

I've been up for a while, especially since nurse Ratchet has been in

251

here every couple of hours. Speak of the devil, she's back again. MJ is still asleep with a tight grip on my hand. "Mr. Rodriguez, you are going to have to let go of her hand and let me do my job. I'm going to need you to sit up and try to get your sea legs. Since it was your hip, I'm giving you a walker to help with your balance. I'll help you to the restroom to get cleaned up. There's a cup in there for you to use." Her smirk is not lost on me.

MJ opens her eyes and smiles. "Good morning, beautiful. This wonderful nurse needs my undivided attention."

"I must have fallen asleep. What time is it?" She gets up stretches and I swear my damn cock just saluted her.

"It's six am and time for Mr. Rodriguez to try to walk to the restroom. I need to get you up and moving before my shift is over." Nurse Ratchet means business.

"Where's all my stuff I came in with?"

"In the closet. If I get it for you, will you do as you're told?"

"Yes, ma'am." She goes over to the closet and pulls out a bag with what's left of my clothes and hands it to me. I'm reduced down to a clear plastic bag. I find my wallet and hand it to MJ.

"Hey, I'll make you a deal. I'll get all jazzed up for you, if you can find coffee and something to cover my ass, please."

"Sure, coffee sounds good, I'll be back."

I don't need MJ to see how much pain I'm in. When she's gone, I let nurse Ratchet help me up. "I don't think I need the walker, it's not that bad."

"You need it, so behave and we can get this over with quickly."

When I try to take a step, putting some weight on my right side, I nearly buckle and grab the walker. Nurse Ratchet is smiling. "Do you believe me now?"

"Why the hell does it hurt so much?"

"Probably because bullets and bodies don't mix," her comment spares no sarcasm. I take baby steps to the bathroom and, when I

252

get there, I'm ready for a nap. She helps me with everything and I mean *every*thing. I have newfound appreciation for nurses. She helps me to the recliner and puts a pillow down for me to sit on.

"Is there anything I can get you before I leave?"

"No, thank you. Hopefully, I'll be sprung from here soon."

I'm sitting here, waiting for MJ to come back when Gail walks in. "Hey what are you doing here?"

"I was in the neighborhood and wanted to check on you."

"You can't lie to save your life. You were worried about me," I call her out. She turns beet red and I laugh.

"Yeah, keep telling yourself that. Hart filled me in on everything that went down. I'm glad I didn't have to do an autopsy on him. Do you think his wife Nicole knew anything?"

"Honestly, I really don't know. That's up to the FBI to figure out."

"What will happen to the kid?"

"That depends on Nicole's part in all of this. Who knows, maybe Mark's sister will take the kid in? Did Hart tell you that it was your information on the dresser that led us to identifying him?"

"Yeah, who would have thought my love for shopping would actually save lives. So what's next?"

Before I can answer, MJ comes in with coffee and I hope some food. "MJ, meet Gail, we work together."

"Hi, nice to meet you." She hands me my coffee and praise God—it's normal, Starbucks coffee.

"What's next for me is some much needed time off. After that, I'm not sure. I'm just going to take it one day at a time."

"Well, I need to get back to work. I'm glad you're okay. I hope you finally take some of that vacation time you've been stockpiling; you earned it. Nice to meet you, MJ." She waves and walks out.

"I got a couple of muffins, but you can't eat until the doctor says it's okay. I couldn't find any place open at this hour to buy you pants," her voice trails off.

"Hey, you okay?"

She looks away from me and shrugs. "Yeah, I think everything is finally hitting me."

"Come here, babe." I reach for her and she backs away.

"I'm not getting in that chair with you. I could hurt you."

"MJ, don't be so damn stubborn." I give it all I've got and hoist myself out of the chair.

"What the hell are you doing?"

"I know how crazy everything has been, and I know how you hate anything upsetting your apple cart. We are lucky, we both made it out of this mess in one piece. Everything happened for a reason and this has given us a chance to finally be honest with each other. I don't know what's going to happen next, no one does. I only know that wherever this journey in life takes me, I want you beside me the entire way. All of my tomorrows begin today, with you."

The doctor chooses now to walk in the door. I hold my hand up, "Please wait a minute." I turn back to MJ and continue. "MJ, I love you, I always have and always will. You're a dream I never thought possible, all the stars in the sky can't shine like you do. I would get down on one knee, but I don't think I would ever get back up. So, with my bare ass hanging out for the world to see, I have one question for you. Will you marry me?"

She takes my hand and places it on her heart. "Always home, Fitzy, yes." She kisses me and there it is—gooey cinnamon buns.

EPILOGUE

Four Months Later

FITZ

EVER SINCE MY BARE ASS proposal, the last four months have flown by. I healed up pretty quickly, but took some extra time off to spend with MJ. I made her a deal: I would give her any wedding she wanted as long as it was before the first of the year and Father O'Connor married us. She finally agreed.

Two days before the wedding, Dad asked to speak to me alone. I didn't think I was in trouble, but I was still nervous. When I showed up, Mom was nowhere to be found. Only Dad was sitting in the living room, waiting for me.

"Hey, Dad, is everything okay?"

He smiles which is a comfort for me right now. "Have a seat, son." I quickly sit down, still a little nervous. Oh, who am I trying to kid? I'm scared shitless.

"I know for a long time you blamed yourself for everything that happened with your mom and dad. You did nothing wrong and you're not to blame. You could not change the outcome, no matter how hard you tried. You're good man and I'm proud to call you my son. I know someday you will be a better father than me. As a parent we lay down the groundwork and we hope that our children will build upon it. Your mother was a good woman with a heart of gold, and I see so much of her in you. I'm proud that you and Makenna have finally figured out what we all knew, that you two deserve each other." He lets out a chuckle.

"I mean really, son, she is high-spirited and you are one stubborn man. I think this is going to be an interesting ride, to say the least. I know that you sometimes let the job consume you—don't.. That's how secrets stay hidden. Please find that balance and know when it's time to walk away. I didn't and look at me now." There's an envelope on the table, he picks it up and hands it to me.

"All these years you've lived in the basement, you've given me a monthly check. I never wanted it, but you always insisted. I wasn't sure what to do with it; I felt blessed to always have you here.

"So over the years, I invested the money, knowing someday, I would figure it out. Finally, last month with the help of Stephen, since he is the only one in this family who can keep a secret, I purchased the house across the street from Andy for you and Makenna as a wedding gift. I won't be around forever and at least I know my children will all be together." I open the envelope and sure enough, there is a deed for a house and a set of keys.

"Dad, I can't take this. That money was supposed to be for you to have a better life."

"I do have a better life and what would make it even better are some grandkids." He gets a huge smile and I can't help laughing.

"That ball is in Makenna's court, I'm just waiting for the green light."

"I understand that you are going to wait till the spring to go to Ireland. That will give you time to work on the renovations. I'm sure Andy will want to be knee deep in them. Have you decided when you are going to go back to work?"

"I got my clearance and I'll start back after the first of the year."

"Make sure you're really ready." I know he speaks from experience and I love him for caring so much. The physical scars heal but the psychological ones take longer.

"I will. When can I tell MJ about the house?"

He laughs and wipes away the tears. "I told you, you couldn't keep a secret!" He waves. "Go on, she's probably at Andy's house."

I get up and hug him, "I love you, Dad." I race out the door and stop in front of my old house, where it all began. I always thought my life ended in that house, but I know now . . . that's not the case.

I will never be crippled by fear again. I will teach my children to love unconditionally. I will never let a day go by that MJ doesn't know that I love her more than all the stars in the heavens above. I cut through the alley and find MJ bundled up, sitting on Andy's stoop.

"What are you doing out in the cold?"

"Dad just called and said to meet you out here."

I laugh, sly old dog talks about me not keeping secrets. I hand her the envelope. "Dad gave us this for our wedding." She opens it and begins to laugh hysterically. "Yep, we are now the proud owners of that." I point to the house directly across the street.

"It needs a lot of work, Fitz."

"Yeah, but that's what we have Andy for. Oh, and Dad wants grandkids. I told him as soon as you give me the green light." I kiss her and savor that sweet taste I've come to love. I never ask why she tastes like that. Some things are better left to the imagination.

Two days later, before God and our family, Father O'Connor married us on New Year's Eve, right before midnight. At thirty-eight, I finally married the girl of my dreams.

THE END

ACKNOWLEDGEMENTS

I am truly blessed with a wonderful family. I have friends who support me and always have my back. It really is the best gift in the world. I would like to say a very special thank you to Detective Louis Georgetti (Retired). You put up with my constant crazy questions and late night calls. Do you miss me? 😉

About the Author

Theresa Sederholt was born and raised in Brooklyn New York. She is a graduate of Campbell University in North Carolina, with a degree in Criminal Justice. Theresa now calls North Carolina home, with her husband, a professional chef, and her two dogs.

Experiencing life first hand is what she does best. Believing she can do anything has put her in many crazy situations. Whether it's babysitting a pig farm or cutting the top off of a mini truck; nothing is ever out of reach. Her list is endless, A to Z.

Theresa's beliefs are pretty simple. There isn't a luggage rack on the hearse, and give a girl Nutella and espresso and she can change the world.

Theresa enjoys connecting with her fans. She can always be reached through her website at:

www.theresasederholt.com

OTHER BOOKS

The Unraveled Trilogy

The Unraveling of Raven
Darkness Into Dawn
Shattered Lies